KINGS
IN THE
COUNTING
HOUSE

BY HERBERT MITGANG

FICTION

Kings in the Counting House
The Montauk Fault
Get These Men Out of the Hot Sun
The Return

BIOGRAPHY

The Fiery Trial: A Life of Lincoln
The Man Who Rode the Tiger: The Life and Times
of Judge Samuel Seabury
Lincoln As They Saw Him

CRITICISM

Working for the Reader: A Chronicle of Culture, Literature,
War and Politics in Books, 1950s to the Present

REPORTAGE

Freedom to See: Television and the First Amendment

EDITOR

The Letters of Carl Sandburg
Civilians Under Arms: Stars & Stripes, Civil War to Korea
Washington, D.C., in Lincoln's Time
Spectator of America
America at Random: Topics of The Times

PLAY

Mister Lincoln

KINGS
IN THE
COUNTING
HOUSE

A Novel by
Herbert Mitgang

ARBOR HOUSE
New York

For S. M.

Contents

The government of your country! I am the government of your country: I, and Lazarus. You will make war when it suits us, and keep peace when it doesn't. You will find out that trade requires certain measures when we have decided on those measures. When I want anything to keep my dividends up, you will discover that my want is a national need. When other people want something to keep my dividends down, you will call out the police and the military. And in return you shall have the support and applause of my newspapers, and the delight of imagining that you are a great statesman. Government of your country! Be off with you, my boy, and play with your caucuses and leading articles and historic parties and great leaders and burning questions and all the rest of your toys. I am going back to my counting house to pay the piper and call the tune.

—Bernard Shaw, *Major Barbara*, 1905.

PROLOGUE

NOW dawn began to fringe the prickly leaves of the hemlock and tamarack trees, rising over the scarred mountains that formed a natural, radio-quiet shield in the protected valley at Earth Station One in Andover, Maine. The lights of home places in the small logging town began to blink on softly. Men with windburned faces wearing heavy plaid lumberjackets revved the engines of their Ford and Datsun pickup trucks and headed for another day in the shadowed woods, first dropping off their sons in front of the ten-story control tower of the ground-station complex. The cold winds coming down from Canada blew bracing air into morning lungs, crossing the unmarked border stealthily, without visas.

The sons started to monitor the frequencies, adjusting the antennae and rerouting the channels. They captured the fleeing signals from the satellites and retransmitted the messages and pictures to their destinations around the United States. In a birch forest not far away, beyond the clearing for Earth Station One near the Atlantic coast, deer and elk wandered, safe for a few months from the seasonal long guns. The station's dish-shaped receivers rotated in azimuth and elevation in thousandths of a degree, tested and calibrated by the radio emissions from the star Cassiopeia A, light years away.

In these heavens, international communications satellites triggered from the earth circled in synchronous orbit above the North American and European continents. On these grounds, the mortals in command locked in the latest words and images: sometimes for information, more often for amusement, and covertly, for intelligence. The searching telemetry antennae stalked the man-made, sapphire-studded stars: the new Emperor's Nightingales. The firmament itself was pure and mindless. But the false stars cast no shadows and sang no songs...

In the modest village of Goonhilly Downs in Cornwall, fewer than fifty miles from Land's End, the Post Office's earth station provided commercial, or quietly concealed, telecommunications services over the British Isles. Its own geostationary satellites were positioned above the Atlantic spectrum. Three aerials probed for signals reaching the isolated village, a fourth sent television images to the orbital satellite controlled by the European Space Agency. Goonhilly Downs was linked, by private and public communications consortiums, to the earth station in Andover, in the state of Maine. Not to forget the transponders of far-ranging international conglomerates in the business of communications, getting and sending heavenly bulletins to ground stations linked all over the Continent, including...

Pleumeur-Bodou, an otherwise picture-book village inhabited by fishermen, on the northern coast of Brittany, almost directly opposite Goonhilly Downs across the English Channel, whose baited antennae could reach for the catch in the hardware skies, from the Mediterranean Sea to North Africa...

Except for the polar regions, the entire surface of the earth could be covered for whatever purpose by the roaming international satellites: televising, telephoning, banking, surveillance, spying.

The iron birds of the new era of communications seemed lofty and invincible, above the mundane battles below, but they soon began to spin off the familiar sounds of domination.

These earth stations could be grounded by determined outsiders pursuing their own nationalistic aims; in the old world of avarice, the new terrestrial wonders were vulnerable to anarchic human lightning.

A few men, each for his own reasons, picked up ambiguous early warning signals in the corridors of intelligence and in the broken temples of the news...

PART I

CHAPTER ONE

Death of the Paper

IN the autumn, the newspaper died.

"Jumped, fell or was pushed": for the last time the familiar cover-up phrase used by cautious reporters and instructed editors for known suicides was right on the mark. Round up the usual suspects for the first edition; beat the tabloids and afternoon scandal sheets. Only this was the final edition after a hundred-and-something years. The story a newspaper or magazine never really reported to its readers: its own death by corporate *diktat*. With great regret, the board of directors regretfully announces that... and the rest of the baloney. For Christmas's sake, said a seasoned copyreader, shaking his head under one of the few green celluloid eyeshades left in the sanitized newsroom, none of the high-powered flacks knew enough to edit that second "regret" out of the chairman's official communique. Not that they had to, up in their cloud-capped towers, their realms of gold. For the network now ruled over more than the disciplined words and wordsmiths; it owned the bats and balls on the playing fields of the national mind: the video display terminals that had replaced the typewriters, the silenced printing presses and the spiked stories. Eventually, the corporate language would be revised and polished by the next level of group vice-presidents at the network's headquarters hard by Rockefeller Center. The chairman's ghost-written phrases would come out with elegant deception in the only place where print counted anymore: the network's glossy annual report.

What the hell, Sam Linkum thought, why not turn up at the wake, and join in the threnodies at the farewell party in the evening for the final edition. He was among the mourners, too; with all its faults, the newspaper deserved a measure of devotion . . . a few last prayers for ink.

He was a man of middle years, of a little more than middle accomplishments, attractive to the men and women he worked with, considered a pro by his peers. He had grown up in these harsh streets, run coffee and pints of brown-bag whiskey for the big bylines covering the waterfront and police shacks, dreamed of his own name over a story some day. The bylines had come slowly. Over the years he had paid his dues—like so many of his beached friends on other papers that had been killed by hired guns with Master of Business Administration degrees—in the city and Washington, becoming wiser and worldlier after a stint in Air Corps intelligence and as a war correspondent, learning about censorship firsthand while reporting from magic carpet datelines in second-string countries.

Linkum had even earned the right to that contagious newspaperman's disease, cynicism; yet, beneath the surface, he still harbored idealism. And now, a thousand buried bylines later, he found himself walking in the direction of Union Square again. There were bound to be a few laughs during the unofficial obsequies for the paper. He had joined in the gallows humor himself when the New York *Herald Tribune* and the Washington *Evening Star* had jumped, fallen or were pushed.

In the gloom of the night he knew there would be a few people around that he admired and loved; and one in particular . . . Jennie

Ives. He had heard (but not from her, not lately) that she was back in New York, and he wondered if she too would make an appearance, drawn by the magnet of memory, the pull of their working and personal lives in the past. Hoping, he played out their encounter in his imagination but he couldn't fit the parts together; he did not know if they would embrace, or shake hands, or nod across the room, or turn for a final wave as they once did, parting.

When the network first invested in, then inched up on the board of directors, and eventually gained the controlling shares in the venerable paper, it was all but curtains for the era of serious news. The happiness boys with lockjaw grins wearing newly brevetted corporate stripes turned the paper into a subsidiary of the leisure-time division in the neat little boxes of the network, making it compete with video games and gourmet foods. Compared to the millions paid for minutes of TV time, the newspaper's figures didn't add up. The network's news was interlarded with commercials cleverly designed to sell sexy soap and light-calorie, no-belch beer, cosmetics for the plain faced and deodorants guaranteed to obliterate every normal body odor from the armpits to the crotch to the corns for at least twelve romantic hours, cars photographed to look like winged phalluses from Pompeii and breakfast cereals with crunch peddled by overgrown jocks talking baby talk, flattering pantyhose to conceal the bumps and grinds of housewives and brassieres to elevate sagging bosoms, and designer jeans worn by nymphets promising that you, too, could aspire to be rich and famous and sinuous by having Gloria Vanderbilt's signature imprinted on your ass.

Going up against the network's own elemental competition, the newspaper subsidiary languished on the bottom line. For a while, the marketing senior vice-president decreed that the newspaper should become supplementary reading for the network's major news shows, concentrating on what the media surveys called the personality side of the news—"the up-front, up-scale folks, the take-charge guys and gals, the movers and shakers in business, the Now Generation in the arts." Under the network regime, the real news was simplified and relegated to the back pages. Rather than serve as editor of their lifestyles section, which had become a glorified gossip and advertising come-on for the nouveau strivers in hot pursuit of the latest consumer software, Linkum had quit the newspaper subsidiary. Not long afterward, "with great regret," the network announced that its newspaper would cease publication.

Walking downtown from his small apartment near the United Nations enclave toward the old newspaper plant below raffish Union Square, Linkum thought of something that one of the British press lords had said after buying a broadcasting franchise: *It's a license to print money.* Whereupon one of the columnists on a faltering opinion weekly, temporarily subsidized through an American oil magnate's tax shelter, had taken off on Lord Acton: *Radio tends to corrupt, absolute television corrupts absolutely.*

Maybe the Brits were a little threadbare in the pay packets, and their suits were beginning to shine and poke out in the elbows, but they could still clothe themselves handsomely in the English language they had created.

And now the new temporal lords in mufti were carving up the cities and the heavens into privileged fiefdoms: landlocked by cable on the ground and dominated by communications satellites in the skies. In a little over a generation—Sam's, and Jennie's, and that of most of their friends who still revered the printed word—the broadcasters had delivered the *coup de grâce* to the newspapers. The purveyors of casuistry smiled and served up the goods, selling their signals across the small screens of the Western world.

"How they hanging, Lou?"

"Hanging loose, Mr. Sam."

In the outside office past the elevators that never arrived, where the flacks and crazies had been screened before being allowed to enter the premises, the former news analysis section editor and the ancient copyboy-receptionist exchanged a ritualistic greeting for the hundredth, and last, time.

Suddenly Lou raised his head and then came out from behind the desk and pumped Linkum's hand.

"Jesus, it's you, looking just fine. For a minute there I didn't know that you were gone, like old times, Mr. Sam. Hanging *loose?*

Balls. No, hanging *low*. You know the score, don't you?"

"Yeah, I read about it in the Washington *Post*. Yesterday. As usual, twenty-four hours late. This bunch didn't even have the guts to report its own big story. They'll probably streamer it in the final edition—and then sell souvenir copies for an extra buck...write in to your local network station. The TV carried it, but they forgot to report who padlocked this place."

Lou nodded. "The television cameras are inside now. They're all over the joint with their wires and lights. They say it'll make the eleven o'clock news. Wanna be in the movies?"

"Sure, but not this one. I want to wear a top hat and be a hoofer like Fred Astaire or I'll even settle for being the guy who walks off with Ingrid Bergman in *Casablanca,* what's-his-name, the husband she doesn't love. I don't want even my mug in their feature story and be interviewed by some character wearing a razor-cut hairpiece and grinning on cue for fifty memorable seconds."

"You working, Mr. Sam?"

"A little here and there, mostly on my own. I've been looking into a few things. How about yourself—got something lined up?"

Lou laughed and said, "Hell, no, nobody would want me, first I couldn't get a sit-down job until the affirmative action came in and we brought the lawsuit, and now I've gone and turned fifty and that's a second strike against me in the hiring halls, you know?"

"I wish I had a paper, Lou, there'd be a spot on it for you somewhere—"

"Appreciate the thought. I'd give my left tit to work with you again. But the severance pay shouldn't be too bad because of the Guild contract. I'll visit the old folks down south, and then something's bound to turn up, I've still got a few muscles left in my hide."

Linkum took a step toward the newsroom, then hesitated at the threshold. The blinding lights and camera and sound crews and assorted spear carriers with clipboards blocked his vision, but these alone didn't stop him. He couldn't bring himself to reenter the network's newsroom; it was alien, hostile territory.

He stepped back. "Any of the old crowd around?"

"No, most of them cleaned out their desks as soon as the news became official, took most of their junk home and left tonight right after the first edition. About the only ones inside are the brass hats on the masthead and a few of the young eager beavers who're transferring over to the TV news and the private security guards. They wanna make sure nobody walks off with a box of paper clips."

"The editorial brass still sticking it out loyally, even after what's happened to the staff and the paper?"

"I hear they've been offered pretty good jobs in public relations and speechwriting over on the corporate side of the network."

Linkum nodded. "Anybody else from the old crowd I would have recognized?"

"No, I didn't see her."

They exchanged knowing glances, and Linkum tapped Lou on the shoulder.

"Wouldn't be at all surprised if some of the old gang was over at Mannie's Place tossing back a few beers to chase the blues away."

"That's what I figured. I could use a couple of chasers myself."

Linkum extended his hand. "Keep in touch in case you need anything—anything except money, friend."

Lou laughed and gave Linkum a high five with his fingertips.

"See you around the quad—and hang loose."

"Right." He turned to go. "And one more thing, Lou."

"What's that?"

Linkum crossed his flexed arm, pointed his upraised, clenched fist toward the captured newsroom in an old Sicilian gesture, and said:

"Up theirs."

Mannie's Place was almost the last of the newspaper hangouts that hadn't just collapsed from a combination of tired blood and high rents or been taken over by a restaurant chain and turned into an upholstered, disguised spaghetti and hamburger joint for the plastic-money, expense-account crowd. Dinty Moore's, Lindy's, Artists and Writers—all the spots where the gags and *gemütlichkeit* were served up with the good food and drink, where if you knew the bartender you could get a refill by asking him to put a little head on your glass, and fake lunch if you were broke by nibbling the cheese and crackers—they had all been laid to rest in that great big pizzeria in the sky or wherever pastrami and cheesecake were buried in some heartburn heaven. Mannie himself was not, as some of his customers surmised, a descendant of one of the tribes of Israel because he had once been an argumentative waiter at Lindy's who had parlayed a long-shot daily double into a place of his own; the Yiddish he spoke was sprinkled with the brogue of County Clare, and, as he was the first to confess, in his youth he had never caught let alone stripped a pickled herring in the River Shannon. He had been nicknamed Mannie by the jokers at the front comedians' table in Lindy's so long ago that nobody remembered his real name. Mannie swore that the authentic blackthorn shillelagh hanging like a warrior's battle emblem in front of the mirrored bar had been given to him by Ernest Hemingway, to replace the original one that Papa had cracked over his own or John O'Hara's noggin (the tale changed from season to season), in a display of might to prove his literary superiority.

Halfway down the block, Linkum could hear the clinking of heavy beer mugs and voices raised in song and shouts of laughter but not, of course, the bitterness in the sounds of silence. He entered the interior swinging doors and was immediately greeted by Mannie:

"It's the lad, it's Himself! I knew the best ones would show up here tonight, for the Kol Nidre service before the Yom Kippur fast."

"You pouring tonight, Mannie?"

"Wherefore is this night different from all other nights? But for you, Sam, I can make an exception."

"Only if you have one with me, and I buy the next one."

Mannie pulled down the wooden handle on the good Carlsberg that he always kept on tap and blew off the Coney Island head and they touched beer mugs.

"Whenever there's a hanging, I'm on the side of the guy on the wrong end of the rope. You got out just in time, Sam."

"It's always just in time these days. In the last couple of years, you were warned on the day you joined and congratulated on the day you resigned. You know when you could smell that things were getting worse? When the network lieutenants shook your

23

hand and said, 'Welcome aboard!' In the TV chain of command, you salute the captain's bridge and get their permission to come on deck. For chrissakes, the paper began to sound like the white-shoe navy after—"

"Wrong, that came later," Rodney Rappaport, the architecture reporter, interrupted. "The welcome-aboard bullshit was the end, not the beginning. The walls. When the corporate art designers and interior decorators knocked down the walls and killed the bulletin boards and pictures, they sent us a message. Nothing personal, one big happy family, everybody on the team. Three guys seen talking together in a concealed corner of the newsroom and the stock-option editors figured you were conspiring outside their Kremlin Wall."

"Damn right we were hatching a plot to overthrow them—and a lot of good it would do us," said Robert Licata, who had a conspiratorial mind even before covering the Statehouse in Albany. "Hey, how you doing, Sam? Look everybody," he said to the group holding up the long dark-oak bar, "Sam Linkum. Mannie, charge one to my former account and lemme buy Sam a drink. I used to make money off of him writing the same analysis piece session after session about the upstate hustlers in the legislature and their tradeoffs with City Hall—"

"And another thing that burned my pretzel," continued the architecture writer, knocking back his third Scotch, "they walled off the offices except for the ensigns, separated the working press from the stock-option editors, and stuck up these Sheetrock partitions all over the joint. The partitions were part of the process, and don't you bastards forget it. I asked one of the design idiots what the reasoning was, and do you know what he told me? *Eye contact*. What's eye contact? Exchange of vision and ideas between editors and reporters, says the boy genius, keeps you in touch. Learned it at Harvard, M.B.A. I don't want to be in touch, all I want to do is have a little privacy and work my phone and typewriter, but the little asshole says it'll be good in the long run. Well, you know where we are now? We're *in* the long run."

"But didn't you enjoy living snug inside an egg crate?" said Eddie Ruskin, the British head of the foreign copydesk. "No, gentlemen,

I suggest you look for symbols. What turned the paper on its rum bottom was when our revered stock-option editors started to go to lunch with Henry the K. and take his self-serving 'on deep background only' phone calls seriously. After that, you may have noticed, the good Doctor K. only got Good Conduct medals in print. The editors even kissed the arses of the *National Review* and *Commentary* neoconservatives to get themselves dinner invitations. They partied with the people *we* avoided. Eventually, the paper stood for nothing—except careers."

"Hey, you call *this* a party?" asked Ellen LeMoyne, the travel writer who had led the women's case against the management. "You're depressing me—I may have to turn to drink."

Standing next to her, Doris Florian, the movie listings editor, recited:

> *Christmas is coming, the geese are getting fat,*
> *Please to put a penny in the old man's hat!*

"Change the old man to old lady and I'll buy it," said the travel writer. "Anybody want to come to my first rent party? I should be sending out invitations in three months. That's how long my money should last unless some of you rich swells take pity on a lovable newspaperperson."

Licata came up to her, squeezed her waist. "Call yourself a newspaperman or woman and I'm yours—I'll share my last sou and bed with you. But you can't possess my body or my bank account if you use that friggin word person. No more chairs or chairpersons or person-persons, get it, baby?"

"The last of the red-hot Sicilians," she said, removing his hand. "Here, I'll give you a dime to call your wife and lie to her."

"Okay, girlperson, you don't know what you're missing," Licata said, retreating, and looking toward the end of the bar for some of the live ones from the secretarial pool.

LeMoyne ordered another Calvados and said to Mannie, "You ought to post this notice at the entrance—I brought it along as a souvenir. It should be good for some laughs around here." The souvenir, a memorandum from the network's legal department, included a mild warning about sexual harassment on the job. Mannie put on his bifocals and read aloud:

"It is forbidden to make unlawful sexual advances, requests for sexual favors or other verbal or physical conduct of a sexual nature as a condition of employment or as a basis for decisions on pay and promotion."

He pocketed his glasses. "Wonder what the difference is between lawful and unlawful sexual advances?" Returning the memorandum, he went on, "What do you want to do, drive me out of business? If I ever had to police all the pinching, they'd suspend my liquor license for neglect of duty. As my sainted grandfather used to say in the old country, It's all right to have a toss in the hansom as long as you don't frighten the horses."

Linkum craned his neck to see if the woman he had come to see again was in the narrow room with the checked tablecloths beyond the long bar and the clouded reflecting mirror. Mannie used to save them the quiet booth in the back, where the old framed photographs of the River Liffey and Joyce's Martello tower were spattered with Lea and Perrins Worcestershire sauce. Nobody could notice if he reached for her hand there. Now his view was blocked. He delayed elbowing past the bar, savoring the anticipation of coming on Jennie as if for the first time.

On the inside of the swinging doors, voices suddenly lowered. Silence rolled down the bar like falling tenpins.

"Jesus, Mary and Joseph," Licata muttered. "Unless my eyes are playing tricks it's the she-devil herself."

Jane Twining Delafield, the network's vice-president who had supervised the paper under the leisure-time division of the broadcasting group, studied the scene through circling eyes above her Ben Franklin glasses. She fixed her gaze on Linkum, walked toward him. The crowd parted before her.

"Hello, Sam," Miss Delafield said, smiling in her tight-lipped way.

She extended her hand but he did not take it; instead, he waved his whiskey glass in a half-acknowledgement.

"The last time we spoke," she said, still politely, "you told me to go fuck myself."

26

The barflies around them looked up, embarrassed in their cups and glasses, and several moved back a few steps, out of the line of fire.

"Correction," Linkum said. "If I remember right, and I ought to, I rehearsed my exit line pretty carefully, I told you to go fuck the *paper* yourself."

"Oh. Is there a difference, Sam?"

"At the time I thought so. Not now."

"Nothing personal, then?"

"Well, I wouldn't put it quite too sweetly. But never mind the nuances. By the way, how's your bottom line?"

"My what?"

"You're the original *bottom-line girl,* aren't you? Vice-president, bottom-line, leisure-time division? It's your phrase, not mine. Nothing personal, of course."

"I don't blame you for sounding bitter. It was my job. I think it's a little unfair to blame me for what happened to the newspaper."

"Who should we blame, God or the stockholders? You know, the way the network PR flunkies have stagemanaged this reminds me of the parliamentary investigations after a state railroad accident in France. First, there would be accusations against the president of the railroad, who would point his finger at the regional department chief and then the town mayor where it happened and then the engineer and conductor and, finally, the investigation would put the blame on the poor *lampiste,* the little guy at the end of the line who forgot to wave his lantern at the crossing just before the head-on collision. So the culprit was just an anonymous nobody, he was retired early on a half-pension and everybody on top was cleared of responsibility... You *were* in charge, weren't you?"

"*Were,* indeed. Okay, Sam, I was up there in the network chain of command, I wasn't just your little lamplighter—"

"Bullshit," Licata interrupted. "You were a ball cutter and you know it, you did their dirty work, baby."

Miss Delafield's smile turned cold.

"Licata, don't call me baby or anything else, you asshole. Everybody knows you eat it."

Miss Delafield did have a way with words, but that was not why she had won her corporate rank. In the network's carefully calibrated vision of a clean, consumer-targeted Middle America, she represented the superiority of the WASP patriciate. Jane Twining Delafield: her ethnically balanced name could reach into the heartland of the country without offense to any group. Whenever her language cracked the primness of her exterior, the words always came as a surprise. Linkum thought of the schoolteacher's admonition, You should have your mouth washed with soap, and then of the sponsor's brand, Dial or Dove or, better still, Safeguard, the cleanup hitters of the network's Evening News.

The air in the smoky barroom crackled with tension; now the party had become rough. Mannie sensed that there was something wrong and asked Miss Delafield if she wanted a Perrier. She ordered Haig & Haig Pinch. She glared at Licata and smiled at Linkum, turning herself off and on in an instant. After a deep swallow, she said:

"In case you haven't heard, Sam, I've been reassigned myself."

"You've joined the ranks of the unemployed too?"

"Not quite, I'm still on the payroll and I'm still a vice-president, but I'm no longer on the broadcast end of things."

"I thought you'd have received a big promotion after the newspaper subsidiary was folded."

"No, it's what we call a lateral move in the network chain of command. No reduction in rank or rights, just change of station."

"Are you still involved with news? I thought you were having a good time with the lifestyles section, translating it into television and—"

"No, I'm out of news altogether. They've put me in charge of the electronic games division. Interplanetary warfare, tennis and chess and backgammon and the Indy 500, asteroids and space invaders and missile command and air-sea battles and warlords—"

"Congratulations. It sounds as if you're running World War Three."

"Sam, be fair . . . it's all good clean fun, home video games played alone or against a partner, and it's pretty educational, too."

"Oh, that makes it okay—as long as it's called education. What division does it come under, the network's professional school and publishing end game?"

"No, we're in the gourmet food division." She smiled and added, "The idea is that while you're playing you nibble on the network's munchies."

"Everything but the squeal, as they used to say around the Chicago stockyards on the way to the slaughtering—"

"Sam, what I'm trying to tell you is that *I'm* out on my ass, too. But I don't expect you to feel sorry for me. What I'm trying to say, and not doing it well, is that we all have to adjust, you fuck or get fucked, it's a changing marketplace."

Miss Delafield tapped the side of her glass, and Mannie refilled it. Linkum watched as she downed the Scotch quickly.

"Even you, Sambo," she went on. "Gotta look out for Numero Uno. Just stopped by because I heard that you and a few of the others I admired would be here. Wanted to wish you well in all your future endeavors. Look, the chairman of the board predicts that in the next two years video games will be as big as long-playing records. More profitable. All age groups. I may have room for someone as smart as you in my division—"

"It's out of my line of work."

Linkum clinked his glass against hers.

He moved away from the bar, leaving her standing with the neutral Mannie, and nobody came up to her; after a few minutes, Jane Twining Delafield, who had ruled their working lives, who with a stroke of her network felt-tip pen had marked some for life and some for death, drifted out into the night, alone.

A group of reporters blocked the entrance to the dining room, stopping Linkum. They stood in a circle of disjointed laughter, exercising their inalienable right to condemn the copy editors who had cut their good stuff and their pride, alongside the critics and correspondents called in from abroad, all in the same state of gloom, still not believing that it had really happened, that their well-known names would be out of the paper forever and that the telephones would stop ringing because the producers and politicians, the publishers and promoters no longer needed them, and in the morning they would be supplicants themselves, on the asking end, the ass-kissing end, their power only derived from the paper.

Waving his glass of port, the Pentagon correspondent, beloved of admirals for advocating more battleships, recited,

> *They've taken of his buttons off*
> *an' cut his stripes away,*
> *An' they're hangin' Danny Deever*
> *in the mornin'!*

"Not me," announced one of the political affairs columnists, who had once served in the White House *judenrat,* "they ain't cutting mine away. I've been offered a job by this President, and I'll be doing business back at the same old candy store."

"Doing what—shining the cowboy's riding boots?" asked his former Washington editor.

"Not quite, dummy, you're talking to the new White House telecommunications counselor."

Whereupon the Washington editor threw a beer in the columnist's face, then bowed to the reporters. They clapped.

"The bastard's had it coming for years," the editor said, acknowledging the applause. He started in again, "And you milked the paper for all it was worth, you made money on our reputations and now you're going to get punched out."

His friends pulled him away before he could take a swing, and they all watched the face of the despised columnist for a reaction as the creamy suds flowed down his designer tie and soaked shirt-front. But he stood there, wordless for once.

"At least you proved one thing, prickface," yelled the Washington editor. "Never trust a rich journalist."

Loud enough for the damp columnist to hear, the ex-Congressional correspondent (but everybody now was an ex-) said, "It took the last edition to tell off the fucking White House stooge—that's too high a price to pay for a small moment of truth."

"Be philosophical," said one of the editorial writers. "We won't have to run any more editorials from the big oil companies telling the world that the way to save the environment is to drill it full of holes."

"Yeah, it became necessary to destroy the town in order to save it, as the bird colonel told me at Ben Tre in the Nam," said the Pentagon correspondent. "Shed no tears for big oil, friend. They'll get their tales of woe across on the tube and a big fat credit as sponsors of British shows on the public television network. You've heard of the Petroleum Broadcasting Service, haven't you?" Then, swinging his glass like a conductor, he sang throatily,

> *Why does the front rank breathe so hard?*
> *Said Files-on-Parade,*
> *To turn you out, to turn you out,*
> *The color-sergeant said . . .*

and added, "Stick with Kipling, he'll never let the troops down . . .

> *And they're gonna hang us all*
> *In the morn-ing! in the morn-ing!"*

The Pentagon correspondent was the political affairs columnist's only known friend on the newspaper. Now he went up to the drenched writer, took his elbow, and they both shoved their way through the bar crowd and out of the place.

Marty Goldfarb, the lead writer on the old analysis section, inched forward to shake Linkum's hand, then turned to Licata, the authority on matters sexual in Manhattan journalistic annals.

"Look, Licata, I've been meaning to ask you and Mannie this for a long time—and tonight's the night." Goldfarb was standing next to his date, Dorothea Willow, the garden editor, who sipped her usual nonalcoholic Sprite.

"Did the biggest tool contest between the *Daily News* and the *Herald Tribune* ever really take place here?"

Miss Willow blushed.

"This may be too raunchy for your delicate little ears, Dorothea, so please excuse yourself and reserve us a table before they're all gone." After she left, Goldfarb said, "And I want confirmation, too."

31

Mannie said, "Not from me. I'm pledged to secrecy—confidential communication, priest to confessor, barfly to bartender. On pain of excommunication, my lips are sealed—and I'll deny the truth, too."

"It's the least you can do for an unemployed newspaperman on his last night out. I'll need something to keep my soul warm—even a story I can't print."

Licata grinned. "Okay, Marty. It so happened I was on the *Herald Trib* myself then, a kid reporter working the three-alarm business insurance fires and Saturday night knifings for a fast C-note a week. I'd do at least two phoners an edition, with laughs and a little vice squad action in between—"

Linkum interrupted, "You know, they used to say that the curse of the *News* was drink and the curse of the *Trib* was sex."

"Like most clichés, true," Licata said. "Well, after the bulldog edition came out and everyone was stealing stuff out of everyone else's stories—we had terrific rewrite men, you think those TV razor cuts would know how to handle a phoner?—a bunch of us would meet at Mannie's for a snort before going home. So late one night, while we're playing the match game for beers, the *News* city editor turns to the *Trib* city editor and says that he is ready to wager a large bet that nobody on the *Trib* has as big an instrument as one of their young printers."

Mannie and Linkum smiled, Goldfarb told Licata to go on.

"It so happened that the *Trib* at that time had a common pissoir where you couldn't take a leak in privacy. The management was never too generous in the plumbing department. There was a nice old gent who wrote the stamps column under a pseudonym, San Marino Liechtenstein, you could look it up, that was duller than the knives in this saloon. But he did have one unusual asset. In the philately game, he was known as the Terrible Tool. This was confirmed by reporters in the newsroom john. Well, the *Trib* city editor accepts the challenge and collects fives and tens and twenties from the guys on both papers—there must have been a grand riding on each man. The match was set for the next night after the closing hour at Mannie's. The city editor had a hard time persuading our tiger to make a public spectacle of himself, but he was told it was for the greater glory of the *Trib*—and his job was on the line. Only the two city editors were allowed to be present—except for Mannie."

"Me?" said the proprietor of Mannie's Place innocently. "I must have been off that night."

"Yeah, you probably had a bet down yourself. So we're all back in our newsrooms waiting for the result. A ten-spot meant something in those days. Here is this thirty-year-old printer, prime of life, going up against our seventy-five-year-old flyweight. He was a little guy otherwise—we didn't know if he could even get it up. Well, it's two in the morning and suddenly in walks San Marino, his pockets stuffed with two thousand bucks. Everyone starts slapping the little guy on the back and he's licking his chops and grinning. It must have been one of the finest moments in *Tribune* history— in the great tradition of Horace Greeley. Our city editor turns to San Marino and orders him to describe what happened—"

"This part," said Mannie, winking, "I never heard before."

"'Well,' says San Marino, 'this nice young lad from the *News* opens his fly, lays his instrument out neatly on the bar, and strokes himself into quite a respectable erection. He manages to work up to about an eight-inch salute, give or take, though a bit on the thinnish side. And I, gentlemen? I simply reached down, unwound the Terrible Tool and put out *only enough to win*.'"

Goldfarb punched Licata, spilling his drink. "For that cock and bull story, the next round is on yours truly."

"At least the *Trib* had the winning bull," Licata said. "All right, so you won't find it in the *Guiness Book of World Records,* but it happened right here at this bar."

"It couldn't have happened at our old paper," said Linkum.

"How do you figure that?" Goldfarb said.

"Because nobody high up there had the balls to resist the network take-over."

"What turned them into mice?"

"They had thirty pieces of silver where their well-knowns should have been."

Near the free lunch end of the bar, where dead meatballs had been soaking in ketchup, the head of the women's page copydesk stood, surrounded by feature writers he had broken in in more ways, if possible, than one. "You know what I'm going to miss the most? Saving you broads from double entendres. I remember when the millinery editor returned from Paris and the lead on her annual spring hat story went: 'Every girl looks good under a big black sailor.' That was before your time, most of you. She was out twice a week having matinees with one of the vice-presidents from Saks Fifth Avenue, and then would put in an overtime slip for working late. She was quite a number." One of the copypersons asked him if he had ever had what she called "sexual relations" with the millinery editor himself. "You mean, did we screw? I never talk about such matters in front of company." But, on this final night, they pressed him, and he said, "Okay, we did make it in the sack once, and don't listen if you find this X-rated, but we were laying there, ass-naked, and she was fooling around with the tip of my thing. Out of the blue, she looks down at it and says, 'You know, it does resemble a Poiret cloche.' Well, kiddies, you can imagine what happens next—it goes right down and I can't get it up again."

"That'll be the day," said the furniture columnist, whose colleagues called her "Bloomingdale's Basement" because she looked like an unmade bed.

"All right, it only happened once, and that one really didn't count. I couldn't blame myself—I never thought of my cock as research for the latest from Paris. She broke the mood and I resisted all future offers."

"Bragging again," said Bloomingdale's Basement.

"Cross my heart," he said. He reached for her glass and drained its wine.

"So the moral of the tale, kiddies, is: Never mix business with pleasure in the sack and never call a cock a cloche."

Linkum overheard the end of the story and joined in the laughter, not quite knowing why, not even knowing these lively people except as elevator faces; but he was glad that not everyone's tail was dragging, time enough later.

"You know what I'm going to miss most, Sam?" asked Martin Palewski, coming from behind and shaking Linkum's hand. "The perpetrators. The 'poips,' as the Brooklyn precinct boys called them."

"How you doing, Maxie? It's been too long."

The byline said Martin but he was Maxie to the editors and even that was an abbreviaton of a longer Polish name. When he had first hit the bricks as a police reporter in the district shacks, the paper wasn't wild about foreign-sounding bylines.

"The telex from police headquarters," Palewski said, "it was poetry, it was Dickensian. Used to read it with the first cup of coffee in the A.M. I took this morning's telex as a souvenir. I never realized how beautiful this stuff was, they invented a new grammar, sound of the city, O. Henry's Four Million plus, and now only television actors in wigs and greasepaint will be able to read the PD wire. Listen to these entries, my bread and butter:

THIRTY-SECOND PCT: HOMICIDE WITH NECK WOUNDS DOA AT SCENE MALE PERP IN HALLWAY APPREHENDED. SEVENTY-THIRD PCT: HOLDUP CHASE MANHATTAN BANK ONE MALE PERP ARMED SHOTGUN HURDLED TELLER COUNTER MADE OFF WITH UNDET AMT OF CASH NO SHOTS IN-JURIES OR ARRESTS VIA ALL KEYS BELLS. SIXTH PRECINCT: UNIDENTI-FIED MALE ARMED SAWEDOFF SHOTGUN ENTERED CITIBANK TOLD TELLER GIVE HIM FIFTIES AND HUNDREDS TELLER GAVE PERP APPROX $10,000 FLED NO SHOTS FIRED NO INJURIES ALL KEYS.

"It goes on like that, the homicides and bank robberies and bur-glaries and wife beatings. And this was just for starters, the real goods I got for the paper, I knew every precinct captain and how to read the blotters backwards and which deputy commissioners could be reached because they owed me one for keeping their names *out* of the paper."

Palewski's voice trailed off. Linkum put an arm around his shoul-der. Then one of the junior reporters Palewski had started to break in on the police beat took the old boy's elbow and steered him home.

"Perfect!" Licata said to Goldfarb. He was still working over the secretarial pool, floating back and forth between them and his former deskmates. "Tell Sam what you just told me about why some of the no-talent broads with their all-American overbites and long blonde hair got their jobs on the paper. Jesus, it's Ziggy Freud and Ann Landers rolled into one."

"It's not original with me—Dorothea Willow has to get a byline for figuring it out. I'm not talking about her, gents," Goldfarb said.

"She can put a story together better than most of us. No, it's something she discovered from talking to the girls in the locker room." He paused for effect. "You know what test the stock-option editors used for taking on new women reporters? Dorothea said: 'They hired the *shiksas* who looked like the girls who wouldn't date them at Subway College.'"

"Terrific," said Licata, laughing. "So that's how the fuckers got their rocks off."

"Not bad," said Linkum. "Anyway, the Breck shampoo reporters shouldn't have much trouble landing new jobs in videoland."

"Everybody's on the Titanic now," said Goldfarb. "The Titanic Broadcasting Corporation brings you the eleven o'clock news, after this word from the Jolly Green Giant. Doesn't matter if you were one of the jigglies or one of the jockstraps. If you were waiting for the corporation to kiss you, you were dreaming. These companies know how to screw—but not how to kiss."

"I won't have any excuse not to be home on time," Licata said. "You know, late-breaking story bullshit, got to stay on overnight. What the hell am I going to say now?"

"Custer died for your sins, Licata," said Linkum. "I'll still put my bets on you as the greatest matinee man in the history of the late newspaper."

"I take that as a compliment," said Licata, "so I won't blush and the next one is on me."

"You know what made Licata get laid more than he got slapped?" said Goldfarb, half-seriously, as if warming up to one of his news analysis leads pulling together military assistance to dictatorships on several continents into a coherent story.

"Tell me," Licata said, passing them fresh shots of Canadian Club. "This party is getting interesting again, my favorite subject, me and broads—how come this good stuff never got into print?"

"From my longtime study of your mating habits when you weren't turning in your pieces on time," Goldfarb said, "your success had to do with your remarkable tolerance. If one of the new fashion reporters had fat ankles, for example, your attitude was, *Mamma mia,* what a pair of ankles, how would you like them wrapped around you? And so to bed, with various other flaws in the anatomy never standing in your way. Your positive approach was admirable, and effective."

Licata held up his palms and said, "Thank you, thank you, no more applause, please. Jesus, I didn't know you gentlemen were watching me that closely. And now, if you all will excuse me, I'm working on that seasoned women's page writer. Never let it be said that I discriminated against someone who was overage in grade or rank. Experience counts, too."

They watched him shoulder his way to the women at the bar.

"An equal opportunity cocksman," said Goldfarb.

"Hello, Sam."

The voice belonged to her, throaty and a little cool, as he remembered it.

It hovered in the air behind his shoulder, calling up the grace notes of their past . . . as if nothing had intervened.

For an instant, he felt his heart pounding; and then he turned and saw her, her lips slightly parted, suggesting a smile. The light from the lamp in the ancient wall fixture burnished her cheeks and reflected a golden glow in her hazel eyes.

"Hello, Jennie."

He extended his hand, and then he looked at hers, remembering the veined elegance he admired and she deplored; and as their fingers touched, he held her hand for a moment of intimacy.

Goldfarb and another writer from the old analysis section moved away from them discreetly, aware of their former relationship. It had never been concealed; and, anyway, the big newsroom was a leaking sieve for any attempt at privacy.

"It's old home week at Mannie's Place," Linkum said, and immediately regretted that he had not thought of something more original. "I couldn't help showing up—to see some of the old crowd . . ."

Jennie Ives had her coat on, over one of her green open-throated blouses; she had always looked wonderful in green.

"Have you been here all evening? I was stuck in the bar, listening to all the tall tales, and I couldn't break away to get to the dining room. I thought—"

"I thought—"

They both laughed.

"I wondered if you were in town," he said.

"Just briefly—I'm about to go abroad on assignment."

"I heard that you were doing some pieces for National Public Radio."

"And one or two other places—the opinion and art magazines."

"I'd like to hear more about it. Dammit, I'm sorry I didn't break through the mob and get to you sooner. I guess you've already had dinner."

"I have, and it is getting late."

She started to walk toward the swinging doors.

Mannie stopped her and said, "Hey, how you two kids doing? Good to see you together. Been a while..."

"Good night, Mannie," she said. Nothing more.

Mannie looked puzzled. Linkum reached across the oak bar and shook Mannie's hand. "Drop in again, Sam," he said.

The crowd began to thin out, crossing the city's rivers to home.

He caught up with her outside. The air was cool.

"Are you here alone? I mean, with someone—"

"Yes and no. I'm here alone and I'm not here with anyone."

"You're being very accurate," he said. "As usual."

"Is there something wrong with that?"

"No, of course not, not at all."

Suddenly, they were measuring each other's meanings, adversaries distanced by words.

Once, their narrow world had been divided between outsiders and themselves. They could devastate someone beyond their circle on the paper with a wisecrack, even with nothing more than a gesture or a glance. Language, casual and critical, had been their bond; now it was a barrier. Their biggest word had been a small one... *us*. Then, like a star disappearing in the dawn, their world had winked out.

"You're still at your place in Gramercy Park?" He knew she lived there; it was a way to keep talking and walking with her.

"Until it turns into a cooperative. How about you?"

"I've still got the same studio near the U.N. building. Room with view, overlooking Pepsi-Cola sign."

It began to drizzle as they moved along the edge of Union Square, avoiding the shadows in the center of the city. She looked at her watch, but he was in no hurry.

"If you want, I can try to hail a cab," he said. "You were always better at spotting them—"

"Stealing them, you mean," she said, half-smiling. "Lousy time to get one."

Three fat Checkers passed by with the usual signs reading "On Radio Call" and "Off Duty." The other cabs were occupied, and they continued to walk in the rain. He touched her elbow lightly at the street crossings, waiting for a signal of warmth, for her to take his arm.

"Licata was funny tonight—dirty-funny," he said.

"What brilliant remark did he make about his favorite subject?"

"One of his old favorites: 'A cock has no conscience.' Used it to titillate the young things, trying to get a rise out of them."

"That's not original with him—and those young women can spot his line a mile away. Someone said there was a fistfight—"

"Better than that—the Washington editor threw a beer in the face of the White House true believer columnist."

"Now that's more like it. That's one I'd like to see on instant replay. What's the job scene like—any of our friends land on their feet?"

"Where are they going to go? If you're from the networks, you can always bounce from one to the next but there aren't many choices left in these one-newspaper towns."

"Maybe it all comes down to the tube, and we didn't realize it—"

"Or wouldn't admit it."

"There's one thing I've learned in my years as a newspaper-woman."

"A lot more than one—but which do you have in mind?"

"That newspapermen are as dumb as anyone else in any other

business who feel superior because of their company."

"Another true believer has been heard from," he said.

He was glad that they had not caught a cab.

He hooked his arm into hers as they crossed the two-way traffic on Park Avenue South.

"Well, Ives," he said, "I assume you mean to include newspaperwomen, too. But never mind. How do you like the newspaper game—if I may call it that? Do you have some philosophical statement to make for the cameras?"

"Sure—if you'll give me a moment to apply my pancake makeup." She paused. "The newspaper business is the last Children's Crusade."

They had arrived in front of her old limestone building.

Standing outside, he looked up at the bowed windows. On warm evenings, she would throw open the louvered shutters and they would stand there, arms entwined around their waists, staring at the skyline, the twinkling sparkle of the towers. Dimming the lights, they would deliberately slow themselves, prolonging the anticipation, and then begin to unfasten each other's underclothes, laughing as the last button and hook always got stuck in their fingers, and then they pressed their swollen flesh together, unable to hold back any longer...

And now, he could not bring himself to reach out and touch her, as if it would be an intrusion. The passage of time had brought shyness, building an unseen wall between them. Still, he wanted to be near her a little longer.

Linkum said, "Did you see the Dragon Lady?"

"No—did she really show up at Mannie's? She's shameless—I thought she'd be in hiding."

"Criminal always returns to scene of crime. Gutsy of her, in a sort of way. At least the stock-option editors didn't—they were too busy doing their number with the network undertakers at the newspaper. They've been offered positions as flacks and speechwriters with the network PR department."

"Serves them right. What did Jane Twining Delafield have to say?"

"She's moving into another branch of the leisure-time division.

Video games. You want to write tech pamphlets on how to win in interplanetary warfare? You got it.".

"I don't think I'm ready for the big time yet. I couldn't bring myself to write . . . neutral words."

Neutral words.

The phrase was one of the reasons why first Sam Linkum and later Jennie Ives had quit working for the newspaper, months before the network had decided to shut it down. The editors running the show for the network had said that too much opinion was creeping into news stories, that newspapermen and women tended to take a liberal stance, and that hereafter they would have to find "neutral words" in the name of objectivity.

As calmly as he could, Linkum had asked the top editors to tell him which words and ideas were prohibited under the new network rules. But they declined to spell out what they meant, saying that it was up to every reporter and subeditor to know for himself when his stuff was sinfully subjective.

He knew that the very act of inquiring would be considered hostile so, as a parting shot, Linkum said, "I'll define what I think you mean by objectivity: If you're writing the anti-Auschwitz side of story, then you're supposed to balance it with the *pro*-Auschwitz side, right?"

They blew their cool; when word got around he was a twenty-four-hour hero in the newsroom and his definition turned up in the press columns of *Newsweek* and *Time;* and then he walked out. Before he was thrown out.

"It wouldn't really have made a difference if we had kept quiet at the time," Jennie said. "They only wanted their clones around — the neuters of neutral words."

"Well, the clones are out now, too. They thought the network gave time off for good behavior and they're going to have a lot of time to think that over. Life evens itself out. At least we knew we were riding off without a horse under us. It's the last of the ninth, two out, and no designated hitter around to save the game and the paper."

"You're mixing your metaphors, sir," Jennie said, smiling. "Better stick with the neutral words."

She looked at her watch again.

"I've got packing to do. It's been good seeing you, Sam, but I'm off to *bella Roma* in the morning—"

Suddenly, he said, "Where does that leave us?"

Jennie looked at him, said nothing for a moment.

"Does it matter?"

"It still does—to me."

"Let's leave it this way," she said. "You always want to punctuate everything, Sam."

"I never thought about our relationship as a grammar lesson."

"Well, not everything, or everyone, has to be punctuated."

She leaned over and brushed her lips against his cheek, quickly . . . as if they were only automatic friends.

Jennie turned the keys in the doorway's double locks.

"Where are we now?" he said, more to himself. It was her advantage, somehow; parting, without invitation.

In her voice that he loved when she lowered it, her smoky voice, Jennie said, "How about calling it the semicolon stage?"

"Okay," Sam said. "As long as it's not a full stop."

She smiled, and waved from the other side of the opaque door.

Linkum started walking in the direction of his apartment, toward the East River, wanting to clear his head of the night's thoughts and booze. Across the seasons he had learned to handle almost any story in any corner of the world: the rise and demise of dictatorships, the frailty of monarchs and superficiality of presidents, the insolence of office and corruption in corporate suites, the companionship of combat and long grief of war; not being fooled *too* often, distrusting the high and mighty. That took a sort of arrogance, he realized.

Lately, he had traveled in small rhomboids: the office, the newspaper hangouts, the theater, the studio apartment, all within walking distance of each other, the uneven geometry of his life. And then his familiar routine went flying apart.

Okay, Jennie, no punctuation marks on the psyche.

Instead of heading home, he reversed course and instinctively wandered toward the newspaper plant where the presses were spinning out the final edition. The anonymous midnight men, in their folded paper caps, were bundling up the sections and sending them away. He stood across the street and noticed that others, in the doorways, had also been drawn to the death watch. Nobody wanted to be observed; it was a private experience, not to be shared, a shadowed night with no sunrise. Now came the chaotic miracle moment when it all fell together, the dispatches from the foreign outposts, the phoned pieces from stringers in unheard-of towns in the American boondocks, the police precincts describing the misbehavior of alleged perpetrators in the great metropolis, the reviews by critics passing instant judgment on long-term creativity, and the signals bouncing off the communications satellites for the last regional editions.

The street seemed to rumble beneath his feet. Far below, the presses groaned and screamed, speeding up production, and then it was all over, human voices could be heard again, and the trucks bearing boastful slogans about the newspaper sped away down the choked street and onto the long, potholed avenues, spreading out across the city, catching the country's trains and planes, recording one spin of the earth: disasters for breakfast, laced with the lifestyles of celebrities, twenty-four hours around the sun.

One habit remained. Linkum glanced up at the ornate tower clock above the entranceway to the newspaper. Its black old-fashioned Roman numerals and intricately carved hour and minute hands glowed against the illuminated pale green glass. You could see it a block away. The clock was driven by weights, hung from an endless roller chain, and its striking and chiming mechanism tolled on the half-hour and hour—a lordly carillonneur above the concrete.

After the American Civil War the newspaper's first editor had ordered it built in England. It had been scaled down by the same designers who had erected the great clock at Westminster overlooking the Thames, only with a visible pendulum and escapement for fascinated spectators. Then it was shipped across the Atlantic to compete for attention against a dozen morning and evening publications crowded along Newspaper Row. On the journey uptown from lower Manhattan, the timepiece had been moved twice as the paper expanded. Early in the new century the clockworks had been electrified; but its face was still polished with beeswax by hand several times a year as a protection against the city's grime. It remained a symbol: of the paper's long-held love of things British, and of its own independent traditions.

Sam Linkum checked his wristwatch against the great outdoor clock for the last time. He was only a minute slow. Or maybe a lifetime.

CHAPTER TWO

The Pentagon Calls

THE telephone on his bedside table rang insistently for a fourth time and he thought it must be a wrong number because it seemed to be the middle of the night, his mind was still glazed by the good whiskey from Dublin and the good beer from Denmark, but when he finally lifted the receiver on the seventh ring a familiar voice on the cheerful end of the line said, "It's 0700 hours—drop your cocks and grab your socks!"

Linkum replied sleepily, "If this is World War Three calling, tell them I'm not in and to wake me when it's over—this is a recorded message."

And he hung up.

After a few minutes, the phone rang again.

Linkum shook the night and the pillows out of his head, picked up the receiver and said, "Hello, Hap, can't you take a hint? It's only seven bloody o'clock. Has the Pentagon been bombed or are you?"

"Correction, it's now 0710 hours and counting. How the hell did you know it was your old asshole buddy, Sam?"

"Because I could smell that Romeo y Julieta you're smoking all the way up the line from Washington."

"Correction again, but pretty close. It's a Montecristo this time, but it's from Havana, all right. You must have picked up a few things from hanging around with me in intelligence. You're not as dumb as I think you are."

"What the hell are you calling me about at this ungodly hour? Why aren't you turning around some Russian diplomat or destabilizing some democratic government in Central America or whatever you're up to in Air Force intelligence, mischief division, these days?"

"Sam, who killed Cock Robin?"

Linkum sat up in bed, puzzled. "Is that some sort of code? If it is, I'm slow on the uptake—"

"No, nothing like that, Sam. This time I'm talking about your racket, not mine. I pick up the New York and Washington papers at the drugstore in the Pentagon basement and it says that your old rag is finished, final edition, kaput. The Washington *Post* story seemed to have more of the inside doings—"

"Hap, you're not calling out of plain curiosity, are you? I think we know each other too well to play games before the first drink in the morning."

"It's personal *and* professional. I'm damn interested in what's going to happen to you next, old friend—somehow, I always thought the network would come to its senses, keep hands off and let someone like you run the paper. Professional? Yeah, for reasons I'll tell you about face to face. This is the last phone call I'll make to you in the clear. I can tell you it's urgent. For my business, Sam, which you know a little about. I need you, and maybe you need me even more so this time—for your *own* sake. What time can you get here this morning?"

"Today?"

"There's a Lear jet at Butler Aviation waiting to fly you to Andrews Air Force Base. No markings on it—it's part of my private fleet. Don't bother looking for the departure time on that chalk blackboard. *You* will be spotted the moment your taxi pulls up past the main entrance to La Guardia at the old Butler building. The pilot will be wearing a three-piece suit. The vest is bulletproofed. Try the one he offers you for size—always like to see my boys well dressed."

"I can't make it this morning, Hap."

"And why not?"

"Because I've got a long-standing appointment with my periodontist—"

"For God's sake, do you want to save your country or your goddamn gums?"

"My goddamn gums!"

They both broke out in laughter.

"If it's really that urgent, I could probably get to Butler at noon and still keep my ten o'clock appointment. But I can't promise to be bright-eyed and bushy-tailed—"

"Okay, Sam, but don't blame me if Castro invades Miami Beach while you're at the dentist. Take along an overnight bag—you can stay with me at the farm in Maryland. In the meantime, I want you to think about why the paper was killed—I have my reasons. Who killed Cock Robin?"

"Not I, said the sparrow. It was the powers that be."

"I'm serious. Bring along any documents about what was going on between the paper and the network *electronically*—I'm particularly interested in that aspect . . . the use of the big bird."

"Cock Robin again?"

"No, chum, the *real* bird—the communications satellite."

"Oh. That new Emperor's Nightingale."

"I'm not kidding, Sam. The documents, interoffice memos, tech manuals, policy papers, anything you've laid your hands on. I know you're like me, a pack rat. It could all be useful background stuff. For something that you may be interested in . . ."

Linkum hesitated, thinking of his last experience with Hap at the

Pentagon. He could still taste the bitter ashes. Neither said anything for a moment; knowing why the line was silent. Then Linkum said:

"How about if I bring a copy of the First Amendment?"

That autumn, a terrible thought invaded the mind of Sam Linkum. He began to believe that his words no longer could move mountains.

Oh, he knew most of the tricks of his craft: how to throw the curves and change-ups in the English language, bunt or hit the long ball, even how to tip his cap afterward in pretend-modesty. These came quickly enough—almost *too* easily.

But in the new pacification programs imposed on the network-dominated newsrooms, he constantly heard the echoes of the Vietnam era Presidents and generals: Grab them by the nuts and their hearts and minds will follow. Poll them and rate them and give them what they want. You better believe it; but he never could.

A different dream remained fixed in his memory: that the tidings from the fields of action, defiantly pursued and artfully arranged, could somehow right an injustice, end a wrong war a second sooner, keep the flame of a lost cause crackling.

Linkum realized that there was a degree of self-deception in that dream. You could overstep the line of a crusade and become a poseur with self-important paragraphs; become like *them*. Yet without the undying hope that words still counted, there was nothing. Now even that almost-ordinary dream had been pierced in the heart.

In a strange way, the call from the Pentagon came at a vulnerable, dangerous moment in Linkum's life.

He entered the Pentagon's outer ring on the Arlington side. The moment he mentioned his name, a plastic clip-on ID badge was handed to him. His photograph was already encased in it. Unescorted, he remembered the maze: first up, then around the second ring, down the long corridor with the wild blue yonder photographs of the bombers and interceptors in flight, Cobras and Hornets and Eagles and Blackhawks and Tigers and Tomcats; their names evoked the denizens of a zoo, not the machinery of a killing business. At the far end, above the chief of staff's offices, a gold-painted slogan was emblazoned: PEACE IS OUR PROFESSION.

Linkum stopped in front of the first office to the right of the chief of staff. Room 3224-AF. There was no identifying sign but he remembered the number. A bird-colonel and a leaf-colonel sat in the outer office typing personal letters. As Linkum entered, they snapped to attention, covering their asses in case he was somebody. Between the paunchy field-grade officers, the flirting and the endless coffee breaks, Linkum always felt reassured that war was unthinkable here.

"Greetings, chum."

"Hello, Hap."

Henry H. (Hap) Chorley, civilian director of the United States Air Force Security Service, all six-foot-five, two hundred and forty pounds of him, rose from behind his souvenir-strewn mahogany desk and embraced Linkum in a bear hug. Without bothering to introduce him to the colonels, Chorley ushered Linkum into his private office and closed the door.

"Time-serving fuck-ups," Chorley muttered. "Twenty years in and then they begin double-dipping on pension after they get jobs with Rockwell International or Boeing."

"Thanks for the buggy ride on your shuttle service. And for the bulletproof vest. Didn't have to use it."

Linkum began to remove the vest but Chorley touched his arm.

"It's all yours, Sam. Lambswool on the outside—it can go with your best set of threads and nobody'll notice. You might find it useful some day. It'll stop anything up to a nine-millimeter Luger. After that you're on your own. Consider it a present from your old asshole buddy."

"I see you're up to your old tricks, Hap."

"We don't do dirty tricks here."

"No, *ordinary* tricks."

Hap looked puzzled. "What do you have in mind?"

"This thing," Linkum said, pointing to his phtograph on the ID badge.

"Oh, that," Chorley said. "I thought you'd like seeing your mug shot when you walked into the Pentagon. A way to greet you in proper style—your own picture instead of just an ordinary visitor's pass. If you wear that fancy badge, you can buy your favorite Irish whiskey at the PX at half-price or—"

"I'd rather pay full price and not have my mug and a fat dossier in the government files."

Chorley raised his hands. "Come on, Sam, you know it's just an old shot that we made last year when you took on that little job for me."

Linkum shook his head but kept quiet.

"It was an honorable assignment, Sam."

"I'd rather not talk about it now—we've both had our say about that. Honorable or questionable, it's a closed chapter for me."

"Sure, Sam, whatever you want. That isn't why I broke your hump to get down here so quick. There's something else I had in mind."

"So I thought. I didn't think this was just a reunion."

Linkum respected Chorley; they went back. At his own insistence Chorley was the only civilian intelligence chief commanding one of the Defense Department's services. As director of USAFSS he was entitled to a lieutenant general's rank, equal to his opposite numbers in ASA (Army Security Agency) and NSG (Navy Security Group). The three intelligence chiefs dominated the National Security Agency within the Pentagon, swung their weight in the White House and were respected in the Senate. The Central Intelligence Agency had the glamor boys who made their payoffs to bush-league dictators and played games on paper; but NSA owned the real resources—the machinery of the armed forces, the advisers in every embassy, the covert and visible weapons, the counterintelligence stations and, above all, the message and monitoring satellites circling the globe.

"Let the CIA take the credit," Chorley said. "Because with it comes attention. I'd rather work behind the scenes in our own way. We've got the resources and the specialists—we're *operational.*"

"And you still don't want to wear your equivalent of three stars?"

"Nope, I outrank them all—I'm a *civilian*. They know I can tell them to go to hell and walk out any time I want to. When I sit down with the intelligence chiefs I don't salute and they know it. I came back to the Pentagon—on my terms."

"But why did you sign up with this funnyhouse, Hap? I thought you enjoyed your math research at M.I.T., and you'd end up in a nice comfortable endowed chair."

"For the same reason I could never get you to join me here as an intelligence reservist—*belief*. Remember President Eisenhower's parting shot warning against the military-industrial complex? Well, I thought I could fight the military overkill in the country better from the inside. Maybe you thought you could do it better from the outside, as a journalist. I didn't want to wind up on campus just talking professor talk. That's why I decided to come here after the Vietnam War—I believed the career boys in charge and the White House security advisers blew it. They thought they could win the war with B-52s and a dose of Agent Orange medicine over the rice fields and a slide rule computing the body count on the electronic battlefield. Sensors don't bleed—but a lot of grunts did. They left out the people equation—the lessons of our experience, yours and mine, when we were in counterintelligence during the Good War."

The Good War, World War II: one they believed in. As young officers they had worked side by side in the djebels and wadis of North Africa, on liaison duty with the French *Deuxième Bureau* and the Sixth Regiment, Algerian Spahis; moved across the Mediterranean to the unnamed, numbered hills of Sicily and Italy, recovering art treasures stolen by the Fascists and Nazis; had affairs with the same Red Cross girls and contessas, and then had gone their separate ways, Chorley to the university, Linkum to the newspaper. To second and third lives...

Linkum walked over to the tall double windows and looked through the iron-barred view facing the Potomac. He picked up Hap Chorley's field glasses that always rested on the seat-bench, focused them and watched the classic landmarks and profiles of Washington swim into sight in the distance.

"Beautiful view. Is there one for the enlisted men?"

The line still delighted Chorley. It was the caption on one of their favorite cartoons by Bill Mauldin, showing two pompous young American officers studying an Alpine sunset in southern France; and they tried to recall some of the other Mauldin drawings that revealed the human, antimilitary side of their war in the Mediterranean Theater.

Until Linkum said to Chorley, "Okay, *che cosa?*"

"*Capitano!*" Chorley replied, lapsing into their army Italian with its *mezzogiorno* flourish.

"Sam, before I tell you what gives, it's damn good to see you again, gums and all. You bring back the fun times, old cock. Look, worse comes to worse and you turn me down, at least you'll wind up smoking one of my heaters and carrying a few back to New York for later."

He handed Linkum a couple of Montecristo Number 3s from a cedar humidor. "*Habana*. Fidel's best. From my Cuban connection. *No,* put that butane lighter away, the gas clashes with the aroma. Here..." He lit their cigars with two wooden matches, letting the tip of the flame lick the tobacco. Then he settled back in his deep leather chair and blew two smoke rings, watching them perform half-Immelmanns in the blue-gray clouds over his Pentagon desk. He closed his eyes.

"You look as if you've just been eaten alive by the centerfold bunny of the month," Linkum said, and Chorley replied from his reverie, "Well, it's more like post-coital *tristesse,* so relax and enjoy it." He paused. "You know, I once knew a woman, Ph.D., University of Chicago, sort of half in love with her until she wanted to get married, who I cherished all the more because she once told me that she wanted to be buried, when her time came, in a black lace negligee. When I go, Sam, I want to take along a box of long Churchills, natural leaf, with one stuck in my mush."

They puffed away, aware that they were delaying the reason why Chorley had rushed Linkum to the Pentagon, but wanting to catch up. They waved their Montecristos like wands, mocking themselves, close enough friends from a hundred experiences to be able to kid each other.

Chorley looked at his chronometer. It had two faces that simultaneously told the time in Washington and western Europe. American time; enemy and allied time.

"All right, you've got one hundred twenty seconds to tell me what the hell happened to your old newspaper before we get down to business. Believe me, it's relevant. There's a real link now between your racket and mine. The thing you call the Emperor's Nightingale has brought military intelligence and newspaper intelligence together—"

"Too bad."

"I mean the whole field of communications—not just papers but radio and television and banking and oil and all the information that's carried around the world by the satellites for the international cartels."

"Is my time up yet?"

"I'm sorry, chum—go ahead."

"Okay, Hap, I'll let you have it in shorthand. One of the Harvard M.B.A.s who studied the paper just before the network took it over admitted that it would lead to an updated version of Gresham's law—a debasement of the news currency. When he had three martinis straight up, he put it bluntly: news doesn't *sell*."

"Meaning what?"

"Oh, that the network applied its numbers game to the paper and tried to get some of the same stuff in print that it put on the air. They replaced the news analysis section with the lifestyles section, they had all the old pros covering parties in the plush restaurants instead of politics and the government agencies. Eventually the reading public didn't see any difference between what the paper and the telly had to offer."

"I was under the impression that once they had a monopoly—"

"So were they, and the other networks started to shop around for papers, too. It worked for a while, circulation went up, the shit floated. That's when some of us who resisted were fired or forced to quit. It didn't take too long before the readers got wise. The moment the profits began to take a slide and the advertisers turned to the tube, the network's guillotine descended and the newspaper's head fell into the basket."

Chorley nodded, relit his cigar and put his size twelves up on the desk, next to the cut-down seventy-five millimeter shell that served as his ashtray. He stared at Linkum for a moment, holding back his thoughts, searching for words.

"Sam, let me ask you something personal—but don't take it personally. I have a professional reason—so no offense. Are you *respected* by your colleagues?"

Linkum shrugged. "Nobody's ever asked me *that* before, thank God." He hesitated. "Respected? Feared? Looked up to? You never know if you're in a position of authority. That doesn't help you very much. Okay, I'll guess. Respected, maybe; loved, by a few people I've brought along..."

"That's what I wanted to hear. Even though you walked out before the network shot down the paper?"

"If anything, I'd guess because I walked out. They gave me a party and said that I acted on principle and was their conscience. That was flowery crap, but I admit I was flattered. At an informal farewell last night at the old newspaper hangout when everybody got a little drunk, I at least seemed to be accepted as a fellow rebel, one of the boys."

"What about overseas? In the European and third world? Do you have some standing in those places?"

"Well, I've met foreign journalists here and there over the years. And my stuff was printed in the British press and syndicated in some of the papers in the third world, I'd see clippings now and then, but no big deal. I think my name might ring a bell but it wouldn't set off any alarms."

Chorley said, "That checks out with my impression," and Linkum said suspiciously, "Have you been doing your checking number again, Hap?" and Chorley said, "Come off it, I only heard about your paper's final edition by reading it this morning in the Washington *Post*. I'm fast, but not *that* fast. I've got your number without having to check you out, chum. And you've probably got mine by now, too."

Linkum said, "Okay, I'm listening...but first let me ask you a question, Hap. Are *you* respected by your Pentagon friends?"

"Touché."

Both men smiled. Chorley added, "Hell, I hope not—I prefer to keep my distance from some of the characters around here. I don't pass out friendships too easily, not that I can in this line of work."

The USAFSS director got out of his chair and walked to the tall windows and peered through the field glasses, toward Washington.

"Here's the gen, Sam."

Chorley turned and faced Linkum, a rare frown furrowing his brow. "There's an intelligence war going on twenty-two thousand plus miles up in space, out of sight and therefore concealed. A vital part of it is about to be joined right here on earth in the open between ordinary diplomatic types, not Star Trek invaders. A few weeks from now there's going to be a world information meeting in Algiers. It's sponsored by the U.N. International Information Agency. Sounds very lofty, but it's full of booby traps. Number one, there's a resolution the third worlders are trying to push through to license Western journalists—meaning censorship. *It's got to be stopped.* My concern is selfish. If it sneaks through, my intelligence people on the scene won't be half as effective. Some of my best sources are living in those sensitive countries and they'd be given the thumbscrews more than ever—probably be a crime to talk to western newsmen. Number two, the satellites. Messages in and out of half the world would be controlled through licensing, too. You've been out of our old racket for a long time so you can't imagine how these roving eyes have changed the nature of intelligence. Every time those satellites pass overhead, my computers track them, monitor them and decode them—those belonging to some of our shaky allies as well as the other side's. Which brings me to Number three, the Russkies. If the licensing resolution is okayed in Algiers, it's red meat for them because they've got better lines into those countries than I have. You know, Sam, nobody's waving a banner for Tom Jefferson in Africa, Asia or anywhere else on the map. The Russkies have pockets of hard-core believers who are willing to risk for them ideologically. Marxists in the universities, anarchists who talk like theologians and plain old opportunists who go where the money goes and the arms are for sale. So the KGB operatives in the Fifth Directorate in Dzerzhinsky Square remain in the background and pick up the pieces. I could give you Numbers four and five in detail, but instead I'll just mention them—both sides rely mainly on ELINT, electronic intelligence, and the laser weapons both of us have in the works are hooked into the satellite systems. I have to keep them away from our ground stations. So it comes full circle back to that licensing resolution and what it means to me—and you."

"Whatever happened to invisible ink, microdots, garroting and the rest of the family arsenal? All those nice tricks of the trade we once learned in training—are they obsolete or in orbit, too?"

"Oh, I think I could still rustle up a nice wire garrot for you from the dirty tricks section but that's not my game. I'm interested in the big stuff, the high-level threat."

"You've got that much riding on the Algiers meeting and how those votes line up?"

"More than I can reveal to you—so far." Chorley paused. "Which is why I want Sam Linkum there as the delegate representing the United States."

Linkum stiffened. "Just like that."

"Yes—just like that. You're the ideal person for the job. If you'll pardon the expression, you're *respected*. You'll be among journalists and can speak their lingo. Many of the delegates are from Mickey Mouse countries who don't know shit from Shinola about news except that it has to come out favorably for the regime. They speak for whatever government prick happens to be in office: the colonel-of-the-month club. With information chiefs in uniform and censors watching too-inquisitive reporters from the American and Western press." He stood up. "Do you want to know another reason why Sam Linkum isn't just an ideal delegate but the *only* one who can try to tip the scales to our side? Because Moussi Ali is going to be there."

Linkum looked puzzled. "Moussi, the young guy we nicknamed Moose? Our old liaison friend from the *Sixième Régiment, Spahis Algérien?*"

"The same. He's now a columnist for *El Moudjahid*, the main French-language daily in Algiers. Nonpolitical and literary stuff—that's how he's survived the twists and turns. I haven't had direct contact with him but some of my people inside a friendly embassy confirmed that he'll represent Algeria at the big meeting. Right in his own backyard. Before then, he'll attend a preliminary cultural warm-up at the Mediterranean-American Foundation on Lake Como. The Mediterranean-American Development Corporation has its own private reasons for sponsoring the junket—to make friends and influence votes. Of course, it's hardship duty—you'd have to go to Italy for several days and sit on your keester at the lakeside villa. It would be a good way to renew old times with Moussi Ali and see which way the wind is blowing. It shouldn't be too hard for you to pretend that you're cultured, chum. You can always fake it—"

Linkum fingered Chorley with the cuckold's horns. "That'll cost you another Montecristo." Chorley reached into his humidor and pitched one.

"By the way, Hap, are you running the U.N. or the State Department these days? Since when does the director of Air Force Security Services decide who the American delegate should be? Wouldn't that look a little fishy?"

"Don't worry, your appointment wouldn't come through me. It will all be done properly through the right United States Mission to the United Nations channels."

"And you can name the delegate?"

"Sam, I don't want to sound immodest, but I've got my lines into places way beyond the Pentagon. I think I proved that to you once before. You didn't really believe that I could plant operatives in your old newspaper, remember?"

Linkum remembered; Chorley had picked up the phone once in his presence, dialed a private number in the office of the network chairman, and heard him "request" that certain names be dropped from the bottom-line cut list prepared by Jane Twining Delafield...and the "request" was honored.

"No, Sam, that's only a detail. My problem is to convince *you* that what you're doing would square with your own beliefs about the press. You're the one who made the joke this morning about bringing me a copy of the First Amendment."

Linkum smiled. "What's your angle, Hap? You've talked about my business—what's *yours?* You didn't fly me down here so that we could recite our paternosters together—"

"Correct. It's one for you and one for me. I'm glad you're asking me to show my hole card. My angle isn't to save the integrity of reporting, though much to your surprise and maybe mine I'm concerned about that, too. Sam, my interest is saving my intelligence network, making sure that the big birds and ground stations are functioning. I want to know what the Russkies are up to. I want to know what certain of our esteemed NATO allies are up to. I want to know what the A-rabs are up to. What happens at that Algiers conference—how the votes go on a few key resolutions—can help me or throw a monkey wrench into my machinery."

"Star wars?" Linkum said, his skepticism showing.

"I'm not talking Buck Rogers, but by next year the Russkies may be able to deploy laser weapons into space that could cripple my communications. They could orbit a manned space complex that would be capable of attacking ground, sea and air targets by 1990 or before. But right now it's my intelligence network that's at stake. Unless I have my eyes and ears up there, I'm light years behind them. But this isn't just a Soviet-Americanski confrontation scenario—that's always an easy out to justify things nowadays. In a peculiar way, we've got a modus vivendi going with the Russkies in satellite country. Satellites pass each other, tip their helmets politely and lower their spears. It's a helluva lot better than the who-blinks-first scenario in the unreal world on earth. No, the Russkies aren't the *immediate* threat. There are other forces at work, more dangerous, more uncontrollable—"

"Is that why you called me down here, Hap? You're sure trickling this out—"

"Okay, my electronic intelligence boys have picked up something that would blow me out of the water or, rather, out of the skies. Make for chaos in the transatlantic world, civilian and military. I can't give you details unless I know you're in with me—"

"I'm not, Hap. I can't see the relationship between the U.N. conference on news and censorship and your birds and ground stations."

"You will, Sam." Chorley sounded confident. "You will when I fill in a few additional facts."

The USAFSS director glanced at his chronometer, snapped his fingers impatiently. "Grab your overnight—you'll be staying with me at the Maryland farm later. But first I've got something I want you to observe. It's ordinarily out of bounds to unauthorized personnel, except for a few technical dragomen, and the list is very short of even those who are authorized to see what you're about to. If you decide not to come in with me on the new assignment, you can forget that you ever saw it—"

"Is this a not so subtle form of pressure, Hap?"

"Who says I'm subtle? Actually, Sam, most people working in this building, uniform or civilian, don't know this place exists. So, either way, you just weren't there and never heard of it." He looked at his chronometer. "We've got fourteen minutes and counting. What time you got?"

Linkum replied that he was sixty seconds slow.

They descended to the first ring of the Pentagon, circumnavigated the ramps to the basement floor and crossed under a bridge walk adjacent to a helicopter pad, where a VIP chopper could be lowered below ground and hidden. Next to the hangar's exit was a green door. Chorley inserted a notched aluminum card and opened the door's lock. They walked a hundred yards through a dimly lit tunnel and came to another green door guarded by two Marines and a police dog. Chorley pulled a tiny button from his pocket and passed it over a signal box; the right clicking sound was emitted for the next ten seconds. The marines saluted, without saying a word, and Chorley and Linkum walked past the restrained animal. "He's with me," Chorley said. A buzzer broke the stillness in the musty tunnel. The doors slid open, they ducked their heads, the doors slammed behind them.

They entered a brightly lit arena resembling a medical school's surgical operating room but miniaturized, with a circular bank of plush chairs elevated above the center of activity. Reflecting mirrors revealed three-dimensional screens, closed-circuit monitors and computers. They slid into the deep chairs overlooking a group of "dragomen," Hap Chorley's peculiar Middle Eastern term for these technical interpreters. Only four others were seated in the bank of spectator chairs—the army and navy intelligence chiefs and their aides. The chiefs nodded to Chorley from the other side of the room but no word of greeting passed between them.

Linkum looked up at the overhead clocks that showed the world's time zones against a flashing globe of the earth.

"Where the hell are we?" he whispered.

"Launch Control Center—Pentagon Green," Chorley said quietly. "We've got the ability to abort a mission right from here for intelligence reasons. And the power to watch seventy-seven million dollars go up in smoke." He touched the tops of two telephones built into the armrest of his chair. "This one leads to Mission Control, this one to the White House."

The digital clocks were labeled GMT—Greenwich Mean Time—and AMF—Apogee Motor Firing. Other clocks on the lighted globe showed the time at ground stations in Tanguá, Brazil; Zamengoe, Cameroon; and Carnarvon, Australia.

"We're counting," Chorley explained. "Putting up a two-hundred-pound bird, kicking it thirty miles out and into a geosynchronous orbit above the Atlantic, way the hell and gone, from a hundred and twenty-three miles to over twenty-two thousand miles. See that new light on the globe?" A signal was being sent from the ground station in Fucino, Italy, from technicians in direct contact with Intelsat, the communications satellite. "That's the final shakedown pass, our fail-safe point. It looks good. This bird went up two nights ago in the nose of an Atlas Centaur rocket. Now it's about to go into a transfer orbit. Mission Control is making the big maneuver in ninety seconds. Keep your eye on the AMF clock." Linkum watched the second hands jump. In the center of the arena the dragomen communicated with ground stations around the world. "If the rocket didn't fire at the right angle—if it was off by tenths of a degree—the orbit would be cockeyed and drift off into the space graveyard. The last thirty seconds will tell the story."

The minus-second hand reached zero. The mirrored images on the large screen in front of the spectators showed a magnified stylus, unwavering, and a vertical stream of graph paper unwinding. The tense bodies of the technicians suddenly relaxed under their headsets. The bird was flying on course. The stylus moved up the paper in a consistent, diagonal line—the signature of satellite success. They checked the status of the orbit as the satellite began to make its steady passes over the ground stations. The consoles and computers in the secret room began to process thousands of pieces of information signaled back from the satellite. They added up to exact placement in the scarred heavens. Linkum saw that it had gone well in the satisfied faces at Launch Control Center—Pentagon Green.

There were no cheers; no thumbs-up signs. Linkum had witnessed demonstrations of delight following space shots in the past; he wondered if the presence of cameras in public spectacles encouraged acting, if the glory of television altered the naturalness of an event. Now, in the privacy of the unreported Pentagon, there was no need to play games for the network evening news.

Nor were there introductions offered as the intelligence chiefs walked down the tunnel and peeled off to their separate service areas. Linkum remembered the unspoken rivalry from his last time in these corridors; the barely concealed jealousy that the generals and admirals held for the civilian director of USAFSS in their theoretically integrated National Security Agency. Rivalries within rivalries: the CIA vs. the NSA, the Security Adviser in the White House vs. the Security Branch in the State Department, and everybody trying to gain the ear of the President, their Commander in Chief, so eager to divert funds from social programs to fill the bottomless hole of the military.

Hap Chorley opened the green door from the inside with his aluminum key card, and they emerged like moles coming out of earth tunnels into the harsh afternoon sunlight, blinking.

"Are you impressed, chum?"

"Of course not—how could I be when my orders from you are that I saw nothing, was never here."

Chorley laughed. "Okay, I'm canceling your seat on the next launch to study the nude beaches on Mars."

"In that case I was impressed," Linkum said. "By the way, don't you speak to your intelligence buddies, or they to you?"

"They're not my buddies, they're my colleagues in uniform. As the Mafia puts it, they made their bones during the Vietnam War and they know I wasn't a fan of that little adventure. I preferred our learning experience with M.I.6 and the *Deuxième Bureau.*"

Chorley walked to the parking lot on the southern ring side of the Pentagon. Before opening the trunk of his ancient Bentley he ran his fingernail below the lock and removed a piece of invisible dental floss, then felt for a second piece on the driver's door. Linkum recognized the precautionary measure. Cars were inescapable, fat targets for planted explosives. Still, he wondered why Hap was taking no chances even in the Pentagon's VIP parking area. And why Hap was so up front about it, deliberately letting him know that the car was clean.

"Hop in," Chorley said, tossing Linkum's bag on the back seat. "I have a little surprise for you at the farm." He paused, waiting for a response. "There'll be three of us for dinner tonight."

Linkum said, "Let me guess — a new girl."

Chorley said, "You're close, but she's not a girl. She's a *woman.*"

"You've been educated by the feminists, I see."

"Not exactly. Don't forget I said it — she — would be a surprise. That's all you're getting now."

He pointed the Bentley toward the road that went past the Vietnam rows of crosses at the national cemetery and then across the Arlington Memorial Bridge. The afternoon traffic clogged the exits of the Pentagon. All the navy commanders and army and air force colonels were knocking off early and heading for the tax-free PXs and golf courses instead of taking a restful midday nap like their Commander in Chief in the White House. To avoid the outflow from the District, Chorley drove alongside the Potomac, crossed the Chain Bridge into Virginia, then recrossed farther west and picked up the River Road toward Maryland. The pin oaks and sycamores cast long shadows across the country road.

"Okay, you saw Pentagon Green, you may as well know more," Chorley said.

As they drove, Linkum relaxed in the cracked blue leather seat of the comfortable Bentley.

Chorley glanced at him. "No, I'm not twisting your arm. Whether or not you take on the Algiers assignment, this is stuff you ought to be familiar with as a journalist. The special bird you watched go into geosynchronous orbit belongs to my intelligence operation. Intelsat is a consortium of interests—the television people, the telephone people, certain cartel people and yours truly. I have a space detection and tracking system that can spot and classify every piece of hardware circling the earth. Ours, and theirs, too. Remember those sensors that could pick up the sounds of elephants screwing a hundred miles away on the Ho Chi Minh Trail in the Nam? Well, we can code and decode who's doing it to whom up there in the wizard altitudes. Of course I always have to keep in mind that the other side can use their birds exclusively for intelligence if they want to. I have to do a certain amount of sharing and fighting for circuitry. It's the price that has to be paid for having civilian control—"

"Don't forget you're a civilian, Hap," Linkum broke in.

"Yeah, but it doesn't always make it easier being a maverick," Chorley said. "This stuff can get damn competitive—you want to know details about our transponders, their Intersputnik, my electronic countermeasures?"

"Thanks, no. I get the picture—for now."

They continued driving in silence for a few minutes. Linkum recognized the turnoff from the macadam highway and then the winding, rutted dirt road. Along its edges barbed wire embroidered the old stone fences. They were only a mile or so from the hillside farm.

"One other thing," Chorley said softly. "I'll have to clue you in on the ground stations—"

"Those big mothers that bring in the wonderful world of commercials to your living room?"

"Not only, Sam. I'm aware of your feelings about the networks— especially after what happened to you. But I'm not just talking about television. In the Intelsat game we're all plugged together." He paused. "You and I have shared a couple of capers around the Mediterranean in our time. You know how to clam up—don't forget you were a spook before you were a journalist. Remember those telltale rubber stamps we used at Allied Force Headquarters when we worked with M.I.6 and were hiding papers from the French? No, it wasn't TOP SECRET then. It went: U.S. SECRET EQUALS BRITISH MOST SECRET..."

"I always liked the symmetry of that line, Hap."

"What I'm sharing with you is right up there with that classification. It's so sensitive I can't even tell the dum-dums in the White House because someone may leak to score brownie points with the Big Chief in the Oval Office."

The farmhouse was visible through a break in the trees. Chorley suddenly pulled over to the side of the road and shut off the motor. He looked at Linkum and said:

"ELINT has picked up information that certain third worlders— I won't tell you who or where, not until I have to—are plotting to blow up one of our key transatlantic ground stations..."

The four dynamiters squatted on the ground in the walled private garden overlooking the Corniche and the great port of Mers el Kebir west of Oran, nibbling roasted locusts from a wicker basket lined with oily newspaper. The carapace and wings of the locusts crunched in their mouths. They picked their teeth with plastic toothpicks.

The leader of the Algerian group, who called himself Tlemcen, wore a double-breasted striped suit, white shirt and no tie. Like his companions he had a two-day growth of hair on his face but his mustache had been trimmed. He opened a satchel and removed the tools of the dynamiter's trade: detonating cord, tetryl caps, safety fuses, flashlight batteries, a galvanometer. He did not open a second satchel that was locked with a diplomat's chain but explained that it held half-pound blocks of TNT for the thermite explosives. He took a box of condoms from his jacket pocket and rolled them carefully around the safety-fuse igniters, then knotted the ends of the rubber.

"Everything must be waterproof," Tlemcen said. "Even a single drop of water on the core of the time fuse or on the blasting cap can cause failure."

Tlemcen, Batna, Arzew, Tebessa—none were their real names.

As a security measure, they called each other by the names of their places of origin in Algeria.

"There is enough explosive material here for one operation against one satellite ground station. Which one will be determined by political events and by the opportunities available to ourselves and our loyal students in England, France and the United States. Events may dictate that we hold this material in one of our safe locations in the Oran region in case we have need for it during the U.N. meeting in Algiers."

The dynamiter called Tebessa asked if additional material could be obtained quickly to expand operations.

"Yes, but at a high price. This came from some of our followers working on the French pipeline south of Touggourt. It is prime quality—the Du Pont Corporation brand known as Tovex 220 dynamite together with Du Pont electric blasting caps. But we cannot depend only on stolen material because of the risks for our men. We must make our own explosives."

Tlemcen passed the others a typewritten list of instructions about the ingredients for straight-gelatin dynamites, ammonium nitrate, black powder, mercury fulminate and plastic explosives.

"These should be memorized and never found on your person because they are prima facie evidence," said Tlemcen, who held a law degree from the Sorbonne.

Now the lawyer turned to Arzew, who had served with a chemical warfare company in the French Army when it surrendered at Dien Bien Phu, and asked him about the most effective explosive for their planned operation against the earth stations.

Arzew pointed to the locked satchel. "The straight dynamites— they deliver a sudden, shattering effect. The ammonia dynamites produce a heaving instead of a shattering action. The gelatin dynamites do have a high strength and can unhinge the hard rock below the ground stations. But they also produce toxic fumes in a confined area that can cause deaths—"

"No, that is not our aim," Tlemcen interrupted. He was considered the politically sophisticated member of their cell. "Except for any traitors who betray our cause, we are not in the business of merely killing people. Remember, we are not butchers or so-called Moslem fanatics. This is not *jihad*—we are not engaged in holy war. Our Independent Moslem Brotherhood is made up of activists as well as true believers in the faith. We are like elite Janissaries, not assassins—"

"What is wrong with assassination?"

The dynamiter called Batna broke into the lawyer's speech. He had once led the anarchist student association at the university in Constantine and been jailed three years because of his unlicensed writings. "There are historic grounds for murder. An enemy can have a memory like a computer and know too much about our comings and goings—he must die. A man can be much hated and no one will weep for him—his death will save the lives of others. Assassination can be the only recourse for a great cause."

"It can also set back a cause," Tlemcen said brusquely. *"Vive la mort, vive la guerre, vive le sacré mercenaire.* We are not just a group of mercenaries looking for victims. This is a different battle. We fought with arms for our independence against the *colons* inside our country. Now we must do so again against the European and American *colons* invading our homes and lives from afar. We must protect the independence of our Arab and Berber brothers from the new colonialists. We do not want Marxists from the east or capitalists from the west destroying our way of life. Already the television programs sent directly from France, England and the United States have reached into our social and political affairs. That is what we must stop."

Batna said, "But which way will the wind blow at the U.N. meeting in Algiers? How can we overcome a hundred voices when we have none at the table?"

Tlemcen rose from the ground. He handed the satchel with the tools to Tebessa and held the satchel with the explosives for a moment. Then, without passing him the key, Tlemcen turned over the locked satchel to Arzew. "If the wind is blowing the wrong way in Algiers, if it looks as if the Americans and the other foreigners will be free to make their profits and impose their programs and news reporters on our country with no restraints, well then"—Tlemcen shrugged. "Then we shall strike them on their home grounds.

They will hear us speak loudly enough when the time comes in the only language they definitely understand—the language of our dynamite."

The four dynamiters shook hands and kissed each other's stubbled cheeks, then entered separate cars driven by bodyguards carrying Chasseur nine-millimeter semiautomatics stuck in their belts and took different routes down the serpentine roadways past tangled carob trees and Alepo pines, the Mediterranean in the distance, toward their everyday lives.

Hap Chorley turned on the Bentley's ignition again, listened to the purr of the engine, affectionately tapped the instrument panel in front of him.

"Inlaid walnut," he said. "I've always been a sucker for these old British touches. Somehow, whenever I'm in this ancient little toy of mine, I'm carried back, I'm a kid again. It's the Battle of Britain, all those daring young men going up in their flying machines, the Spitfires defending London against the Luftwaffe, the ack-ack banging away like crazy, and a Messerschmitt twisting downward in a ball of flame over the Thames." He closed his eyes for a moment. "She loves them, too. Maybe that's why we're in synch—"

"Who's *she?*"

"The woman who's cooking our dinner tonight, chum. The woman your old friend is engaged to. Helen Wyandanch—my girl, dame, broad, and I don't want to hear any wisecracks out of you."

"Hey, I'm too surprised to say anything. So you've finally been grounded."

"And if you want another surprise, she's part Indian, too."

"Indian Indian?"

"Nope, American Indian. Or as the current phrase has it, Native American."

"How—where—did you meet her?"

"In Santa Fe. We were both staying out of town at an inn that Willa Cather mentions in *Death Comes for the Archbishop*. See, I'm literate too. Anyway, there's a chapel on the property built by the real-life bishop. We both went inside carrying copies of the novel, looked up at each other and laughed. What the hell else was there to do? I was there holing up and she was at a meeting of amateur cryptanalysts—she's a math whiz. We began talking and clicked..."

"Whatever happened to all your nymphets, Hap? All those southern belles at the Pentagon with rolling haunches in high heels who had two names like Marybelle or Luluanne from Agnes Scott College that you used to charm into the sack?"

"I figured it was time for me to become a grown-up—at least in minor ways. You want another shocker? Helen is forty-nine, going on fifty next month. I told you she was a *woman*." Chorley's face reddened slightly, and for once he appeared shy.

"Now I've seen everything," Linkum said. "It must be love, Hap. You're blushing."

"Anyway, I've got a few years on her. It's all systems go, for both of us, but nobody's counting."

"If I hear you right, congratulations—I never doubted that you could still put it into orbit."

"I'm glad that you're the first one of my friends to meet her. We can discuss our business—my proposition—in private after dinner."

Helen Wyandanch was standing on the porch of the antebellum farmhouse waiting for them as the Bentley pulled up. Linkum almost immediately sensed her warmth: something about the way she looked directly at you, listening as if what you were saying was really interesting when you knew otherwise. She was trim and tall, close to six feet but somehow just right for the huge Chorley, and, yes, her smooth skin did have a coppery hue.

All through dinner—a crown roast of lamb, for which Hap had sprung with a bottle of 1966 Margaux—she smiled as they talked of their wartime adventures in Italy and France, tracking down paintings that had been stolen by the Einsatzstab Rosenberg, the official art looting organization, for the private collections of Hitler and Goering; and they drifted off into the Atlas Mountains of Morocco and Algeria, recalling how they bought the loyalty of the Arab chieftains who scouted for the highest bidders; and later, in Greece, parachuting at night on a field lit by flares outside Megara along the Gulf of Corinth, saved by partisans who unarmed the planted mines that bore the Krupp insigne, *amen,* liberating Athens with the British Red Berets and being greeted with conversational *vins ordinaires:* Do you know my first cousin who runs the Greek restaurant on Avenue Atlantic in the City of Brookyn? They stretched out their stories, and Helen loved them.

It was an evening of detached past, not personal past, which was safer. Helen made a casual reference to a divorced husband in her youth and a joking reference to Hap's long bachelorhood, but she avoided asking Sam about his family, and he wondered if Hap had told her, if she knew . . .

Somehow she also knew how to carry the silences between the small talk, yet there was a coil of awareness when she did unwind. Out of habit, they watched the eleven o'clock news as if something important was in the air — as if the world or Washington or a saving new idea for mankind would flash on — but the anchorperson and the weatherperson offered the usual laundry list of sponsored highway crack-ups, captured felons and two-headed calves, plus scattered showers.

Afterward Helen kissed them both goodnight and climbed upstairs to the master bedroom, leaving the two men alone. For a moment Linkum thought of Jennie behind her closed door . . .

Chorley poured two fingers of Calvados into water tumblers, then lit their Montecristos with a kitchen match.

"What do you think, chum?"

"You're a lucky bastard, Hap. I don't know how you measure it or exactly what it means but you're right — she is a *woman.*"

"Thanks, Sam. You and I have been on the same wavelength on so many of the things that really mattered." He paused. "I hope all goes well with you and Jennie, too. Anything changed?"

Linkum shrugged. "It's a little complicated," he said.

Chorley knew enough not to follow up the personal questions with Linkum; things that were "complicated" were best left unsaid.

"Sam, let's talk about the assignment. Now I'm putting on my

USAFSS hat again. Did you bring down any of the electronic tech manuals from the network?"

"Sorry, but I threw all that stuff out when I walked away from the lifestyles newspaper. I never thought I'd have use for it. Nothing much there anyway. Mostly instruction manuals that you can get free from manufacturers. Just buy one of their computer terminals with the built-in obsolescence. You get stuff on how not to lose a story or blow a fuse—"

"There's a helluva lot more involved that you obviously don't know about—"

"Or care about." Linkum poured himself another from the Calvados bottle.

"Look, Hap, I promised myself that I wouldn't take an assignment again. I haven't changed my mind. Nothing personal. I'm not in the intelligence game anymore, this is Maryland, not North Africa, and I prefer it here."

"The circumstances were different then, Sam. What you did was important, and you did it well. You were the one guy who knew the curator at the Hermitage so that we could pass along certain information and get it into the hands of my opposite number in the Fifth Directorate of the KGB. Honor among the thieves and intelligence chiefs. It was absolutely essential for me to break channels and let them know that our doomsday weapon was equal to theirs— that we knew what they had in store for us and vice versa. So what did we accomplish, with no small help from you? A stalemate of sorts of geological and chemical warfare weapons. It's held so far. And that's what it's all about, Sam—stalemate against doomsday."

"But what happened to my curator friend at the Hermitage? He's no longer there. I can't help feeling that they put the skids to him because we made contact. I tainted him, and he's probably now got the colored postcard concession in the Gulag."

"My information is otherwise, Sam. He was on the shitlist for a while, no doubt about that, but he had friends in high places, including making it with the wife of a member of the Politburo. The latest word is that he's working anonymously in the Pushkin State Museum in Moscow. He was too expert to be put out in the boondocks. Don't worry about him—he's a survivor."

"I'm glad you told me that, Hap."

"I wanted to clean the slate. Incidentally, the fact that we know where he landed is not for publication."

"I've got no publication to publish it in, have no fear."

Chorley came over to him, relit their Montecristos. "Sam, you've got nothing to lose on this one and everything to gain. You can pick up background for your own writing assignments later on. You'd be up front about the whole thing, nothing to hide, you'd be going as a journalist—as yourself. The resolutions on licensing reporters and any other controls they spring at the Algiers conference I'm sure you can handle. I don't have to give you the government's party line against foreign censorship—you can give *me* lessons on what the American position should be. All I'm saying is that as the American delegate, you'll be standing up for what *you* believe in."

"Back up a minute, Hap. You said there would be nothing for me to hide. What about *your* connection to what I say and do at the . . . what is it? . . . Mediterranean-American Foundation conference at Lake Como and the U.N. show in Algiers?"

Chorley kicked off his low boots and rested his feet on the oak coffee table. He glanced toward the staircase landing; not a sound came from the room he and Helen shared.

He lowered his voice. "I'm not to be mentioned at any time to anyone. Your appointment will come through the U.S. mission in New York after formal approval by the State Department section in charge of U.N. affairs. They'll give you briefings and position papers, and there'll be backup types at the embassies in Italy and Algeria in case you need anything."

"So you're behind the scenes—"

"I wouldn't put it that way. Once there, you're pretty much calling the shots. Be prepared for attacks."

"Who?"

Chorley grinned. "Your former colleagues in the press. The columnists and television commentators will be lecturing you from afar, rewriting your speeches and telling you where you went wrong. You'll be called either a scapegoat for the striped-pants tea drinkers in State or a pawn of the Kremlin—*unwitting pawn,* I believe your phrase goes—"

"I always said the press couldn't be trusted."

"Good for you—get a taste of your own medicine. Learn to swallow your pride and keep your yap shut if you're dealing with name-brand columnists. I know most of the lines by heart from reading the newspapers and newsmagazines. It'll give you some perspective to see what it's like to be on the receiving end."

Linkum hesitated. "Well, let me think it over and tell you in a couple of days—"

"Sorry, Sam, I haven't got that much time. I must put this into motion first thing in the A.M. The other intelligence chiefs have their candidates, too. It means calling in some credit, making a few trade-offs. But it'll be worth it—for both of us."

"What's your quid pro quo, Hap?"

"Information—*my* kind. I want to know where Moussi Ali stands—and if he can be tilted our way. I want to find out which of the third world countries can be detached from their blocs—some of them hate each other more than they hate the U.S. I want to get a handle on which cartels and conglomerates control which delegations—and how much money is changing hands. I want to know the gossip—who's into a heavy drug scene and who's into whoring—"

"Sounds like the old newspaper gossip section," Linkum said.

"Well, I don't have to tell you why that kind of gossip can come in handy in our line of work. But the immediate thing I need to know is if any of the anarchist groups or whatever they call themselves are planning to take out an Intelsat earth station. *Especially if it's one of ours.* The Moose should be able to steer you in Algeria—if you play your cards right in the meeting with him in Italy beforehand. He's bound to know the names and serial numbers of the activists with arrest records. You'd have to signal me directly if you discover an A-rab hit plan—any specific signal about time and place. It would help our counterstroke to know if they're going to use dynamite or *plastique* when they try to blow up an earth station. That way, I could send in some of my people to clobber them, or at least lessen the damage—propaganda as much as physical damage. The two go together in this game. Otherwise, on the general stuff, I can debrief you like this, with our feet up, when you get back."

"Feet up or feet out?"

Chorley nodded. "Look, in that part of the world nothing isn't a risk, including breaking a leg by slipping in camel flop on the Boulevard Che Guevara."

"International terrorists?"

"If you mean manipulated from Moscow, forget it. They're not that dumb in the Kremlin. Intelligence professionals, ours or theirs, don't rely on terrorists—they're too unstable, fuck-ups in business for themselves who always leave their calling cards. It's not the internationalists we're concerned about, it's the *nationalists*. They're the true believers who act like crazies. The people we've tracked carry briefcases, plus bombs. The most dedicated, as usual, are the most dangerous. But I'm not telling you anything you don't know."

Linkum nodded. Chorley's intelligence estimate reminded him of the series he had written for the newspaper on the resurgence of the Mafia in Sicily and how it had spread its code of conduct to the Italian mainland. The editor of the *Giornale di Sicilia* in Palermo had explained that there were two Mafias, white and black, clean and dirty: the black Mafia did the shakedowns and kidnappings, the thug work; the white Mafia sat in the city halls and regional legislature, delivering the contracts and wielding the real power. He had often thought about the white Mafia while covering Washington.

"Sam, I wouldn't ask you to take on an assignment for USAFSS that involved any *clear* danger," Chorley went on. "In fact, the major health risks could be to your throat and ears. You could lose your voice debating freedom of the press, and you could be kept awake listening to long-winded speeches on why the western press should be licensed. You can take along the bulletproof vest to ward off the verbal attack." Chorley refilled their tumblers with Calvados. "What do you say, chum?"

Sam Linkum was thinking that Jennie would be in Rome, reporting, she'd said, for National Public Radio at the same time he'd be warming up for the Algiers session at the foundation on Lake Como. He didn't mention her; still, if he decided to take this on, Jennie would only be an hour's flight away...

Chorley stole a glance at his two-continent chronometer.

Linkum walked over to the window, looked out toward the Maryland countryside, then turned.

"Okay, Hap."

Chorley stood up and extended his hand.

"In for a penny, in for a pound." Linkum tried to sound more offhand than he felt.

Chorley walked over to the wall opposite the fireplace. On it was mounted a beaded and painted elkskin robe. "Taos Pueblo, done by a modern artist," he said. "A present from Helen."

The green and yellow robe covered a wall safe. Chorley twirled the dial, reached inside and removed something, then concealed the safe again. He held his hand open.

"Have you still got yours?"

In his hand was the bronze emblem of the *Sixième Régiment, Spahis Algérien*—a silver scimitar set in the blue enamel rectangle; in the left-hand corner a gold-colored crescent and the number 6 set in a blood-red enamel square. He turned the talisman over and read aloud, "Drago Paris, depos 25 Rue Belanger."

"No, I gave it to someone"—someone he'd loved a long time ago—"and it somehow disappeared," Linkum said.

They both had been awarded the regimental emblems after serving as liaison officers with the Free French.

Chorley placed it in Linkum's hand. "Take mine along with you—it could be useful around Algiers. A reminder of the time everybody hung together."

"I should have it back in your hands in a month, right? Give me an incentive not to go native and join the Camel Corps." Linkum yawned. "You yanked me out of bed—and that's where I'm going now. It's been a long day—"

"Oh, one more little matter, Sam...I'd like you to get a sort of technical briefing before you take off for the Mediterranean-American Foundation encounter sessions. Remember I said there are private as well as intelligence interests sharing the communications satellite that you saw launched at Pentagon Green? Well, I've given you my reasons for needing you as the delegate. Now you ought to hear the private side—directly from them."

"Who's *them?*"

"Robert Farron and Walter Whipley—"

"For crissakes, Hap. I hear you out all day, you know my feelings about the network, and now you pull this—"

"Hold your fire, Sam. You know that I didn't pick them as my partners in this show—"

"But the two octopuses of networks and newspapers here and in Britain?"

"They're also the main shareholders controlling the circuits on the commercial side of the communications satellites. They've pooled their resources and interests—Farron gains access for his broadcasts, Whipley for duplicating his newspapers by laser across the Atlantic and, eventually, all the way to Hong Kong and Australia. In return for controlling the circuits, they've got to lease time to their competitors under the Communications Satellite Corporation rules. But they're in the catbird seat so far. Oh, they're a couple of beauties, all right."

"And *I'm* supposed to stand up for *their* interests?"

"Sam, how much say do you journalists have in a shrinking market? Forgive me for mentioning that, but nothing's black and white. The new technology is light years ahead of our ability to sort it out—or choose our partners. Want to know one actual alternative? Petrodollar control. Do you know that three billionaires from Kuwait, Saudi Arabia and Abu Dhabi own a multistate bank holding company in New York, Tennessee, Virginia, the District of Columbia—the country's capital—and Maryland, right in my home state. You know who the sheiks of Araby have hired as their lawyers to lobby for a piece of the action on our satellites through their hidden banking control? A former secretary of defense, a former United States senator and a former presidential chief of staff. At least I know what motivates Farron and Whipley...good old apple-pie American greed. With the sheiks, we'd have greed *plus* political leverage. How you like them apples?" Chorley lowered his voice.

"Sam, if you think you can't handle it, or whatever, you can still change your mind and forget—"

Linkum shut him off, tried to concentrate on where things stood. Where he stood. He was either going to get into the action, take advantage of the opportunity to say something—for *himself*—or let their people do it, their bought-off *condottieri*. Where were the front lines, the zone of combat in these new wars? He was damned if he knew, but all his working life he'd at least risked... "Hap, it'll cost you another box of Montecristos."

"Good. Farron will be on his Long Island estate this weekend. I don't know if Whipley will be back from London yet. He's fighting with his top editors—wants to be listed on the masthead as both publisher *and* editor-in-chief."

Linkum laughed. "Meaning he wants to pick the next prime minister or president *and* the cheesecake shots for page three."

"But Farron may surprise you. A charmer. Brilliant in his own way. Listen closely to him—you could learn something."

They climbed the stairs to the bedrooms.

"Sam, thanks for sticking with me. I don't want one of their handpicked clones from management on this one. It's too important."

Chorley paused before entering Helen's bedroom.

"Just remember this when you're dealing with Farron or Whipley—now or later," he said half-smiling. "These guys take no prisoners."

CHAPTER THREE

In the Enemy Camp

ONCE Sam Linkum had seen Robert Farron from a distance.

In the world of big-time mass communications, it was more than possible for one man to work for another man and never once communicate with him directly.

Of course the perennially cloaked face of the chairman of the network that had first absorbed and then demolished the newspaper was familiar. Linkum had watched Farron testify on television in congressional hearings against the regulation of his airwaves by the Federal Communications Commission—and later hired the pliant commissioners as his Washington lobbyists; he had seen that strong face peering from the society pages and people columns of the newspapers and newsmagazines for years. But he had only observed him in person, in an elevator at the network's headquarters hard by Rockefeller Center, when he had visited Jane Twining Delafield to discuss the new party line for the unlamented lifestyles section. All conversation had stopped the moment the chairman stepped into the elevator; he wondered then if Farron had shared in the embarrassment of silence.

But there was no reason now to hold back, no reason not to talk as an equal. After all, he was the one who had been summoned, who would be on the firing line.

Almost immediately after they shook hands, Farron said, "I believe in a free and responsible press—in print as well as in broadcasting." Like a written speech.

Linkum quickly replied, "And I believe in a free and *irresponsible* press."

Farron frowned.

"I see you have a sense of humor, sir."

Anyone who called you "sir" from a known position of superiority placed you at a disadvantage, and knew it.

"I meant what I said, Mr. Farron."

"Robert. Mind if I call you Sam?"

Linkum said he didn't mind.

"If you're acting *responsibly,*" he went on, "then you're letting something get between your story and your typewriter. You begin to think of the effect of what you've discovered—if it might make a president or some pooh bah or government agency look bad. The next thing that happens, you're ... well, temporizing."

"Temporizing? It's a matter of balance, isn't it, Sam?"

"I don't believe so. That's another way of saying that you should lean over backwards. I'd rather it all—or at least almost all—hung out."

"That could be *irresponsible,* all right, Sam."

Linkum wondered if he was pushing the network chairman too hard. But he had thought about it for a long time, had seen too many stories that had been so-called balanced to death.

"What I mean is that by being quote irresponsible unquote, you use your freedom to be quote responsible unquote. I don't think it'll help if I mouth platitudes in Algiers."

Farron looked at him.

Linkum saw the anger and thought that he had overreached himself, that he'd allowed his feelings about the network's role in the shutdown of the paper to show when he really wanted to make a point about the press.

The chairman resumed his friendly posture on his home grounds. Apparently no need to take prisoners yet.

"I hear you're an old Air Corps Intelligence friend of Henry H. Chorley's," Farron said, obviously changing the subject. "A distinguished public servant. He could have been the president of a university or some multinational company, considering everything he knows. A very *responsible* person. He spoke highly of you."

Linkum heard the word again; Farron didn't let go easily. "Yes, Hap and I had a few adventures together around the Mediterranean. He knew I was stranded without a paper and I guess he thought I might be of some help in that part of the world again." Linkum paused. "How do you know him?"

"Oh, from here and there," Farron said.

A good reporter, Linkum knew the answer before asking the question but he wanted to see how Farron would respond. Hap Chorley received "cooperation" from the network, could look at unused film and even plant people in the news department. He heard what he expected from Farron: nothing.

"Well, Mr. Farron, I guess what we were talking about a moment ago is a matter of semantics."

Better to cool his approach and wait for the meltdown. Hap was right; he had something to learn from this man.

"Oh sure, Sam," Farron said, the corners of his eyes crinkling. "When it comes to dealing with the other side in Algiers, I'm certain we'll be on the same wavelength. You wouldn't let us down..."

Sam Linkum had glimpsed Robert Farron earlier that Saturday standing alone on a knoll—playing a kite in the wind. The line from him to the violet-and-black cloth bird with its knotted tail appeared to be connected as if by some secret pact. Farron teased it around the feathery breeze, letting out string and forcing the cloth bird to glide and flutter and climb swiftly, sending it soaring three hundred feet above his head, below the air channels he revered and ruled as few men of his time, sliding paper messages that jerked upward into the countervailing currents; and then, when the spirit moved him, a wraithlike figure far beneath the dancing kite, he suddenly plunged it like a mortar shot gone wild toward the ground.

That morning, Linkum had rented a compact Ford at the weekend discount rate, realizing again that he had cut himself off from the credit-card life, and pointed the small car to the Queensborough Bridge, saving a dollar and a quarter crossing the East River, then driven along Northern Boulevard, lined with fast-food franchises and hand-lettered evangelical churches, till the city's potholes became macadam on the Long Island Expressway. After an hour, where the houses of the mortgaged strivers were fenced off from their neighbors and the towns bore Indian and colonial names, he had turned sharply and taken a country byway under a bower of quaking aspen and shagbark hickory that formed a natural canopy of twisting silver and green leaves. A copse in the middle of the road diverted curious motorists, sending them back in circles to the main highway. Linkum had been told to look for a fading blue-painted fence, the color of washed denim, and he followed it for nearly a mile until he came to a break in the enclosed estate. A small gold-on-black wooden sign read "Trade Entrance." And Linkum thought to himself, this is the way to enter, in Farron's world I am a tradesman. A larger rectangular nameplate proclaimed: "Farron Fields." Only a crest was mssing above it, with a mythical lion rampant; but none was needed to proclaim the power of one of the American lords temporal.

The lone figure on the knoll playing the kite waved to him. Linkum circled several dwellings that housed servants and two greenhouses and reconverted stables that contained a small fleet of automobiles. It was still early enough for Linkum to be embarrassed by the throaty rattle of his rented car. He turned off the motor and walked up the manicured lawn, his feet sinking in the Zoysia grass.

Farron stood there, winding the string on an elaborately carved wooden reel.

"It's from the Orient," he said, "the real China, an antique, maybe two or three hundred years old. It's in the shape of a carp. See these notches carved in the fish for the string? That's just the way I got it—it was always used as a kite reel. A present from the minister in charge of the foreign-language broadcasts in Peking. Mahogany lasts. It must have been made for a son of one of the old emperors— maybe the emperor himself. Flying kites there was a skill, not child's play, and it's still not a dishonorable pastime."

Farron extended his free hand and smiled broadly.

"I hope you didn't get lost finding the farm—all you have to do is follow the blue fence. Appreciate your taking the time to visit with me here. Haven't we met before?"

"I don't believe so, Mr. Farron."

"Guess I heard of your name from Jane Delafield." He seemed to study Linkum's face for a reaction. Linkum assumed that the network chairman had gone over his dossier in Corporate Records. "A bright woman," Farron added. "All business."

"I worked for her on the paper—briefly."

"So I heard. Sorry that the paper had to be folded—it just couldn't hack it in today's marketplace. Lost some good men and women, I was told, but we hope to absorb those who can adjust in other parts of the firm...Well, *c'est la vie*. That goes for a business or a person. Sometimes I think that all I've been working for is a one-column story on the front pages instead of the obituary pages. With my picture—unless someone more important dies that day, isn't that the way it goes?"

"I don't think you'll have much to worry about," Linkum said, suddenly feeling uncomfortable.

"They asked me if I wanted something prepared in advance in the network news department and I said, why not? No use slapping something together at the last minute. I let them have some of the old stills and newsreel shots, the transition from radio to television and the next step—cable and satellites. No need to be squeamish. What do you think of the title they put on my mini-documentary: *Pioneer and Patriot?*"

Linkum understood that he was being tested.

"It's a little out of my field—I don't know much about documentaries. Anyway, friends don't have to be impressed—"

"Friends? No, I'm thinking more of my surviving enemies. You know, it's a rough ride staying on top in television. If you go the whole course you find yourself doing certain things to survive. My taste, and yours, is different from the general public's but they're the boss. My responsibility is to the shareholders. It was different when I owned the shop myself, back in the radio days. I could take risks . . . but it's no sense looking back, we've got to meet the new challenges before the wrong people gain control. Still, I sometimes read what they write about me, rough character and all that, and I wonder whom they're writing about. Even my correspondents who've become wealthy because I gave them a showcase, who knows what they'll say? One thing I've learned, kindnesses are not retroactive."

Wondering if he sounded churlish as the words left him, Linkum said, "Well, it's over and done with as news pretty quickly—they say death is a one-day story."

"You're right," Farron said easily, "and life is a one-day story, too."

For a moment, both men stared at each other. Then Farron finished winding the string around the mahogany carp. The violet-and-black kite in the shape of some extinct prehistoric bird lay dead at his feet. He lifted it with unexpected tenderness, gathering the broken ribs and pierced cloth that he had smashed to earth and walked without another word to the toolshed next to the converted stables.

On the long sweep of lawn approaching the columns of the three-storied Greek revival mansion, Linkum noticed a score of hitching posts, each a foreshortened iron jockey, with babylike blunt hands clawing rings that had once held dropped reins. Not long ago, this part of Long Island had been polo country and, once a year for some charitable cause, a sentimental game was mounted by men of girth living in the past.

Peering toward the windows of the toolshed, Linkum could see other kites dangling. It was a private enclave Farron reserved for his sport. When he emerged, Farron again seemed a spectre at a distance. There was a hard shading in his countenance, lights and darks that Linkum had not noticed at first. His bearing was newly erect and the informality had vanished. Linkum waited for Farron to say something as they walked toward the mansion, and then to break the silence he asked Farron about the row of jockeys.

Farron suddenly revived. He patted a jockey's cap.

"They're the real thing, not made by some cheap iron works in Long Island City. Could be a hundred and twenty-five years old. The managers of the network affiliates in the south combed half the Confederate mansions in Alabama, Georgia and Mississippi to find them. All I had a few years ago was one on the lawn and a couple at the barn. Then the president of the affiliates began collecting them for me on his rounds, wherever we broadcast. At first I thought my wife and daughter would find them ostentatious—sorry you won't meet them, they're shopping in the city today—but they decided to place them in this antebellum pattern along the lawn. If you look closely there's a call letter below their feet telling which stations they came from. I had them scraped and redone so that they're dressed in the racing silks of friends of ours—they seem to enjoy seeing their colors when they drive up to the house."

Above the distinctive squares and diamonds and polka dots and Maltese crosses on the silks, the heads of these nineteenth-century pickaninnies looked as if they were mongoloids. Southern iron-mongers of a dying slave era had exaggerated their features, bulging out eyes and thickening lips. But Farron had their faces and hands repainted to conceal their blackamoor appearance, cancelling their ancestry with whitewash.

Linkum recalled a quotation that the network chairman had placed in his biographical folder in the newspaper's morgue: "I'm a liberal among conservatives and a conservative among liberals." If nowhere else, the changed image of the once-black stable boys proved Robert Farron's liberal-or-conservative instincts and his ability to roll with the times.

The two men walked under the porte-cochere and entered the mansion. Farron signaled his housekeeper to bring them drinks. They leaned back on wicker chairs in a glass-enclosed veranda overlooking the Fields of Farron.

This, Linkum thought, is a bizarre scene. A few nights ago I was standing in Mannie's Place, clinking beer mugs at a wake with editors and reporters, and now I'm sipping a slightly chilled Saint Emilion out of Baccarat crystal in the center of the enemy camp.

If only Jennie could see me now...but he would not want her to, not until they were alone and he could plead guilty with explanation.

"Walt Whipley will be here by lunchtime," Farron said. "The Concorde has landed and he's coming directly from JFK. I thought it would help—and so did our mutual friend from the Pentagon— if he briefed you on the print media side of things."

No wonder the newspaper had been pushed over the edge; in the eyes of the Farrons and Whipleys it was something called *print media*.

"I don't quite understand the relationship between you and Walt Whipley, Mr. Farron."

"Well, Sam, I can assure you that Whipley and I aren't partners, not by a long shot. We're what you might call allies of convenience. We're both watching the other side and the third world as well as each other's back." He laughed hoarsely. "Covering each other's rear end, to put it more accurately."

A black limousine slowly circled the crushed-stone driveway below the veranda. The chauffeur parked and ran around to open the passenger door. A stout middle-aged man stepped out, looked up toward them and waved. He bounded up the stairs and pushed open the glass door at the far end of the veranda.

"Breakfast in London, lunch on Long Island," Walt Whipley said. "I hope you have something besides kippers."

"This is Sam Linkum," Farron said.

Linkum tried to size up Whipley, checking out his style against what he already knew about the Commonwealth press owner's reputation as the piranha among the lords of international newspapers and magazines. The man's thinning reddish hair appeared to be tinted. He was sudden in his movements, aggressively short.

"I've got a package for you from your network office in South Kensington, Robert."

Whipley handed him three jars of "Violet Shaving Cream" from Trumper's of Curzon Street. Farron explained that his favorite brand was not easily available in the States. "Just had time to stop by for a fitting at Benson, Perry, my Cork Street bespoke tailor, and pick up this blazer," Whipley said, actually turning himself around to be admired. It was light green. Linkum recognized the brown suede shoes from Peal's (he had once bought a pair himself on an impulse during his stint as a correspondent) though he noticed that Whipley's trousers scraped the ground. He wore a medley of brand names.

So this was the gentleman from the Commonwealth who bought and sold newspapers like pork bellies on the commodity exchange. Walt Whipley and Robert Farron seemed to be closer than the network chairman had let on when he described their backsides and business together.

"Let's get down to cases, Sam. First, you may be subjected to talk—propaganda, actually—that the network's position on the communications satellite is a monopoly. Second, that in some way I or my people can censor the messages or programs carried on the satellite. Both claims are false."

"Utterly," Whipley added, nibbling a handful of macadamia nuts.

"This is for background only"—Farron had apparently learned to speak the lingo of a government official—"because it concerns another American firm and I would not want it to boomerang, come back to haunt us. What we have actually done is *broken* a monopoly. The American Telephone and Telegraph Company once owned the whole shooting match—the long lines, the cables, the hardware. You couldn't get a show on the air without paying them through the nose. Whatever fee they set, that was it, and all the public service commissions went along. Protect widows and orphans and lifetime savings—that was their song and dance whenever they raised their charges for transmitting our pictures and messages. Ma Bell! Whoever thought up that nickname was a genius, deserved a million dollars. Made AT&T sound warm and cuddly. Love your mother, love the phone company. You would think—"

"Robert," Whipley interrupted, "far be it for me to say so, being a bloody foreigner, but you sound as if you OD'd on the

New Statesman or one of the other radical rags in London. A real leftie—"

"Liberal among conservatives, conservative among liberals," Farron replied. "Fair's fair. I won't bother you with the figures, but the network paid Ma Bell a small fortune just for transmitting a half-hour of our Evening News show. Multiply that with a round-the-clock service and you'll see why I call them an *uncommon* carrier. If they ever pulled the plug on us, there would be a national blackout on news and entertainment. So don't let anyone tell you that the networks are the censors. We do our work as well as humanly possible, not perfectly but we try to please our audiences—the American viewing and listening public. If anyone has the ability to exercise censorship, it's good old Ma Bell."

"But why should that be for background only?"

"Sam, I don't think one American company should be attacking another publicly at an international meeting. I simply wanted you to know, as a *responsible* delegate speaking for our country, that the networks are not all powerful. You will hear propaganda to the contrary. I want you to be armed with the facts of the real relationship between the networks and the big carrier. That doesn't mean you have to use it. I always like to have a round in the chamber. To understand what's happening in the world of software today you've got to know the hardware, too, the technology."

"And we've got to get into the hardware business ourselves before it's too late," Whipley said. "By *we,* of course, I mean the free western media, television, newspapers, magazines. If news is going to be delivered electronically, we don't want to be second best."

"We know Ma Bell's party line," said Farron, pleased with his pun. "Same with the satellite carriers. Talk only transmission, not about the data base. But the two have become inseparable. Just as we've moved into cable systems, they've engineered experiments to transmit over telephone lines. It's like the history of the old movie industry. First came the movie houses, then came the need to fill them with a steady flow of new pictures. So the people who owned the theaters began owning the movie studios—the writers, actors, directors and producers. I'm not saying it was all that bad. There were many talented individuals, but eventually there had to be divorce. What if the same crowd that rules Ma Bell also ran the networks? It would mean the end of independence as we know it—"

"A single voice," Whipley chimed in. "Now people can twist the dial or go to the kiosk and make their own choices—"

"Not at the newsstands," Linkum said softly.

Farron glanced at him but kept still, started to speak but was interrupted by the voluble Whipley.

"Survival of the fittest is what it's all about. Either you trim your sails for your readership or you perish."

"Is that what you did with your tabloids, Mr. Whipley?"

"Look here, Linkum, I'm not a bloody lecturer—I don't feel superior to my readers—"

"Well, I think it's time to put on the feed bag," Farron broke in, trying to neutralize the charged air. "And there will be no kippers, my friends."

What was it that Hap had said about them? They were a couple of *beauties*. But Hap never said Linkum had to like this penny-dreadful newsmonger even if he played the publishing tycoon. All Linkum was supposed to do was hear them out. He wondered if Hap also knew Whipley personally or only through his USAFSS-Commonwealth intelligence connections.

Lunch was brought to them on silver trays: prosciutto and melon, cold poached salmon, a salad of greens grown on the grounds, another bottle of Saint Emilion. Somehow it made Linkum feel better when Whipley asked for a pot of tea instead of sharing the coffee from the elegant English urn and the no-nonsense housekeeper handed him a plain do-it-yourself teabag.

Afterward Farron proposed that they talk while walking through his woods, but a few moments after they started out there was a sudden thundershower. Two gardeners and a caretaker appeared out of nowhere carrying beach umbrellas imprinted with the network's newly designed logotype—a family gathered around the warmth of a television hearth—and escorted them back to the big house.

They sat in the oak-paneled library. It was lined with leather-bound sets of books that seemed to be color-coordinated with the sofas and chairs and lampshades. Linkum noticed that the very top row of books, also of uniform color and height, had connected false fronts. Farron opened a humidor filled with Romeo y Julietas and passed them around. *They* were real. Whipley took one of the Havanas for later; Linkum declined.

"Transponders, Sam—that's the name of the game in international broadcasting and communications today." Robert Farron lit one of his cigars and a look of contentment spread over his rugged face. "I'm not going to overload your head with too much technical data about frequency bands and hemispherical beams and dual polarization or I'm liable to cause a short circuit in your brain. Just remember the transponders. They're the devices on the satellite that relay signals back down to earth. The signals come to television screens through ground stations. No transponders, no pictures. The transponders reach across a broad area of footprints—"

"Footprints?"

"The area of the earth covered by the satellite's signals. It's not done with mirrors but microwaves. And the video signals are sent by high-frequency radio signals."

Farron turned to Whipley, who kept nibbling the macadamia nuts and washing them down with wine. "Do you have any radio stations?" As if he didn't already know, Linkum thought.

Whipley said that he owned a few in Canada and South Africa— "but only as investments, I don't know a damn thing about how they work. I leave them to my managers, unlike my newspapers..."

"Too bad—everybody talks about television but the basic technology is rooted in radio because that's where it all started for some of us—and we're a dying breed." Farron seemed disappointed not to be able to talk to them as fellow radio pioneers. "I left my youth in radio..."

At that moment Linkum envisioned Farron in his memory eye, with surprising sympathy, recalling him playing his kite in the gusty channels, alone on a hill.

"Dish," Farron continued, coming out of his reverie. "You may have seen one standing outside a television station. The satellite transmits to a dish-shaped antenna that picks up the microwave signals. They're shaped like a big bowl of soup with nothing inside, and right now they're at ground stations on most of the civilized continents—or soon will be. You've heard of ground stations, Sam?"

He had—from Hap, in secret; one reason why he had been summoned to undertake the assignment for USAFSS. But how much was he supposed to acknowledge that he knew? How closely were the network's interests linked to the government's—and should he share with these men? How much was Farron telling him—and how much was he pumping him?

Linkum looked across the couch to where Walt Whipley sat munching and drinking. He wondered if the British publisher was sulking or simply catching up with the time difference in his body clock after the Concorde flight. One thing I don't want to do, Linkum told himself, is spill anything in front of the little piranha. I don't know who *his* partners are . . .

"Vaguely," Linkum replied to the question about whether he'd heard of ground stations.

Suddenly Whipley raised his head from his chest and recited like a schoolboy. "A dainty dish to set before a king . . ."

"A king?" Farron said. "No, more likely a common man and his family. Know why? Because of DBS—the direct broadcast satellite. That's the next generation. Receive the signal or show right in your own backyard, captured directly on your home dish. You won't even have to go through a ground station. It's got the cable people worried as hell because a DBS dish would bypass them. Did I call it next generation? If there's one thing I've learned in this business it's that technological time has to be compressed. Twenty years become five years, next year is this year."

"Well, my publications will be safe," Whipley said. "As long as the human body has to visit the W.C. once or twice a day, people will want to read at least while they're sitting on the john."

"But most people will already have gotten their news and entertainment on television," Farron said.

"How close to reality are these satellite-to-home dishes, Mr. Farron?"

"Robert, Sam," Farron repeated. "Oh, I'd say that as a practical matter in a year or two. The capability is there already, it's a matter of cost. Once the price comes down, all you'll need is a clear, unobstructed view of the southwestern sky. With a couple of hand cranks you can move the dish to receive every line-of-sight North American communications satellite."

"If it works for television, it will work for newspapers."

"Absolutely," Farron said, turning to Whipley. "And that's why we're in this together. Fortunately, the Federal Communications Commission came to its senses and opened up the satellite market to the highest bidders. It's good to have friends. Now my network doesn't have to go through Ma Bell or anyone else for the next seven years. Bought my own place on the big bird. I'm subleasing some of my channels to people who can pay the freight for the transponders. Auctioned them off in the fairest possible way at Sotheby, just like Rembrandts, only a little more expensive. I've subleased channels to evangelical and cable networks, entertainment and banking systems, even to my good friend Walter Whipley here for his international newspapers."

Whipley nodded. "That's why I'm here today, Linkum. Anything you want to ask me?"

Linkum looked puzzled. He thought he was just expected to listen.

"Well, sir, then I have a few things to tell you. Not, mind you, as an American delegate because I am not one of your countrymen but as a journalist myself... You should be aware that this upcoming world information conference is not our idea, it's *theirs*. Nothing good can come out of it for our side. But it's something we have to live with, like the United Nations. Now you will be speaking for the first world—ours, the West—against the second world, the Russians and their bloc, and the third world, the underdeveloped countries—black, brown, yellow and what have you. They don't like that word *underdeveloped*." Whipley chuckled. "They say it sounds aboriginal, ring through their noses, as if their minds and bodies are not fully grown. They prefer *developing*." He glanced directly at Linkum. "What's your preference?"

90

"Call them whatever they want to be called."

"Righto," Whipley replied, to Linkum's surprise. "I would call that a pretty good diplomatic response. Even if most of them are indeed backward, there is nothing to lose by conceding them such a minor point."

With a look of amusement, Farron watched their fencing match. The old charmer knew when to disengage.

Whipley said, "I used the word *against* us deliberately because the second and third worlds simply are not interested in news as you and I know it. Their principal concerns are politics and propaganda. Agreed?"

"So I've heard."

"You can damn well take my word for it. I've lived in their countries and done business with them and the worst ones are those who hold political office—or are relatives of the prime minister. They also think that any criticism of their news methods is criticism of their country. They're awfully long-winded too—I saw that as an unofficial observer at a similar conference a couple of years ago in Kenya."

Linkum thought Whipley could be talking about himself.

"Now, let's get down to hard cases, Linkum. They hate our living guts out there in the third world. Associated Press, United Press International, Reuters, Agence France-Presse—if they had their way in Algiers none of our western agencies would be functioning in their countries. Why? Because they can't buy them, can't make them an arm of their corrupt cultural or information ministries. Without at least one of these news services on the scene, my newspapers couldn't serve our international readership. The Whipley Group is about to take a great leap forward, as the Chinese say, and publish on three continents simultaneously. I've made no secret of that. We have positioned ourselves to deliver a news package in Britain, Canada and Australia by leasing a transponder on Bob Farron's big bird."

Whipley turned to Farron for approval. As if to reassure Linkum, the network chairman said, "The Whipley Group's space on the satellite is not exclusive, of course."

"We all need the wire services—none of us could afford to station correspondents in every capital in every country," Whipley said. "But you'll hear another tune played at the Algiers conference. They want to get rid of our roving correspondents from the newspapers and networks and they want to prevent the native stringers in their own countries from reporting. They can cut down most of the stringers except that the governments find them very useful—as stool pigeons. We know all about them from long, sad experience. Don't kill the messenger if you can threaten him or his family and keep him in line—"

Farron broke in. "Sam, both of us want to be as practical as possible. What you're hearing today can be very useful. Let me be positive: the give and take in this room is good practice even if it is a bit argumentative. No need to look at our discussions any other way except as building blocks for your arguments as American delegate. Now, if I hear correctly what Walt Whipley is saying, it's censorship pure and simple that our opponents will be putting on the table in Algiers."

"Under a different name," Whipley said. "They're not so crude as to call for censorship openly at a U.N. meeting supposedly dedicated to a greater exchange of ideas. No, what they call it is a New World Information Order."

"Spell it out," Farron said.

"It's not that simple because the whole bloody thing is disguised behind words like justice, freedom, human dignity. They want reporters to strengthen peace and fight racialism. Somebody has to be the judge of that, and the somebody is a foreign government's press office. Then they hint that the present system—the way the western press reports—is immoral and unethical. So they want the countries that put up the money for the U.N., yours and mine and a few others, to finance their news organizations—press and television. In other words, help them to buy us. Some of their more authoritarian delegations would like to see correspondents licensed—stick to the government line or your license is revoked."

Whipley paused, reached for the bowl of macadamia nuts, then turned on Linkum. "Are *you* for licensing journalists?"

"Not when you put it that way. But I've lived with censorship, actual and voluntary, covering a couple of wars. There's censorship from the outside and from the inside, self-censorship, and I'm not happy with either one of them. Then there's economic censorship, right from the home office, but that's another story."

The British magnate stood up, pocketed another Romeo y Julieta from Farron's humidor and turned his back on Linkum.

"I'll see you at dinner in our apartment next Wednesday, Robert," Whipley said. "I hope that Roxie can join us. My Christine loves her company."

Linkum remembered that Roxanne Farron was a famous beauty whose face adorned the social pages of *Town & Country*; she was known for reintroducing Fortuny fabrics from Venice in New York for one of her charities. In her photographs, she resembled the enameled terra-cotta of the elegant Ginevra de' Benci from Leonardo's Florentine period, yet she always managed to look distinctly cool American. Linkum was sorry that she wasn't around in the flesh on his first and probably last visit to Farron Fields.

What was the phrase that Jennie had once used to describe Robert Farron's stylish wife? The great stone face.

Jennie... no matter where he was she somehow penetrated his thoughts, a party to conversations unspoken. He wondered if she had already arrived in Rome...

Farron thanked Whipley for carrying his special shaving cream from Trumper's, they shook hands and without a word or a glance at Linkum the publisher disappeared into the plush backseat of his waiting limousine.

These guys take no prisoners...

The network chairman smiled benignly.

"Sam, I wanted to hold back on a few things until our good friend from England had left." Farron was making it appear that he had a confidential relationship with Linkum; the strong scent of flattery filled the library. "You know, in the western countries we're all supposed to speak with one voice but there is mighty competition in the field of communications. What I want is for us to remain first among equals. Sure, we can be united about the growth of our

Intelsat satellite system against the Intersputnik that the Russians have going for them. I think we've both heard that loud and clear from Hap Chorley. Intelligence is his business; business is my business. I'm not ashamed to say that. If I were I wouldn't be employing so many thousands of people all over the world. But I don't want to be stabbed in the back by our partners in the west. I couldn't put it quite that bluntly in front of Whipley—"

"Business is his business, too, isn't it?"

Farron laughed. "But that doesn't mean that he wouldn't switch allegiance if he could save money. There's a satellite sales war going on. Whoever controls the transponders controls the game. The European Space Agency has a new generation of communications satellites that will soon be going head to head against those put up by our National Aeronautics and Space Administration."

"Do you think that subject will come up in Algiers?"

"Can't tell—but it will definitely be background music you should be tuned in to. As usual, the French are behaving nasty. They're making noises about national sovereignty in the skies over their territory. That sort of thing has been recognized for oil and minerals directly offshore because of hundreds of years of maritime law. But airspace is another matter altogether. I don't think they'll be able to get away with it. They're also proceeding on another track— their Ariane rocket is giving Europe its own launching capability. They're pitching for the big contracts already, and I don't doubt that they'll pick some off. Communications satellites are the last unmined frontier—at least on this planet."

So he was protecting his leases and circuits, his back and flanks. The dead newspaper was chicken feed compared to the network's huge stake in the transponder game.

Farron rose from his lounging chair and put his arm around Linkum. He extended the cigar humidor again as they walked to the porte-cochere, but Linkum resisted the temptation. From Hap, yes. Not this guy. Farron escorted him to his coughing rental car that was parked on the circular driveway.

"I hope I've been more informative than self-indulgent nostalgic," Farron said, "and that I haven't overloaded your circuits with a lot of technical stuff."

"I'll try to remember—"

"Here, you won't have to—I've prepared a memorandum for you." Farron handed him a manila envelope. "Nothing particularly secret here but I'd keep it confidential because it does contain some trade material." He winked. "I wouldn't necessarily want some of my European competitors to know what we know about *them.*"

"Including Walt Whipley?"

Farron smiled. "Sorry you two didn't hit it off. He's fairly harmless—just gets a little excitable now and then. Small-man complex, I suppose. Likes to play the big newspaper tycoon." He paused. "To answer your question... yes, including Walt Whipley... Well, good luck representing *our* side. Algiers could be pleasant this time of year. Are you taking your wife along, Sam?"

At least Hap Chorley had not revealed anything intimate about his private life.

"She's dead, Mr. Farron."

"Oh... I'm sorry."

Farron waved as Linkum turned the car around and drove past the row of whitewashed iron jockeys along Farron Fields to the tradesman's exit.

Punctuation marks: to begin again, you had to have endings. Memory could be sublime, a sweet melancholy, sometimes the only leftovers to savor in life. Deep in the recesses of his mind, Long Island held two memories for Sam Linkum. His only son, Antonio, had once been buried in the United States military cemetery in Farmingdale. The considerate government had reserved an as-yet unfilled section for Vietnam casualties who had earned the ultimate Purple Heart for their grieving families. Graves Registration was always thoughtful after the body counts. And his wife, Elena, the longer memory, had once been institutionalized in the Thornhill Residence for the emotionally disabled on a hilltop near Riverhead overlooking Long Island Sound.

Elena Florio, the almond-faced golden girl from another life in his life, had become his war bride. They had met in their youth when he wore a uniform in Sicily and she served as a translator attached to his outfit. She was just out of the university in Catania, with a charming accent a few lessons ahead of bare necessity. Hap Chorley had served as best man at their wedding. In the States after the war, they had grown up together, she as a teacher of handicapped children, he making a modest name for himself as a journalist for the political-opinion weeklies and then on the metropolitan newspapers. Life at that time seemed a big party, with no dreams deferred.

After some difficulty, their son was born. They named him Antonio, after her father, because they wanted the boy to be aware of his half-Mediterranean heritage. Antonio resembled his mother, fair-haired and delicate, almost too polite, his father sometimes thought. Elena was unable to have another child; they cherished Antonio all the more. When his draft number came up they told him to take off to Canada, even to disappear under the Florio name in Sicily, hidden by her sister in the village of Brucia on the slopes of Mount Etna, where the ancient code of silence would protect him. Antonio would have none of it; he had seen too many smiling photographs of his father in uniform, had heard too many sentimental tales about their romance and marriage. And Antonio thought it would be immoral for another young man to go to war in his place, even for a war they all considered immoral. Later, it took months of effort for Sam Linkum to find out how it had happened. Antonio was hit, accidentally, in a napalm attack by American helicopters supporting the secret invasion of Cambodia when Mr. Nixon and Dr. Kissinger were in command of the war.

The golden girl from Sicily died slowly, mourning their son. They visited his grave every Sunday in Farmingdale. After a few years, Elena lapsed into silence and was unable to continue working. The doctors had several names for her emotional breakdown, tried shock treatments but nothing worked, nothing could heal a broken heart. They advised Linkum to put Elena in a secure place, where she could be supervised, with bars on the windows, and he had found the Thornhill Residence. Now he made two visits, alone, on Sundays, to his grave in Farmingdale and to her living death in Riverhead. Once, he had driven her to the gravesite, hoping the place would penetrate her silent world; instead, she had uttered a scream from somewhere deep in her throat and then her eyes had glazed over again. After that, with the sympathetic help of Hap Chorley, Linkum had arranged to have Antonio's remains reburied in the American military cemetery at Nettuno, above the Anzio beachhead he had known in his own youth, overlooking the tranquil Tyrrhenian Sea. Linkum believed that Elena would have wanted him there.

Not long afterward, the call came to him at home in his studio apartment near the U.N. enclave. There had been an accident. Could he come to the residential home as soon as possible? Another voice on the line matter-of-factly mentioned the name of the funeral parlor in Riverhead. It would make more sense for him to go there directly and take care of "the arrangements." So he learned that Elena had drowned that evening in Long Island Sound. She had wandered away from the residence after the dinner hour and they had found her body in the surf below. Was it an accident or was it suicide? The officials at the Thornhill Residence implied that it might well have been a case of self-destruction; but they were more concerned about having him sign the necessary documents holding them immune from responsibility, otherwise the body could not be released. Looking at Elena in death, the memory of her in life overwhelmed him. He signed whatever was put in front of him and then walked along the beach of Long Island Sound, the air salting his tears, waiting for the dawn. Once before he had done the same thing in the city, fearing for Elena's health, on the night that Antonio was born.

The following day Linkum knew what he wanted to do: bring her back to Brucia, to her birthplace and her family. He had none. On the transatlantic phone he broke the news to her sister. Bianca understood, saying that it was God's will to end her final, sad years. She would take care of everything. Of course he would be there, but he did not want an elaborate burial ceremony. And so he went back with Elena to her village, in the province of Catania, on the rocky slopes where the mistral swept down over Sardinia, collecting in the sails above the azure waters of the Ionian Sea and stunning the stranger on the shore. Hobbling on his cane, the gray-haired priest who had baptized her buried her. Afterward Linkum helped him walk down the hill from Brucia's cemetery. Bianca asked her brother-in-law to stay with her family for a few days, but he had brought Elena home to her soil, and he decided to leave the next morning. As they parted at the railway station, tears came into their eyes. Bianca embraced him.

She asked: "What do you wish engraved on her stone?"

He answered: "Elena Florio Linkum, Beloved Wife of Samuel, Devoted Mother of Antonio."

It was over.

After dropping off the car at the rental place on Second Avenue, Linkum passed the strip of East Side movie houses, thinking to clear his mind for a few hours, escape, but saw nothing to attract. He decided to walk downtown to Mannie's Place. It was Mannie's night off, a new bartender said, things were getting slow after dark, the changing neighborhood. He did not recognize anyone standing at the bar. After the elaborate lunch at Farron Fields he decided to skip the meatballs floating in tomato sauce, nibbled on the peanuts and drank a Carlsberg. Then, avoiding the closed newspaper building, he walked home.

The telephone was ringing as he turned the keys in the double locks. He missed making it on time. Five minutes later the phone rang again.

"Doing the town?" Hap said. "I've been trying to get you for the last two hours."

"Yeah, a big night—just treated myself to a jar of Iranian caviar, a magnum of Veuve Clicquot, the usual."

"We'll have to work out another phone arrangement. From now on, you call me on that private number I gave you. How did you make out with the boys?"

"Well, Farron—"

"Don't mention names. I'll know which one you're referring to. So you made one friend and one enemy—"

"How did you know that?"

"The first fellow called—your host. Said he liked your style and open-mindedness. He's the one that counts. The second fellow isn't exactly our responsibility. He's just hooked into the first fellow for rations and quarters. I've never met him. Did he mention my name?"

"Don't think so."

"Good. Did you get a chance to look at that stuff the first fellow told me he gave you?"

"Not yet."

"Mail me a copy at the farm. I understand it's not very long. Photocopy it yourself—don't let it out of your sight. The post office usually has a machine."

"Anything else?"

"Yes. Hang up and call me from the outside. I'll be at that number."

Linkum fished in his pocket for change and the slip of paper stuck between his useless company credit cards and Blue Cross-Blue Shield identification papers that he meant to renew. He went down the steps of his building and walked around the corner to a street telephone. He dialed collect.

"That's better, Sam."

"I've got my name back. Good. May I call you by your first name, Mr. Chorley?"

"Don't be cute, chum. I don't know who's tuned into your line. It's not unknown for newspapermen to be tapped."

"If they have newspapers. They've broken me to civilian."

"Well, you're with me so we'll try to be secure. It's good practice, even in this country. Is there anything particular you want to tell me before I tell you something?"

"Oh, just that you were right. These guys take no prisoners."

"Anybody waiting to make a call outside your phone booth?"

Linkum told him no.

"Did either of them mention ground stations?"

"Farron did, but only in passing. I didn't press him on that subject and I think it went over Whipley's head. I'm not sure. The little bastard was more interested in giving me a lecture on how he keeps the western press honest."

"Here's what I want you to know, Sam. Those characters I mentioned have just blown up a satellite ground station in Oran. The dynamiter who was caught alive killed himself. Did a pretty good job of it—it'll be out of operation for months. Including when the Algiers conference meets. It's not that vital a station, which makes me think this was more a demonstration job, a show of power."

"Any American tie-ups there?"

"Indirectly, through a consortium of leased interests. Hard to untangle, but from what I've been able to learn through ELINT and my people on the scene the Oran station was controlled by the French and Saudis through Swiss companies. I don't know the full ownership yet—but I will."

"What does it mean to us?"

"To *you*. It means that everything's accelerated and the game's on. They're not just going to be talking in Algiers, there are some who are going to be acting out their differences with us. The Russkies meanwhile stand by and pick up the pieces for their propaganda arsenal. I can really be hobbled in my intelligence if more of those birds get roasted on the ground. When will you be ready to leave for the warmup at Lake Como?"

"In a couple of days. I have some personal stuff—"

"Not your friendly periodontist again. You're going to have to leave *yesterday*—I want you to pick up what you can from the Moose and anybody else you run into there. My plane is waiting for you at Butler. Get there in the next few hours. You'll be flown to Andrews in the dark. I've arranged for you to get to Milan tomorrow. The transatlantic clock is working in our favor. Come to think of it, don't mail that stuff from Farron to me. Give it to my pilot, I'll get my copy that way. You can study it on the flight down here. Most of what he told you should be in your head anyway. Oh . . . one of my people will be on your tail."

"So when do I turn in my bulletproof vest?"

"You don't—like I told you, it's stylish, goes with anything."

100

"Thanks a lot."

"I won't see you for a while so good luck. You'll be hearing from me. Oh, another thing—keep in mind that fine old Venetian expression: *Prima di parlar, tasi.*"

"Before you speak, be quiet. Okay, Hap, that's the shortest advice your new American delegate has heard all day."

Also, he suspected, the most useful.

PART II

CHAPTER FOUR

A Warning in Dongo

FIVE bullet holes indented the iron railing along the waterfront facing the grand piazza in the town of Dongo where Benito Mussolini in a German lorry and his mistress Claretta Petacci in a Hispano-Suiza were captured by Communist partisans and executed against a stone wall farther down the western side of Lake Como before being hung heads down with her undergarments exposed in the Piazzale Loreto in Milan.

It seemed a fitting place for the Mediterranean-American Development Corporation's cultural foundation.

Instead of taking the swift, surface-skimming *aliscafo,* Sam Linkum decided to go up the lake by the small steamer. From a slatted wooden chair on the upper deck, he could see the clouds mirrored in the shimmering aquamarine waters. High above the perfumed gardens and groves of the villas clinging on the hillsides, the snow-fringed Alps rose in the near distance. As the steamer plowed through the lake and circled toward the fragile dock with the grandeur of a transatlantic liner he overheard an Englishwoman who had boarded at the Villa d'Este in Cernobbio say that the captain, the one with the Neptunelike braided symbols of authority on his crushed white cap, could marry you at sea; the Lago di Como was almost like a self-contained country, far from the madding crowd, neither Italian nor Swiss but *civilized*. Dongo loomed before him, its piazza unveiled between the proscenium arches of the town: a suitable operatic setting for the carbines fired by the partisans during the final act of fascism.

Linkum heard someone call his name as he stepped down the gangplank. A hand reached for his bag and, instinctively, he yanked it back toward him. The hand was attached to an elegantly tailored uniform. Across the young man's breast pocket the word *Fondazione* was embroidered. Linkum loosened his grip and allowed him to take his bag. He felt a little embarrassed. His suspicion was unnecessary; he never placed documents in a bag that was checked.

"Welcome to the Mediterranean-American Foundation," said the uniformed chauffeur in English-English. The accents he had heard on the steamer made Como sound like a British lake, and here was another person talking behind his Adam's apple. He remembered that the northern Italian lake country had long been a favorite hideaway for foreigners living off the exchange and a remittance from home. Stendhal and Shelley had played in these lakeside villas and now, like the surviving great mansions along Fifth Avenue's museum mile in Manhattan, only foundations and physicians could afford to maintain them.

The chauffeur introduced himself as "Jon," and Linkum had translated, "Giovanni?" but the chauffeur, with a slight air of superiority instead of annoyance, corrected him, "No, Jonathan, actually, my mother was originally from Stoke-upon-Trent before she married my father the count." Almost anybody could be a count or hold some other nineteenth-century royal or ecclesiastical knighthood even in the fortieth, or was it the fiftieth, government in the Italian Republic.

Jon (not Giovanni) deposited his bag in the boot (not the trunk) of the Alfa-Romeo and raced the Fiats to the summit of the foundation's private hill. Autumn flowers along the winding pathways bloomed in summer bursts of forced color, holding back the season. Behind a wall of Lombardy poplars, on a promontory that extended like a thrust stage, stood the small castle owned by the foundation. An ancient campanile towered over cultivated shrubs in espalier patterns and closely pruned vineyards, and far below, the cottages of the gardeners and cooks and household staff were hidden on the nine hundred acres of secluded, privately owned corporate land. Attached to the campanile, but of a later vintage, were ochre-hued buildings with high windows topped by crenelated stone battlements. The chauffeur bowed politely and turned Linkum over to Brigida, the chatelaine, who gave him a weighted brass key to his suite—"one room for working, one room for sleeping," she said in Italian— with an added word that it wasn't necessary to lock the door, the *fondazione* was safer than Central Park at midnight. Brigida confessed that her knowledge of matters American came from "foreign" programs played regularly on RAI, second channel.

Linkum threw open the windows of his suite. Across the lake he saw another promontory jutting out where Lake Como and Lake Lecco converged before flowing their separate ways around Bellagio. Pliny the Younger, or was it Pliny the Elder?—he never could get his Plinys straight—had lived in splendor on that promontory; but half the villas on the lake claimed to have some affinity to one of the noble Romans. Standing behind the shutters, he looked down the manicured pathways to see if he was being watched. No one was in sight. He ran his fingers below the window ledge, feeling for wires; his hand came away only with flaking plaster and spider webs. Closing the shutters, he enveloped himself in total darkness and collapsed on the bed for a catnap, his body clock catching up with the European time difference.

Something woke him up, nagging his sleepy mind. He had neglected to check out the rest of the suite. He pressed the silent light switch and glanced around the bedroom. His eyes traced the thick moulding that circled the lofty ceiling. A wire could be hidden inside that would be invisible from below. No way to reach the moulding without borrowing a ladder, which would arouse suspicion. Anyway, there would have to be a microphone somewhere closer to head level. He wondered if his fingertips still had the wartime sensitivity. Not likely. His mind was as alert as ever, maybe more sophisticated, but his fingertips were out of practice and he was not in touch with the latest miniaturized devices.

Well, the obvious first. He remembered how that had been hammered home by the Royal Air Force captain on reverse lend-lease during training at the Army Air Corps intelligence camp on the disguised farm outside Westover Field in Massachusetts. The telephone. He unscrewed the mouthpiece, trying to recall the workings of these Italian wonders that were designed more for style than efficiency, then found it difficult to thread again. There was no extra connection for a tap. It wouldn't have mattered much; there could be outlets on the same line elsewhere in the castle. The light switch itself. Using the special blade of the initialed pocket knife that Jennie had given him on a birthday, he unscrewed the plate and examined the wiring behind the switch, flicked the lamps on and off a few times, unscrewed the bulbs, and replaced them in the sockets. He detected nothing unusual and wished that he knew more about wireless microphones.

He leaned back against the bolster on the bed and began to doze off again. On the opposite wall, facing him, were a lithograph and an etching by Henry Moore of Stonehenge by moonlight, the huge monoliths looking like primitive beasts; he had seen the same graphics at the Tate in London. Between the Moores was a canvas he did not recognize in an elaborately carved wooden and plaster frame. He closed his eyes and opened them again; something about the painting was almost journalistic, it had the immediacy of a press photograph: scores of figures in the foreground, richly clothed in veils, cloaks and tricornered hats, watching an object rising in a radiant sky above a Venetian lagoon. He studied it for a moment, then curiosity put him in front of the painting. Its inscription was still more puzzling:

The Balloon Ascent of Count Zambeccari
Francesco Guardi, 1784, State Museum, Berlin

What was a museum work worth at least a quarter of a million dollars doing in his bedroom? Had the Berlin museum loaned it to the foundation, or was it a fake? He tried to look behind the angled canvas without touching it but the painting was too close to the wall. Carefully, he strained to raise the heavy frame; it slipped off one hook and then a second and was free. He leaned the canvas against the wall.

His fingers followed the mauve wallpaper, up and across until they reached a slightly upraised patch in the floral design. He raised the flap in the wallpaper. He was not altogether surprised to see the microphone concealed inside.

For the first time since undertaking the assignment he felt exhilarated. His discovery called up adventures in this corner of the world when the world was so different, so uncomplicated.

All right, what the hell was this "Guardi" canvas doing in Dongo instead of Berlin? He examined it more closely, turned it around and found the answer stamped on the back of the canvas. It was an "authorized reproduction," neither fake nor real, an ingenious print photographed in full color from the original, then reproduced on rough canvas, shellacked, giving the illusion of brush strokes over the surface. The frame was real enough, with flying cherubim on the four corners, possibly making it more valuable than the reproduction itself. He quietly rehooked the heavy frame and canvas on the wall, glanced at the Guardi venture into low-level space with renewed pleasure, slipped into his pajama bottoms and closed his eyes.

The good old Mediterranean-American Development Corporation and its internationally renowned study center for scholars: anything for culture and the advancement of research for knowledge—even a bugged castle on Lake Como.

"Whenever I hear the word culture, I reach for my revolver," said Woodrow Wilson Condon, laughing. It was the foundation director's favorite greeting, and Sam Linkum heard it often during the next few days. "That's the only thing Hermann Goering ever said that I agree with. Well, that's a personal opinion, but I like to deal in specific proposals and not fancy generalities. I trust none of you gentlemen from the world of culture and information is carrying a revolver on your person. All right, you are all fellows of the foundation during your stay here as guests of Mediterranean-American. I trust you will shed your nationalities and inhabit, however temporarily, our independent republic of scholars. Please call me Woody."

The ten fellows standing on the dramatic terrace overhanging the lake watched the late sun caressing the mountains and sipped white wine made from grapes grown in the vineyards below that belonged to the *fondazione*. It was a half-hour before dinner and they were assembled together for the first time. "A moment of reflected light and reflection," said the director, who had once been an associate dean at Georgetown University before becoming an aide to the national security adviser in the White House. The confidential government position—called a branch of the "military-academic complex" in honor of those Harvard stalwarts, McGeorge Bundy and Henry Kissinger, who had occupied the civilian warrior's chair outside the Oval Office for two Presidents—inevitably assured him a berth in the foundation brotherhood that always took care of its own. Woody Condon, not long out of the professorial ranks, lectured the new fellows in orotund, rehearsed phrases that sounded wise on first hearing but soon dissolved in puffs of smoke.

Only a half-hour before, Sam Linkum had been awakened by what he thought was a scratching noise in his room. He was a light sleeper, especially when his motor was running on a story. It was an alien noise that differed from the natural sounds beyond the castle's walls. He strained his eyes in the darkness but could see nothing except the outlines of the furniture and pictures on the wall. He flicked on the lamp next to his bed and wandered in the half-shadow into the sitting room of the suite. A piece of paper had been slipped by unseen hands under the door. He bent to pick it up, unfolded the creases, double-checked to make sure that the door was locked and read it at the desk:

GREETINGS TO CAPITAINE SAM LINKUM.
I DID NOT WANT TO DISTURB YOU BY THE TELEPHONE IN CASE YOU WERE RESTING AND I ONLY TAPPED ON YOUR DOOR LIGHTLY. SO I SEND YOU THIS LITTLE MESSAGE IN ENGLISH. A HEARTY WELCOME TO MY OLD

110

FRIEND. I NOTICED YOUR NAME ON THE LIST OF FELLOWS AND I LOOK FORWARD TO OUR MEETING IN THE FLESH. IF I AM MISTAKEN AND YOU ARE NOT THE SAME PERSON FROM *SIXIÈME RÉGIMENT, SPAHIS ALGÉRIEN*, PLEASE EXCUSE ME. *A BIENTÔT*.

Moussi Ali

Linkum refolded the message and put it in his pocket. He himself would not have put something on paper here, not yet.

Still seated at the desk, he turned and noticed that another piece of paper was being pushed under his door. This time nobody bothered to knock. He opened the embossed, inner-lined envelope that bore the logotype of the Mediterranean-American Development Foundation: the letters M.A.D. in italics, intertwined on a field of green and red inside a monarch's crown. The elaborate message, also crowned, announced nothing more significant than the dining rules: breakfast served only in one's room (menu forms can be found in center drawer of desk), luncheon and dinner meals must always be taken in "the company of scholars." Thanks to Hap Chorley's long reach into the private world of conglomerates and their foundations he was brevetted an official scholar, at least for a few days. He hoped that the others were not there under false pretenses too. And he wondered if all the other bedrooms in the castle also had concealed microphones—to eavesdrop on conversations between the fellows or to monitor the pillow talk of any wandering professors who might be making it with one of the bilingual maids. The bug in his bedroom couldn't be exclusively his own; he was sure it was hooked into a voice-activated system that reported the nonscholarly activities of the company of scholars.

Outside and above his shuttered windows, he could hear the tinkle of drinks and laughter. The cocktail hour had begun on time. The other fellows were already on the terrace when he joined them. Moussi Ali would be a slight problem; he decided to play down their friendship, at least until they could be alone. But how to do that without the others noticing? He walked to the Lecco side of the promontory, as if admiring the view. After a moment, he felt a hand touching his elbow.

Linkum turned. "Thank you for your note—and I think I will pretend that I'm the one and only Sam Linkum."

"How are you, my old friend?"

"Out of uniform and over age for a *capitaine,* but otherwise, okay. You haven't aged a day, just moved some of your hair from your head to your chin, I see."

"The beard is new, the baldness began when I was a baby so I can take no responsibility for it. It has been, how many years now? How do I look to you?"

"Recognizable, and still elegant." Moussi Ali was muscular and carefully tailored. "They're watching us. I'd like to talk with you later, alone. So far as they're concerned we don't know each other."

Moussi Ali seemed puzzled for a moment, then smiled. *"D'accord."*

They strolled back to the table, where Brigida poured wine from a carafe for the fellows. On the promontory's Como side, Woodrow Wilson Condon was holding court and making the introductions.

"We have two Americans here so, as we say in the States, scholars first." He grinned at his own little joke. "This is Professor Elwood Normie, who holds the Distinguished Chair in Iron Curtain Studies at Bronx University. I am sure that some of you are familiar with Professor Normie's seminal work on press freedom in the Austro-Hungarian Empire."

Jesus...that's what you call *really* seminal, Linkum thought. And then something clicked. He had never met Normie but he recalled reading an article in *The Nation* about a group of subsidized New York intellectuals whose ideas resembled the evangelism of the radio and television preachers in the Moral Majority. Both were trying to purify, by their lights, America's behavior, its literature and, for good measure, nuke Moscow.

"We are fortunate that Mr. Samuel Linkum was able to join us on short notice before going to Algiers as U.S. delegate to the meeting of the U.N. International Information Agency," Condon said. "Undoubtedly, you have read his news stories in your own press." Condon fumbled his note cards that listed the *vitae* of the fellows. "Sorry if I've overlooked something. Sam, your present affiliation...?"

"Freelance."

Which was to say, "Unemployed." Condon did not press him.

The director introduced the other fellows: Moussi Ali, columnist for *El Moudjahid,* Algeria...Umberto Trapani, editor of the *Giornale di Sicilia* and Palermo correspondent for the *Corriere della Sera* of Milan...Aleksandr Skopje of Belgrade, foreign editor of *Tanjug,* the Yugoslav news agency...Jacques Maupin of Paris, a director of l'Office de Radiodiffusion-Télévision Française (ORTF)...Robin Jenkins of London, member of the board of the Independent Broadcasting Authority (IBA) that ruled commercial stations...Rodney Lawson, professor of communications at the University of Melbourne and member of the Australian Broadcasting Tribunal...Miyamoto (call me Mike) Tanaka, formerly of the daily *Asahi* in Osaka, now a director of Nippon Hoso Kyokai (NHK), the Japanese broadcasting corporation.

"I expect you all to cross-pollinate your ideas freely," Condon said. "Whether or not we come up with a consensus is less important than that we concretize some specifics." Linkum looked around at the others to see if they also wanted to laugh, but half of them were professors and would be impressed by, or at home with, the jargon. "And now, fellow scholars, unless anyone wants another glass of wine, I propose that we turn to the next item on our agenda— dinner. Do I hear a second?"

Dinner was served out of doors, under a pair of glazed orange and yellow Della Robbias affixed to the castle wall. The chatelaine's staff brought out the meal on silver platters, bowing and scraping and flourishing new cutlery with every course. For a moment Linkum could not think of the last time he had eaten off real silver, until he remembered his final pit stop at Farron Fields. He decided to save the handwritten menu on the regal stationery for Jennie; some day they'd present it to Mannie. Crema di Mais, Filetto alla Wellington, Patate Crochette, Piselli al Prosciutto, Insalata, Torta Fantasia and a wine from the region, Grignolino. A scholar undoubtedly could think more original thoughts after a platter of crocheted potatoes.

The fellows drifted off to their suites after dark. Linkum noticed that Normie had left alone after he had discouraged an exchange of inquisitive small talk. He did not think he had anything to learn from the professor; the state of the Austro-Hungarian press did not much interest him, and he already knew the familiar line of the radical-right think tanks. In the majestic living room the Sicilian journalist tuned the television set and explained how the commercials were bunched together only once for a few minutes in the evening over the Italian state network. The Yugoslav journalist dozed in a velvet chair, the Japanese and Australian broadcasters took notes. Linkum stood up and signaled Moussi Ali with a nod. Both said their good nights independently, as if going their separate ways, and walked down the long corridor toward their suites. At the foot of the massive staircase, they paused.

Linkum told himself it was time to get to work... "We've got a lot to catch up on, Moussi. I'm looking forward to seeing Algiers again."

"You were so short with me on the terrace, I was not sure if you were trying to forget our old times together—"

"I'm sorry—I just didn't want that cheerleader using our friendship to launch into another lecture."

"Oh, Mr. Condon seemed quite harmless. I would not presume to judge our distinguished—is that not his favorite word?—host, and your fellow American."

"It's a big country—I don't take either blame or credit for him."

"Would you like to continue our talk in my suite, Sam? It's a little more comfortable than standing in the hallway."

So the Moose hadn't checked *his* room; apparently he felt he had no reason to.

Linkum shook his head. He glanced down the corridor and then around the landing at the top of the stairway. No one was in sight. He could not invite the Moose to his room, not unless he wanted to share their talk with unseen ears.

"Let's take a stroll into the town. It may be a little chilly down there so I'm going to get a sweater. You might, too. Meet you here in ten minutes." Then, reconsidering, "No, make it the back entrance to the castle, outside the portcullis."

In his room, Linkum unlocked his leather handbag and reached for the camera case. Hidden below the telephoto lens lining was the regimental badge that Hap had loaned him. He slipped the blue enamel emblem into his pocket. He also wrapped a piece of dental floss around the lock so that he would know if it was tampered with.

Moussi Ali was a minute early. They descended the snaking footpath in the darkness, past a wall of hedges that formed the only railing, treading between the roots and stubbing their toes where the moonlight was snagged in the leaves and branches and they could not see, walking tentatively and grasping each other's arms for support until they reached the bend where the footpath widened slightly a hundred or so feet above the toy harbor. From here one could almost touch the spire of the little Romanesque church with its vaults and arches that stood at the far end of the piazza.

"No wonder the castle is still standing after six centuries," Linkum said, after they had opened the locked gate and finally reached the cobblestoned street. "It would have taken a small army of condottieri to come up this footpath and scale the walls against the longbows and catapults."

"Easier to breach the Vichy French defenses at Oran and Casablanca," Moussi Ali said. He had sided with the Free French in North Africa.

They walked across the piazza and found a bench facing the waterfront. The only lights still on in the town were strung along the dock. Dongo had gone to bed.

Except that Linkum was almost sure that he had heard footsteps behind them, at a discreet distance, heels on the cobblestones, stop and go, keeping up with their pace. Deliberately hesitating for an instant, as if to point out some splendor in the square, Linkum glanced sideward, saw a shadowy figure disappearing behind a column in the arcade next to the church.

Whenever I hear the word culture, I reach for my revolver . . . Woody Condon's laugh-line borrowed from Goering came to mind. Which one of them was the target of someone's interest—and whose side did that someone represent? It was damn strange, being tailed in, of all places, Mediterranean-American's cultural foundation.

Moussi looked at Linkum and nodded his head slowly. *"Sixième Régiment, Spahis Algérien.* I never imagined that we would meet again, and now suddenly it will be twice on two different continents. I am glad that we got away from the others up on the hill—they would not understand the comradeship of intelligence people. It has become unfashionable now but it was different when you, *capitaine,* served as liaison officer with the *Spahis* and I had the honor to be assigned to work with you. And also with the gross, excuse me, I mean, heavy Major Chorley. Whatever became of him?"

"Oh, he became a professor at a big university." Linkum thought that would be enough to tell him for now. "I ran into Chorley a while ago and he was still the same—"

"The same fat cigars?"

Linkum smiled. Hap would enjoy knowing his ID was Havanas.

"Do you remember when our information helped capture the six German parachutists?"

"The saboteurs in civilian clothes dropped near Maison Blanche? Yes, and how they were executed, three in the morning, three in the afternoon—a matinee performance, the French command called it, for those who could not attend the first show. As a lesson to both the Vichy sympathizers and the Arab villagers—a warning not to cooperate with the Germans, that they were kaput."

"The rule was, if a soldier was caught spying in civilian clothing, he would be put before a firing squad—"

"Rules of war, chivalry, all those notions are pretty outmoded in the nuclear age, Moussi."

"Exactly what I've written in my newspaper column, Sam."

"Antiwar?"

"What other war *is* there?"

"Well, at least you have a place to express your opinions. Are your censors tough?"

"Absolutely. No criticism of the ruler of the state. But they are less certain about things like literature, television and the arts. You would be surprised how much you can get away with if it's called *culture.*" He nudged Linkum. "We're talking here between friends, correct?" Linkum nodded. "Of course." And Moussi said, "Because I will have to sound more official in the U.N. meeting in Algiers." Which told him something; it was just the sort of information Hap wanted from him.

Linkum said, "We may both have to be less frank tomorrow—even among the other so-called fellows up the hill. Quite a crew the foundation has assembled. Did you know any of them before?"

"Besides you?" Moussi Ali thought for a moment. "Yes, the Frenchman from ORTF, Jacques Maupin. He's a big shot in broadcasting, travels back and forth a lot between Paris, Casa, Tunis and Algiers. They're setting up a system of linking the three countries in northwestern Africa with the commercial stations in Paris and Marseilles. You know, the French are out of their former Algerian Department politically but not commercially. We have the headaches, they have the business."

"So De Gaulle knew what he was doing—for France."

"In order to remain, you leave—oh yes, De Gaulle always knew which way the wind was blowing, in war and peace. I admired the general, he had a sense of history. The Cross of Lorraine may have been a heavy cross to bear for the Americans and British but De Gaulle won out in the end."

"Did you know Maupin as a government official?"

"What do you mean, Sam? That *I* am in the government? No, not at all, I am registered and licensed, of course, but I'm not part of the government. I know Maupin as a journalist knows all sorts of people, as a source. If you write about television, you get to know government broadcasters. No mystery, Sam."

Linkum hoped he was not pressing; he would not have wanted Moussi to ask him if *he* had any government connection... "So we're in the same boat. Amateurs representing our countries. Well, I'm pleased—it's led to our reunion...I suppose tomorrow they'll be talking about the information links between France and North Africa—"

"I'm sure someone will bring it up. I will if they do not. There is one controversial problem—direct broadcasting. Nobody wants it, but it's like trying to stop the ocean tides. Once the technology exists, the engineers and big corporations find ways to move forward."

Linkum nodded. "I think I read something about it in *L'Express*."

"DBS—direct broadcasting satellites. The signals can go from Paris or Marseilles almost directly to a home in Algiers or Oran or Constantine. I say *almost* because ground stations are required.

Naturally, the government does not want Paris or anyone else talking directly to our people. It could lead to mischief, propaganda in the wrong hands."

"That satellite stuff is over my head in more ways than one. I'm still in the old, nonelectric typewriter age, I like to hear the noise of the keys, it gives me a sense that I'm doing something—"

"You have heard of Pleumeur-Bodou?"

"Vaguely..." So far, Linkum said to himself, he had not lied, only concealed.

"It is the big ground station on the Brittany coast that transmits satellite programs back and forth across the Atlantic. By retransmissions, it means that programs from America could reach Algeria or almost anywhere else."

"I suppose that's where Mediterranean-American Development comes into the picture?"

Moussi Ali shrugged. "I don't know much about the business of our distinguished host. I believe that they're more American than Mediterranean but I'm not sure. There is some French money there, maybe Saudi Arabian, too, they are investors in everything else, why not satellites? It is a secretive company. I do know that they have some sort of partnership with the French in the oil pipelines below Biskra. Even if I did know, I would not be able to write about it in *El Moudjahid*. My head of state looks the other way when it comes to foreign investments. You are one of my unofficial state enemies, Sam, did you know that?"

"No, but I hope you have none worse than me."

As they talked in the darkness, Linkum turned his head several times, listening for the footsteps. But he could only hear the gentle lapping of the lake against the piers of the steamer dock. He wondered if Moussi had also heard the footsteps. If he could believe him, Moussi was here only as a junketing journalist representing a country Mediterranean-American had interests in. Which meant the Moose would not be on the *qui vive* for anything out of the ordinary. The fact that he had failed to inspect his room, had been willing to invite him inside without knowing if it was secure seemed to indicate that he was not on an intelligence assignment...didn't it?

Anyway, the beguiling Lago Di Como tended to dull the senses.

He had probed for some answers but left a little over for the next time; the main thing was to gain his trust and make the connection. This palace, the fellows, even the suspicions seemed far removed from USAFSS and those vulnerable ground stations...

Moussi turned away from the lake. "Sam, what did you mean when you called yourself a freelance? I have often read reprints of your articles in *L'Express* and *Le Monde*. Are you not writing for your newspaper any longer?"

"*Ça n'existe plus.*" Linkum shrugged, as if it didn't matter.

Moussi shook his head. "I am sorry." Linkum was not inclined to explain the machinations of the network and his own disenchantment after the newspaper was mortally wounded.

Instead Moussi asked him about his family life. Linkum simply told him that he had been married and that his wife had died in an accident. Moussi asked, "Did you have any children?"

"A son—killed in an accident, too." The half-truths were enough. Drowning from grief and burning from napalm, weren't they accidents?

Moussi touched his shoulder, then smiled when Linkum inquired about his family.

"Ah, my friend Sam. I am afraid that marriage was not for me. I tried it once briefly, an arranged marriage made between our families in the traditional Moslem way. I was a good son, I wanted to please my parents. You know the Koran promises that paradise will be inhabited with dark-eyed virgins, and she was one, quite lovely, innocent, perhaps too innocent for me. The Holy Book teaches that women are inferior to men, fundamentally servants, childbearers and sex objects. It is written: 'Women are your fields. Go, then, into your fields as you please.' But that was my problem, not hers." Moussi looked carefully at Linkum. "I found that I did not enjoy her fields..."

Linkum was embarrassed. He did not want to intrude, yet he was curious about Moussi's private life. He realized that despite their wartime adventures he never knew anything about the man beneath the uniform; the common involvement of the war overpowered intimacy.

"Are you still married to her?" Linkum tried to pass it off lightly.

"Isn't it true that under Islamic law a man can divorce his wife just by repeating 'I divorce you' three times? It could put American lawyers out of business."

Moussi smiled. "She divorced *me* after less than a year of so-called marriage. The Islamic law gives a wife rights, too. Do you want to know her grounds?" Before Linkum could say only if he wanted to tell him, Moussi told him. "Because her husband refused to have sexual relations. It was true. I did not contest the divorce. By that time, anyway, I was seeing someone else."

"Oh...so you never remarried."

"Not in that sense, no...I hope that you'll have a chance to meet my friend. His name is Ibrahim. We've been together now for fifteen years, ever since he left the university. He is now back there again, teaching classics. We share an apartment overlooking Algiers harbor, high above the Casbah. If you don't come to see us for a drink or dinner we shall both feel insulted. Have I shocked you, Sam?"

Linkum hesitated for a moment. "Surprised."

"Ibrahim Nuri and I have had a relationship that has lasted longer than most marriages among our educated friends. What is that interesting word used in the States for homosexuals? *Gay.* I prefer that to some of the other names that are demeaning. For a while there was an attempt to dictate morals by the revolutionary government and we thought we would have to move to Paris—as a veteran, I had that choice—but the head of state had enough problems without looking into private lives. We may not be following Sunna, the way of the Prophet, but we're content. We are what we are."

Linkum felt an urge to return the confidence. He reached into his pocket and pulled out the brass emblem of the *Sixième Régiment, Spahis Algérien,* turning it so that the light of the moon sparkled off the enameled silver scimitar. From the recesses of his wallet, Moussi Ali extracted a tattered cotton shoulder patch: pale yellow wings embroidered on blue field, the emblem of the Fifth Wing, Air Corps. Linkum had given it to him in exchange, departing.

The two men stared at the bits of metal and cloth; and then at one another. Then they climbed the hill to the dark castle.

> *"You cannot hope to bribe or*
> *twist,*
> *Thank God!, the British journalist,*
> *But seeing what the man will do*
> *Unbribed, there's no occasion*
> *to."*

Robin Jenkins, the British board member of the Independent Broadcasting Authority, wore a look of self-satisfaction as the other fellows laughed and applauded his recitation. "I was still in knee breeches when I first heard that old chestnut in the Manchester *Guardian*," Jenkins said. "Of course, we were not referring to our own practices but to those other ink-stained wretches, the Fleet Street Irregulars."

The *fondazione* meeting room on the second floor of the palace was designed to impress the company of scholars. They sat in high-backed oaken chairs, dwarfed by the knowledge that princely behinds had shaped the woven seats across the centuries. Wall tapestries showed scenes of men in ruffs, hunting lions and griffons and other beasties, real and imagined, and severe dukes in dark, cracked canvas looked down on the proceedings. The only modern touch was a tape recorder erected like a totem to be worshiped, directly in front of Woodrow Wilson Condon.

"Gentlemen, this is a freewheeling assembly." The director had turned on the recorder discreetly. "Of course, whatever you say remains in the confines of this room. As we used to say in the office of the national security adviser, everything here is on deep background only. You can't be misquoted. You may wonder why this tape recorder is turned on. Psychological effect—it makes you think about what you're saying before you say it. It's also for the sake of the record. In case any of you wish transcripts of what you have said, please let me know. Otherwise, we're rolling."

Professor Normie spoke up, "Information is as information does— that's what I told my graduate students. I did not come here to criticize my country or countrymen except for those who deserve a rude awakening. What all of us need are a few homilies that are eternal, and factoids. Factoid one: American enterprise has not been given a fair shake in the newspapers—in the United States or, if you'll pardon me, the foreign press that you gentlemen represent. Factoid two: There are too many reporters of the left-liberal persuasion who color their stories with knee-jerk reactions. Lo, the poor Indian. Lo, the old folks on social security who are starving even if they are independently wealthy. Lo, the poor working women who call themselves discriminated against and blame the government if they're not made vice-presidents. Factoid three: Bad news is news, good news is not—especially if it is about the President of the United States and his wife."

Mike Tanaka of Nippon Hoso Kyokai raised his pinky to be recognized. He bowed toward Normie.

"Pardon my intrusion, but what are these factoids you speak of?"

"Factoids are facts, plain hard facts," Normie replied brusquely.

"Oh," Tanaka nodded. "Very interesting." It was almost comic.

"Ah, but are facts factoids?" inquired the impertinent Jenkins, the British broadcaster, his Oxbridge sarcasm showing.

Normie responded with a silent glare.

Linkum decided to put out a feeler. Apart from the American, the fellows around the table in Dongo would also be in Algiers as delegates or consultants to their missions. As for himself: *Prima di parlar, tasi.* Time enough to speak his views later where they would count, in Algiers.

"I'm interested in hearing from any of the fellows who live with licensing or censorship," Linkum said. "How does it work?"

The Yugoslav news agency man, Skopje, immediately answered, "We have no formal censorship in my country. You can publish whatever you wish—"

"And live to tell the tale?" Jenkins said, smiling.

"Can *you* broadcast anything you wish in England? Yes, I can live to tell the tale, but we Yugoslavs are not fools. If you want to publish, you learn to recognize what the Party considers destructive writing—that is the phrase they have used. Since the top press positions are held by Party members, there is not too much trouble. We can criticize government actions, corruption, but we do not challenge policy." Skopje smiled. "In case you were about to ask, yes, I am a member of the Party. It makes life easier for a writer."

Linkum hesitated to ask him how he would vote on licensing journalists, not in front of this company of scholars and Woody Condon's tape recorder.

Normie suddenly turned on Moussi Ali.

"Algeria is one of the worst, isn't it? I mean, if you had your druthers, wouldn't you prefer writing in a free country?"

Moussi replied, "We are free, free from colonization. There was a time during our civil war when the French government banned any Arabic-language newspaper. I do not know what *druthers* are, but I prefer to remain and write in my birthplace." He tightened his jaw; Linkum had seen him do so in moments of stress. "No, I am not a member of the government party, or any political organization, but I do belong to the *Union Algérienne des Journalistes*. Perhaps you can obtain a copy of my newspaper some time and judge it for yourself—"

Condon said. "Gentlemen, this has been a wonderful session. And now, do I hear a second for a drinkie?"

Walking to his suite, Linkum added it up. The Moose, and probably the others too, were inclined to apologize for their own systems of suppression, even defend practices they regarded, in private conversation, as repugnant. Influencing their votes, let alone their spoken ideas, seemed like Mission Impossible. What else could you expect in public discourse by quasi-government officials? The *fondazione* wasn't Mannie's Place, you couldn't let your hair or your guard down here. The broadcasting fellows had kept their mouths shut at the session. All over the world, the United States excepted, television was considered a publicly owned resource, under the post office in one country, a ministry of culture in another, not a beggar with a tin cup. He wondered what might happen if he was called on to defend the commercial exploitation in his own country; would he also feel obliged to make the right noises? *One for you and one for me...*

"Linkum, just the man I wanted to see." It was Professor Normie. "Can I come in for a moment? It could be for your benefit."

Linkum was standing in front of his suite and couldn't think of an excuse to say no. They sat across from each other in the workroom. Normie reached into his valise and placed a heavy suede leather sack on the desk.

"Know what's inside? Gold. Know where it's from, my friend? Lugano, Switzerland. No problem, take the ferry near the post office, drive north to Menaggio, up through a small pass to Oria, the Italian customs point, then go through a couple of tunnels and Swiss customs till you hit Lugano. The whole trip takes a little over an hour and you can't miss the banks, they're up and down the main drag. Swiss cheese and numbered accounts, what a country."

Normie grinned, looking like a ferret with curly hair, his eyes narrow. He unfastened the leather thong and turned the sack upside down, spreading the coins on the desk.

"South African krugerrands—Fyngold stamped, one ounce fine gold. Gold coins of Mexico, with a winged woman from the classics, look at her tits, not her wings, that's what I call truly stacked, one onza oro puro. British gold sovereigns, struck in twenty-two karat gold, eight grams, from the Royal Mint, and this one is a five-pounder, forty grams, only fifteen thousand minted worldwide. You don't like gold coins, maybe you prefer small bars? Credit Suisse, two to five ounces. Pure platinum bars, from Johnson Matthey Ltd., fine assayers and refiners to Her Majesty the Queen, five and ten ounce troy weight, each one with individual serial numbers, registered in the London Gold Market. Doesn't look fancy but more portable and concealable, can be used as weights in a jacket or coat lining, good as gold."

Normie stacked the gold coins and bars like a croupier, covering all bets with the odds of greed and surprise in his favor, and pushed them across the desk to Linkum.

"They're all yours, Sam."

Linkum stared at the pile and then at Normie, not saying anything.

"And there's more where these came from, if you feel it necessary—"

"Who do you represent, professor?"

"Our side—same as yourself."

"I didn't know we were on the same side."

"Come off it, Linkum, this isn't Las Vegas gold, you know."

"No? Whose gold is it—Moscow's?"

"That crack isn't worthy of an American delegate. Don't forget, you're speaking for a lot of people, including yours truly—everybody concerned about all that licensing crap and making sure that there's freedom of commerce. So I'll forget what you said. Be sensible."

Linkum looked at the piles of gold coins and bars. His old reportorial instincts returned; he wanted *him* to respond.

"How much does this stuff add up to?"

That was more like it. Normie rolled back the cuff of his shirtsleeve. He was wearing a watch that told the time, day and month and, right below it, a calculator. "You want it in dollars?" Linkum nodded. Normie pulled out a card that showed the exchange rates. He tapped out the tiny numbers on his wrist, his lips moving and keeping all the figures in his head. After a couple of minutes he said, "As of today, exactly forty-nine thousand seven hundred and eighty-eight dollars and twenty cents."

"You're pretty fast at figures, professor."

"Not bad."

"That's a small fortune, at least for a newspaperman."

"It's not for you exactly, except if you need part of it. It's for the others."

"Oh, I'm glad to hear that. For a minute, I thought it was intended as a bribe."

"Absolutely not. It's for goodwill and expenses."

"Whose goodwill?"

"Mediterranean-American's."

"Are you acting on their behalf?"

"You don't think I'm taking it out of my account, do you? You're not that charming."

"What's your relationship to Mediterranean-American?"

"I don't mind telling you—I'm a consultant in international affairs. Provide a large-scale vision for their executives, give some lectures to the staff, attend a few foundation meetings, perform an occasional service for the firm. Like now. Nothing mysterious, it's all aboveboard."

"I'm not too clear on one thing—who's supposed to be on the goodwill receiving end of the gold?"

"The delegates and journalists covering the Algiers meeting. Especially the third worlders, like the Algerian and Yugoslav and that Sicilian who writes for *Corriere della Sera,* the one who keeps his mouth shut. You know, Mediterranean-American does business all the way from Gibraltar to Ankara. It's important for the firm to have friends at that U.N. meeting—that's why the foundation brought some of the delegates here for a little Rest and Recreation. The broadcasters and journalists are part of the game. You heard that piece of doggerel about bribing and twisting recited by that loudmouth British guy? *He* said it, we didn't. With a little baksheesh in his pocket, a friendly reporter can slant a story favorably. Leave out the nasty adjectives, substitute other ones. You don't have to say a word—"

"Just pass out the money—just like that."

Normie smiled. "Ah, that's my point. This isn't money, it's coins. Money in dollars is crude stuff. Money in coins is called *collectibles.* For our purpose, like a souvenir a friend admires that you give him. You've got to admit that some of these coins are like works of art. And, by the way, they appreciate in value, too."

"You've come up with a new angle, professor. The answer is— no deal."

"Not so fast. I omitted one thing. None of this pile has to be accounted for, including the coins you keep for your personal expenses. I walk out of your room, it's the last anyone knows of it."

"Well, *I'd* know about it. You understand that?" But Linkum knew he wouldn't.

"A lot of influential people would be extremely disappointed by your inflexibility—"

"Really? Name two."

Normie drew himself up. "People in high places in Washington and New York, in government and the foundations, people who could make a difference in your future. Didn't you work on that newspaper that folded?"

"I guess I'll worry about my future, professor, and it doesn't include any krugerrands from South Africa."

"Sleep on it overnight, Sam. If you still feel the way you do, I'll take them back and no hard feelings."

Linkum shoveled the gold coins into the suede leather sack and pushed it into Normie's hands.

"Stick them up your ass, professor."

Elwood Normie turned red.

"I'm not accustomed to being talked to that way. I assure you that people will hear about your manners. You'll learn that I'm not just anybody—"

"You're nobody to me but an academic hustler," Linkum said, thumbing him out the door. "And another thing. Don't call me Sam."

Afterward, before hitting the sack for the night, Linkum stared at the Guardi reproduction and wondered how sensitive the bug was, and who had overheard them.

"I want to get the ball rolling by reading one of the public service ads from Mediterranean-American that I found relevant for our assembly of scholars," said Woody Condon the next morning, his tape recorder turning. All the fellows were present. "The key part of the ad says that the press has misused its power, allowing its skepticism about public officials to turn so hostile that the government's ability to function has become weakened. No code of chivalry allows or requires us to challenge every official action. In other words, the press has to bear a big part of the responsibility for the disarray in the White House, the Prime Minister's Office, or wherever. Gentlemen, what think you?"

The Australian laughed. "Blame the bad news on the press—where have I heard *that* before? Did the Mediterranean-American ad really revive that?"

Condon retreated. "I'm not saying we here have to agree or disagree. I've just raised it for discussion."

"A press is fortunate where it can criticize freely," said the Yugoslav. "Even opinions hiding behind paid advertisements."

"Right," said the Englishman. Most of the others nodded in agreement, except for Professor Normie. "The press has no God-given mandate to sit in judgment. It's not the Supreme Court, only the Fourth Estate," he said.

Linkum doodled on a piece of elegant M.A.D. stationery and slipped a note behind his palm to Moussi Ali: "Let's skip the afternoon session and take a steamer ride up—or down, whichever you prefer—Lake Como or Lecco."

Moussi returned the note with a footnote: *"D'accord* or O.K., whichever you prefer."

Woody Condon put away his house ads for Mediterranean-American, saying that the development company and the foundation were, of course, independent entities. Of course. For the remainder of the session, the fellows exchanged information about the mechanics of publishing and broadcasting in their own countries.

Instead of turning up for the drowsy, lectured lunch served for the company of scholars at the *fondazione,* Sam Linkum and Moussi Ali boarded the lake steamer at the Dongo dock where, the night before, they had caught up with their lives under the shadowed moonlight. The steamer was already bustling with passengers who had spilled out of the nearby mountain villages and tourists talking in lyrical and guttural languages. Crossing the lake, the officer on the bridge announced in Italian only that a stop would be made first at the fishing village of Varenna. "Look at that sign," Linkum said, pointing to the landing. It noted that a certain villa was the home of a study center for high nuclear physics.

"Even on Lago di Como," Moussi said.

"No escaping the nukes any place."

They did not drop off but continued south to a small island in the lake, Isola Comacina, where they ate lunch, freshly netted trout and a swirled egg-drop soup called stracciatelli and a new wine, Cortese di Raggio, that the restaurant owner's wife touted.

Linkum recognized several faces from the steamer, the vague faces of strangers that remain in the memory hole for twenty-four hours and then disappear. The same faces boarded the steamer again on the return to Dongo, as if trailing them. The stop just before Dongo was Bellagio, at the promontory that divided the wind.

It was as the ropes were being flung overboard and caught by dockhands that the shot rang out—followed quickly by a second—and then shouting.

Blood streamed down Moussi Ali's left trouser leg from a spreading stain above his knee. The first shot had missed; the second bullet caught him. Linkum recognized the noise of a small weapon; only the man who pulled the trigger and saw the smoke trailing from the barrel felt the gun's kick. As Linkum quickly turned his head to see the direction of the shot, he was tackled to the ground by a short man in a striped purple-and-yellow rugby shirt. Flat on his face, Linkum swiveled his head beneath the man who had thrown him. The rugby shirt shouted to him to "stay down." Linkum did. The short man jumped up and over Linkum's head and ran after a figure in a double-breasted business suit. He knocked the gun out of his hand but the figure leaped off the deck of the steamer onto the dock, then ran to a waiting small truck with no markings on it, slammed the back door shut and was driven off, disappearing through the narrow streets and the gate in the southern wall of the town. The short man retrieved the weapon and put it in his pocket.

"Are you all right?" The rescuer grinned, exposing a gap between his front teeth. "Sorry about that—didn't know how many of them there were. Wild shot as effective as an aimed one if it lands on target. Bastard got away, had a friendly waiting for him, but I got his gun." He patted his pocket. "Another five seconds and I would have grabbed him too. Lousy shot."

"Where's Moussi? Is he all right?"

"Your friend was grazed. Looks worse than it is."

Moussi Ali stood next to them, a handkerchief pressed against his thigh. "A nice peaceful boat ride on the lake, Sam?"

"Can you walk comfortably, sir? If not, we can carry you off. Here, Mr. Linkum, let's give him a hand going down the gang-plank."

It had all happened so quickly that most of the debarking passengers had not been aware of the incident...except for those who had disappeared into the crowds along the busy waterfront, witnesses to nothing.

"I know a doctor in Bellagio on the Via della Musica. Get any smoke burns out and cauterize the wound and no questions asked or record kept."

The short man in the rugger shirt signaled a taxi and in rapid Italian with only the trace of a British accent told the driver to take them to the doctor's office and wait outside.

While the doctor bandaged Moussi, Linkum thanked the man for his help and then asked him how he knew his name.

"Oh, I overheard your friend mention it during lunch on the island," he said, "and found it unusual enough to remember. If I'm not mistaken, American?" Linkum nodded, aware that the man was holding back. "A lovely little restaurant and an exceptional wine, that Cortese di Raggio, probably doesn't travel more than ten miles in any direction from here."

"You know my name—what's yours?"

"Tweed Jerome. Half-American myself. Black sheep on both sides, going way back. Boss Tweed on the American side, Jack Jerome on the British side, he was an uncle of Chruchill's mother. I was stuck with both names. Actually, could be worse—dual citizenship."

Linkum thought to himself, he couldn't have invented *that* one, it sounded farfetched enough to be true.

"I haven't had a chance to look at this little toy," Tweed Jerome said, patting his pocket. He pulled out the weapon that he had knocked out of the gunman's hand, ejected the clip and held the barrel up to the light to see if a cartridge was in the chamber. Jerome hefted it professionally.

"Not a bad number. Chasseur nine-millimeter semiautomatic. French, carried by officers. Old-style, slightly dated, probably captured or sold and resold in French Indo-China or French North Africa or one of their Caribbean colonies. I take back what I said about that guy in the double-breasted suit being a lousy shot."

"What do you mean?"

"Well, I know a little bit about weapons, Linkum. Sort of a hobby of mine—I'm a collector of guns and bad shots, and that guy knew just where he was aiming with this very effective sidearm. It wasn't a killing but a warning shot."

Linkum hesitated, unwilling to say anything that might reveal what he knew, not to the mysterious Tweed Jerome who had thrown him to the ground to get him out of a bullet's way.

"Do you think whoever it was aimed only at the kneecaps—to maim but not kill?"

"Can't say for sure but it didn't look like a kneecap job that some Italian gangsters use as a calling card. That would put you out of the game for months. No, this was something less, just a grazing wound in the thigh, enough to cause a little discomfort and make you think twice."

Moussi Ali emerged from the doctor's office. "Who gets the bill? I offered to pay him but he refused anything—said it was superficial and I would be as good as new in a week."

"Don't worry about the bill," Jerome said. "The doctor is an old friend. I've sent him a lot of patients."

"When is the next steamer from Bellagio to Dongo?" Moussi said. "I'd like to sleep this off in my room."

"No problem," Jerome said. "I've got the taxi outside and a private launch can bring us back."

When they reached the Dongo dock Tweed Jerome offered to pay for the hired launch. They split it three ways. Linkum asked him where he was staying. Jerome pointed vaguely to the range of hills above the town. "A private villa—been coming to this area for years. I'm sure we'll run into each other again somewhere. Take care." He walked like a man in a hurry to a parking lot alongside the dock and drove off in a two-seater Jaguar.

Jonathan was waiting at the gate of the *fondazione* to take the two wandering fellows up to the castle in the Alfa-Romeo. Woody Condon stopped them before they could slip away to their suites. He offered to get a local doctor for Moussi Ali.

"I heard you had an accident. Sorry you took off—we had a lively session in your absence." He seemed to be reprimanding them. "Too bad you missed it."

Linkum asked, "How did you hear about the accident?"

"Oh, news travels quickly up and down the lake—no secrets around here. But I'm glad it was nothing serious. Probably an apprentice purse snatcher. You gentlemen do look prosperous. Some of them are as bold as brigands. Don't repeat this to our good scholar from the *Giornale di Sicilia,* but the Mafia is in every region nowadays, even up north in the lake country. Well, at least they didn't kidnap you—"

"They wouldn't try that—the ransom would have to be paid by someone beside ourselves. Wouldn't it cost the foundation too much?" Linkum stared at Condon. "We're worth our weight in gold, you know."

The director smiled weakly. So the bug in his bedroom wall was sensitive enough to pick up a conversation in the sitting room. He wanted Condon to know that *he* knew.

Linkum escorted the Moose to his suite and helped him stretch out. The Bellagio doctor had done his work well; the dressing was small and neat and Moussi hardly felt pain. Linkum wanted to ask him the crucial question now but knew he could not, not in this room or anywhere else inside the castle with big ears.

The next morning, after the room breakfast, Linkum steered the Moose out of doors, presumably to exercise his leg. They walked down a path in the sculptured garden and stopped at a stone bench. No one was in sight or within hearing distance.

"Who, Moussi?"

"One of my own people."

He said it unhesitatingly.

Linkum waited for his explanation; pumping him...

"It is complicated but I am pretty sure that he was an Algerian. One of the splinter parties that has threatened me in the past for what I have written in *El Moudjahid.* They're a fanatical group with anarchistic methods. They would not hesitate to shoot guns or throw bombs."

"Has this group got a name, a particular leader?"

"The Independent Moslem Brotherhood—that's what they call themselves but their name does not tell everything. The leaders are a combination of political and religious fanatics with a big following among students, including many in the States."

"Any ties to Moscow?"

"Just the opposite. They're against any form of socialism, they have some dream of recapturing a true Moslem faith of the past.

Neither French nor American colonialism—that is one of their sayings. They hate the Moroccans for providing airfields to the United States bombers. They do not want any American influences—especially by television. American newspapers are unimportant to Algeria. Most of the people in the countryside have no second language. But television does not require literacy."

"But what would they have against you personally? And it can hardly be enough to threaten to kill you."

"Here I am, surrounded by Americans and Europeans, living in a palace owned by Mediterranean-American and—"

"Moussi, are you saying that being seen with me endangered your life?"

"No, I would not put it quite that way, though I am sure they are not happy when I socialize with foreigners."

"So they were warning you before the meeting in Algiers?"

"Yes. They would like me to talk their language there. I am for more contact between us, not less, just as we once had in the *Sixième*. They would have me bury my head in the sand together with their brotherhood. I shall be under pressure as a delegate . . . Tell me who is this chap, Tweed Jerome, who was so kind to us?"

"Never saw him before in my life." Linkum wanted to add, and I don't think he told us the straight goods about his background and why he was Johnny-on-the-spot. "If I learn any more about him, I'll let you know when I collect that drink you promised in Algiers."

Some of the pieces in the puzzle about the shooting and rescue were still missing, but the information about the Algerians with Chasseurs who knew how to use them and their band of anarchistic brothers could be useful. In a crazy way, the Mediterranean-American *fondazione* had turned out to be a challenging puzzle. The idyllic setting was a curious place to be offered a bagful of gold *collectibles* by a bagman from academe working for the international conglomerate.

At the farewell dinner Woodrow Wilson Condon pronounced the session a brilliant success—"one of the finest exchanges of ideas since Pliny the Younger, the Guelphs and the Ghibellines." He waited for his laugh. In the morning the scholars collected the foundation's soap and shampoo and went their independent ways. Those who would be delegates promised to renew their friendships at the U.N. meeting in Algiers.

Linkum hurried back to his suite and packed. The *aliscafo* would skim across the lake, Dongo to Como, and then he would take the train, Milan to Rome. At the last moment he took out his camera and attached a 105-millimeter telephoto lens. Moving back, he took a shot of the Guardi painting, then unhooked it from the wall and set the heavy frame on the ground. He lifted the wallpaper flap and looked around the room for something to hold it up so that the implanted microphone would be visible in its place. The old intelligence phrase was the same as the one in Latin: *in situ*. Funny how the instincts from that time surfaced, tricks long forgotten, but the evidence could be important. He had no pin or tack, not even a paper clip. Then he remembered that he always carried a Band-Aid in his wallet, a habit left over from the time Antonio was a small boy returning home with scraped knees. The adhesive held back the flap. He moved the camera in for a close-up, yanked the small microphone out of the wall and photographed it, front and back, including its markings. He put it in his pocket. After rehanging the picture, he left the suite and walked down the corridor to the director's office.

Woody Condon looked up in surprise.

"I thought you'd already left—did you forget something?"

"No, but you did."

Condon regarded him coldly.

Linkum realized what he was about to do might not be the most sensible thing in the world... well, the hell with it... let the pompous hypocrite have it, this one, damn it, is for me...

He took the microphone out of his pocket and threw it on Condon's desk.

"I believe this little bug is the property of Mediterranean-American."

Condon's jaw tightened.

"Shove it up your cultural foundation."

He turned and strolled down the stunning hillside to the going-away dock at Dongo.

Feeling very good, at least for the moment.

CHAPTER FIVE

Love and Dynamite

THE ambrosia of Rome penetrated the moment he caught sight of the sentinel poplars silhouetted against the skyline; and as the *rapido* approached Termini Station he was moved again by the sight of those muted colors of the capital, burnt orange and dried mustard, that time had smeared on the walls of the ancient buildings and monuments to folly and grandeur.

Linkum glanced around the great railway station, looking for a phone booth, but all were lined with callers. He stopped and bought copies of *Avanti!* and *L'Unità* to see if the socialist and communist newspapers had any articles about satellite television or journalistic licensing, and took his change in a couple of telephone tokens. He found a free booth outside the station on Piazza del Cinquecento. Sliding a *gettone* into the phone, he pressed the button next to the slot, flagged the international operator after less than two minutes of bargaining and succeeded in connecting a minute later. The credit card and the special number in Maryland had both worked their magic.

"Where the hell have you been? I tried getting you at the foundation in Dongo but the director said that he didn't know where you had gone and he hadn't seen much of you anyway."

Hap Chorley came through loud and clear. From the sound of it, Linkum knew he had made an enemy of Woodrow Wilson Condon. Not that he was surprised.

"What time have you got there, Hap? I didn't want to wake you up before you left for your big Pentagon desk—"

"It's 0730 hours and I've been up for over an hour, chum, stuck by the phone. At your age you ought to learn to tell the time."

"You've got a two-faced watch that does your thinking for you."

"Baloney. Add five hours going east, subtract five going west, nothing to it—"

"Yeah, but which is east and which is west?"

"You seem to be pretty frisky this morning. Couldn't go out with Helen for our usual run on the country roads, and it's all your fault. You owe me twenty-five pushups."

"Hold it, Hap, I didn't hear the last thing you said. There are five thousand Fiats going past this phone booth all at once."

"Where in the hell are you calling from?"

"Bella Roma. In the big square outside the railway station. It's secure—"

"What are you doing in Rome? I thought—I expected—you would be catching either the TWA or the Alitalia out of Milan and come right back after the session at Dongo. What's this long way home stuff?"

Linkum hesitated. He didn't want to lie and now kicked himself for not thinking up a good excuse.

"It's just an extra day, Hap. We've still got almost a week before the Algiers meeting. I wanted to recharge my batteries in Roma—always do."

The line seemed to go dead for a minute. Then Chorley came on again. "Well, how did it go?"

"Lago di Como was lovely as ever. One of those places the Cold War forgot—"

"You think so, chum? What about that little incident on the steamer at Bellagio?"

"How did you hear about that?"

"You'll find out when I see you. Didn't sprain your back or balls when you hit the deck, did you?"

"I'm all right. You seem to know as much as I do about what happened. Was *I* the intended target or—"

"Come on, Sam, this isn't the time to speculate. Anyhow, you're not paying for this call, it's the USAFSS nickel. By the way, give me a quick headline. How did you get along with the Moose?"

"Like old times. Looks about the same, except that most of his hair's now on his chin."

"Did you find the old *Sixième* emblem useful?"

"Matter of fact, I did." Linkum thought of the talk in the darkness when Moussi had disclosed the facts of his private life. "I'm glad you remembered it, and I think I'll hang onto it for later... Hap, you don't have to tell me now but when you called that director at the Mediterranean-American Foundation to ask about me this morning, how did you identify yourself?"

"Well, chum, I didn't tell him who I was. You didn't get there through me—your auspices were Farron and Whipley, remember?"

"Because you'd told me not to mention your name and I didn't think you would blow that cover—who were you, anyway?"

"I was calling for Mr. Farron's office. You know how that goes in telephone gamesmanship, don't you? You call for an office, not the person himself. That guy—what's his name, Condon?—jumped when I said I was from the chairman of the network's office. He didn't even bother to ask me for my name. From the way he talked he sounded like he had a hard-on for you. What did you do, steal his vintage wine or screw his housekeeper?"

"Sorry, Hap, that's top secret."

"Well, as long as you upheld the honor of the Fifth Wing... I assume I'll see you one of these days—like tomorrow evening. Call me when you land at JFK. I can pick you up at National Airport. Anything you'd like me to do for you on this end?"

"You might save me the Washington *Post* for the time that I was away. I'm still the same newspaper freak—unless I catch up on back issues I feel like I've lost time out of my life."

"Nothing earthshaking has happened in Washington. I can tell you in advance that the same people who were in charge when you left are still in charge."

"That's what I was afraid of. Well, give my best to Helen."

"And mine to your friend Jennie Ives. Even though I've never met her, I've been listening to her series about the Vatican over National Public Radio." He hesitated for a moment, then added, "She's got an interesting sounding voice and she's pretty astute... have yourself a time, but be quick about it."

"Thanks, Hap. From both of us."

Linkum slipped another *gettone* into the public phone slot and dialed the number of the broadcasting studio that he had brought along with him. After going through two offices that tested his Italian forbearance for light opera, he finally heard that lovely voice come on.

"Jennie Ives, *per favore.*"

He played it like a stranger, for the hell of it. He felt high.

"Pronto... hello, this is Jennie Ives. Who is—"

"This is your favorite semicolon calling."

"Sam? Sam! Where are you calling from?"

"Roma. Here."

"That's wonderful..."

"I'm glad you think so, and said so."

"How did you track me down? I still haven't been able to figure out the phone system, and as for the mail, forget it—they tell me that the only way to get a letter through in any reasonable time is to go through the Vatican post office."

"I'm up to one of my old tricks with you—calling from a street corner. Only this time it's not from a booth on Third Avenue, it's from the Piazza del Cinquecento. I just pulled in on the *rapido* from Milan. I took a chance that you'd be using the facilities of RAI for your broadcasts. I hear you're not too awful."

"Sam, I have no idea at all how I'm getting over or who's listening. It's eerie—I talk into thin air and suddenly it's all over when the clock says time's up. Not like a piece in print that you can touch or read. I don't quite believe it. Who told you that I was doing okay?"

Not Hap Chorley, not the director of Air Force Intelligence at the Pentagon . . . that would lead to all sorts of questions and dissembling. So he would have to be disingenuous; no, he thought, the real word is lie—to lie to Jennie, to *her,* of all people . . . "I got the word from a friend of mine in Washington who heard you. He said your broadcast on the Vatican was quote astute unquote— how about that?"

"Obviously your friend has excellent taste. Do I know him?"

"No, I don't think so . . ."

Jennie paused for a moment, then asked, "What brings you to Rome?"

"If I told you Jennie Ives, what would you say?"

"Sam, you must have a better reason than me—"

"No better one. Well, you're most of the reason. I was in the neighborhood—"

"How come you were in Milan?"

"Junketing—I'll explain when I see you. Can we spend the rest of the day together?"

"I've got another broadcast I'm preparing and that I have to get out this afternoon. And I did have sort of an engagement with the RAI coordinators—"

"I'm only here for one day. I have to be back in New York on the noon flight."

Jennie said nothing for a moment, then, "The coordinators can wait."

"Thank you."

"Where shall we meet?"

"Well," he said, "I'm at the Raphael, just for the location, because it's behind the Piazza Navona in the old part of town that I like, and the piazza is a kind of all-day theater, but I only go there for the ice cream and to look at the Bernini fountain. Where are you staying? Maybe we can have dinner at a place close to you."

"The Scalinata di Spagna."

"I've stayed there, a long time ago." He did not explain that early in their marriage when they were broke most of the time, he and Elena had taken advantage of the pension's modest prices. "It's that pretty little pension on top of the Spanish Steps...have you had dinner at the Casina Valadier?"

"No, mostly I've eaten at one of the places at the foot of the Spanish Steps that take American Express."

"You're in for a treat. The Casina Valadier isn't far from your pension. As you step out the door, turn right and walk straight up, along the Viale della Trinità dei Monti in the Pincio gardens. The Casina Valadier is at the top of the hill. We can eat on the terrace if it's not too chilly. I usually head for that spot first whenever I'm in Rome. The city really does look eternal from there."

"It sounds lovely...what time, Sam?"

"Let's aim for six-thirty. If you get there by then I'll cue the sunset for you."

"Save me my place in case I get lost."

"No sweat. I'll be the one with an iced bourbon who looks like an unemployed newspaperman."

At the Raphael he negotiated a single room with a double bed, then walked into the square and sat down at Tre Scalini for a chocolate *tartufo* with two cups of espresso. Nothing had changed, not even his habit of staying near the familiar squares and seeing his old haunts in Rome. The waiters at Tre Scalini still used some ancient accounting method that Marco Polo might have brought back from China, tearing small slips of paper only halfway through and calling the mysterious handiwork the bill, and the tired-looking lire that he placed under the saucer to keep from flying away still seemed like play money. He looked at his wristwatch. Still an hour and a half to go before meeting Jennie. After showering he strolled along the Tiber, past the Castel Sant'Angelo, imagining the long leap in the last act of *Tosca* from the Castel to the river and listening for the crashing cymbals as the curtain fell. He turned where the Tiber itself curved and walked into the Piazza del Popolo and sensed the vibrations of the city coursing through the spacious square, people motioning importantly, playing out a thousand street scenes. In the Piazza del Popolo it was hard to imagine that this was the land of sudden violence—

He saw her first. She was standing on the terrace, her profile partly shadowed by a low-creased Panama rakishly tilted. Walking up behind her, he tapped her shoulder lightly, and as she turned around he kissed her full on the mouth, opened by surprise, and anticipation... They caught their breaths, smiling at each other.

"You're five minutes early," she said.

"Which makes you ten minutes early."

She was wearing a green blouse that set off her hazel eyes. The antique Victorian pin he had given her two birthdays ago caught the folds of a scarf knotted elegantly around her long throat.

"The management of the Casina Valadier ought to hire you to stand on the terrace. You look great."

"For an unemployed newspaperman, you're not so bad yourself. Where did you get that expensive tan?"

"I didn't know that I had one. Probably in some expensive garden above Lake Como. As soon as I reserve a table and get the Roman version of Mannie to bring us a bottle of Frascati with two straws I'll tell you about it."

They nibbled on slices of salami with mushrooms and artichokes in oil and sipped the wine and were caught by the view from their table on the terrace: the domes and columns and obelisks spread before them, outlined against the sky, and bold swallows dipped low into the sugar bowls on unoccupied tables and then wheeled and darted away in swift formations, their forked tails feathery in the light wind, and in the distance the great cupola of St. Peter's glistened in the sunset.

"Incredible," Jennie said. "I'm so glad you brought me here—"

"You know why I did," he said quietly.

She nodded, saying nothing, and continued to gaze above the tree line to the other side of the Tiber.

When she turned toward him he pointed at her hat. "That's new...I don't think I ever saw you wear one."

"I couldn't resist it, and no wisecracks, please. I'd be too embarrassed to wear it in New York but anything goes under the Roman sun. It's sort of early Humphrey Bogart translated into straw. At least I got the guy on the Via Condotti to take off the red-and-green striped ribbon..."

After the sun went down they moved inside the restaurant and followed the captain's suggestions about the veal specialty, but it was not quite the same as dining at the private table at the *fondazione*. Still, it seemed safer; and the company couldn't be compared.

"Sam, you're the one who taught us at the late, great paper never to go on junkets, remember? So what were you doing living it up on Lake Como?"

"Oh, I was being kept by a little company you may have heard about . . . the Mediterranean-American Development Corporation."

"The big conglomerate that's into everything? I didn't know it was in the foundation game, too."

"I didn't either, until I was invited to take part with some other journalists and academics in a roundtable on freedom, communications and society—some fancy name like that. The *fondazione* footed the cost of the whole thing, airfare, breakfast in bed and even a free stopover in Rome on the way back. Being bored by some professors theorizing on what's good for the American reading and viewing public was a small sacrifice to make for being here with you . . ."

She smiled at that.

"So I decided to break my own rule. It didn't matter anyway because I didn't have any place to pay off anybody in print."

He wanted to tell her as much as he could. "But that's only half the story. I'm a two-stage operation. Next stop, Algiers."

"I thought you were heading home tomorrow."

"I am, to check in and get some guidance and credentials. You know that U.N. International Information Agency?"

"The one that's trying to license correspondents? It's sort of a Mickey Mouse operation, isn't it?"

"More like Snoopy. Well, whichever, you are now sitting next to the United States delegate. Himself."

"You?" She hesitated for a moment. "Sam, I don't know whether I'm impressed or chagrined."

"Try a little of each."

"Well, all right. But you surprised me. I thought that was the kind of Jabberwocky job that went to one of the neo-conservative crowd around the White House and United Nations. Some professorial screwball who knows how to issue grand pronunciamentos... I'm sorry, I didn't mean to—"

"You're right. That may be as good a reason as any for me to serve as delegate. I know that gang pretty well. I've watched them operate for years in the Nixon and Reagan Administrations. There were even a couple of them doing a number for Mediterranean-American at Lake Como. They helped to clear up something for me, something I've thought about for a long time... they're not neo-conservatives or any other brand of conviction. They're opportunists, plain and simple."

Jennie laughed. "So what else is new? They're first cousins to the plain old-fashioned operators we saw working for Farron's network. Careerists whose code was looking out for number one. But how come you were chosen?"

"Frankly it threw me too." Again he had to hold back. "The American and western European delegations have been losing ground at the International Information Agency sessions in the last few years. They've made concessions to the dictatorships and third worlders in the name of unity but everybody really knows that it's game-playing. You remember the ridiculous American argument in the U.N. that goes: it's okay to be nice to authoritarians as long as you're beastly to the totalitarians? Well, the South American colonels and the East European apparatchiks think alike when it comes to suppressing the press—and they vote alike, too. In the meeting next week in Algiers there'll be a big push aimed at licensing journalists. The American delegation—so I've been told—decided that a professional newspaperman could beat down the arguments better than some professional diplomat or professor—"

"So Sam Linkum was picked to pull the sword out of the stone. It sounds like a toughie. I hope they're not setting you up—"

"What do you mean?"

"Sending you out on a lost cause and then putting the blame on you."

Smart Jennie... he hadn't given her the essential info—that he was Hap Chorley's choice and was playing a double game, one for the United States Air Force Security Service and its orbiting intelligence satellites, one for his own journalistic beliefs. And they were intertwined.

"You may have a point there, Jennie. But maybe I can score a few for my side—our side. Anyway, it should be a pretty good story for my notebook if no place else."

The waiter brought them a second pot of espresso and the captain sent over a sweet brandy that tasted of hazelnuts. He behaved as if Linkum was an old, remembered patron. It was also a signal that they were calling it a night at Casina Valadier.

They stood on the terrace after dinner, watching the steady flow of moving headlights crossing the bridges over the Tiber and breathing the cool night air that enveloped the city. Other couples had carved out private corners for themselves on the terrace, illuminated only by the flame of their cigarettes that described arcs like fireflies in the darkness.

"It's been a long time since we were really alone this way," he said.

"The last time was after the farewell party at Mannie's Place, wasn't it? A lot has happened since then. We thought it was the end of the world."

"It was the end of *that* world," he said. "Once a newspaper dies it's hard to bring it back to life, the habit of loyalty is fragile for readers."

"Maybe the disloyalty comes from the habits of television, you keep flipping the dial looking for another shot to your jaded appetite."

"Yes, including all the bizarre stuff heaven-sent by satellite."

He brushed his fingertips across her hand, as he had done so often during their times of intimacy.

She smiled. "I never could understand why you found my washerwoman's hands so appealing."

"Because they're part of you."

"Well, I look at them and think that they're pretty shopworn. Or typewriterworn. Anyway, I never did believe in palm-reading."

"Neither do I. What I'm talking about is Jennie-reading."

She squeezed his hand. "You know, Sam, when you told me that you're going to be a delegate at that U.N. meeting, it occurred to me that both of us are working for the government. What a way to go for a couple of old-time rebels."

"Yeah..." He hoped he hadn't said anything that somehow hinted to her that he was working for that other government, the covert intelligence agency at the Pentagon.

"Well, you're with the U.N. delegation—doesn't that come under the State Department?"

"Yes..." relieved. "It's a wholly disowned subsidiary—all fault, no credit."

"And I'm with National Public Radio, which is funded by—let's see, who *is* it funded by? By the so-called independent Corporation for Public Broadcasting, which gets its dough from Congress if it behaves itself. But wait a second, I'm working for *two* governments, indirectly." She imitated the resonant singsong voice of an announcer: *"This program is brought to you in part by a grant from the German Marshall Fund for international news coverage."*

They both laughed.

Jennie raised her hand as if it held a wineglass: "A toast to I. G. Farben and Volkswagen."

Sam raised his imaginary glass, clinked it against hers. "And to the wonderful folks at the Mediterranean-American Development Corporation."

It was like old times, finding their humor again in the ridiculous.

They meandered along the pathway leading off the terrace, and at the fork he asked her if she wanted to walk toward the Piazza Navona, in his direction, for ice cream and the late show in the lively square. She hesitated for a moment, then said it had been a long day and she thought she'd better head back to her pension. He didn't want to press her, to unbalance the delicacy of this brief time together. But his heart sank.

They followed the Viale della Trinità dei Monti, holding hands but not talking, not *really* talking, until they arrived in front of the pale yellow coach lamps of the Scalinata di Spagna.

"It's been a good evening, Sam. *Very* good."

He waited for a signal, not wanting to make it himself.

"My head's still swimming with all that wine and brandy."

"It'll feel better in the morning."

"Well...is it a long walk back to the Raphael?"

"It is, this time of night...but there are always taxis in front of the Hassler, right up the street."

"Oh...that's a good idea."

It was a rotten idea.

"Good night, Jennie."

She took off her hat and moved toward him. They kissed, then held each other. Close.

He walked away, toward the taxis at the Hassler, not allowing himself to look back.

It really had been a very good evening, he told himself as the taxi pulled up in front of the Raphael ten minutes later. Almost perfect. Almost was a big word...He walked into the lobby, picked up his key and told the concierge to reserve him copies of the *International Herald Tribune* and *Il Messaggero* in the morning.

In his room, he glanced at the large double bed. Its sheets were folded back on both sides for the evening by the chambermaid. Two pieces of Perugina chocolate wrapped in gold foil had been placed on both pillows. Somebody had the right idea.

He stripped off his shirt and tie. Leaving on only the small bedside lamp, he opened the wooden shutters and the window overlooking the courtyard and the laundry flapping in the light breeze, savoring the cool night air. As he stared at the red-tiled rooftops of Rome, the telephone rang.

"Hello."

"Jennie..."

"You forgot to wave good-by. You've made it impossible for me to get to sleep."

He said he was sorry...any way he could make it up to her?

She said that was up to him.

The concierge looked startled as Linkum ran past him and out the revolving door. He was in luck—a taxicab was just arriving in front of the Raphael. As the driver started to explain the night rate Sam told him to step on it going back to the Scalinata di Spagna. He overtipped him when they got there.

He called up from the modest lobby of the pension and when she

got on he said, *"Pronto,* Miss Ives, this is room service calling—
I forgot to get your room number," and she told him, "Come right
up, room service, stairway on left, Number 24."

Jennie had left the door slightly ajar. As he stepped inside he
closed it quietly behind him. The room was in total darkness. Their
arms reached out and found each other. They touched and pressed
together. Their tongues darted between their lips. His lowered to
her throat, her erect nipples. For an instant they parted, catching
their breaths. He played his fingers up and down her spine and
cupped her firm, lovely buttocks in his hands, drawing her closer
to him. He felt her shiver. They fell on the bed, unable, unwilling
to separate, moving together.

When they could no longer wait, they untangled themselves from
their clothes and kicked away their shoes, still talking silently with
their hands and bodies.

She whispered, "Don't wait, come right inside me, Sam." As he
entered her, she came up to meet him. They thrust their bodies
together...joined. Afterward, he stayed inside her, prolonging the
pleasures of their lovemaking. Their love.

She turned on the small lamp next to their bed. He told her to
close her eyes and he kissed her eyelids and she leaned back, smiling
now.

"See, that's what happens if you forget to wave good-by to a
friend."

"Considering the consequences, I never will."

She punched him. He said that he had brought along their dessert.
She said that she'd just had hers. Besides that, he said, and reached
down to the floor and took the two pieces of Perugina chocolate
from his jacket pocket.

"Compliments of the management," he said.

"Mint flavored. Wonderful."

"So you can be had for a piece of chocolate?"

"You think so? Just remember to leave an envelope stuffed with
hundred-thousand-lire notes on the dressing table before you leave."

She started toward the bathroom and he called out, "Don't you
know that people in love never have to go to the john?"

"Only cherubs and angels can get away with it."

She came out of the bathroom wearing her long crimson robe, and he noticed that she had never sewn up its split seam. The charm of imperfection. Perfect.

The robe was a further reminder of their intimate time. Running his hand down her back, feeling her skin, he said, "I feel right at home—your split seam is still showing."

"Something to remember me by."

They gathered up their clothes and arranged their shoes next to each other in front of the easy chair. She removed the robe and put on a lace-trimmed black silk shirt that barely covered her navel.

"Do you like it? It's a camisole." She actually blushed. "I'm trying to keep up with the younger generation. They've brought back the Victorian camisole..."

"You don't have to keep up with anyone."

They made love again, and again, and then, in their cocoon of darkness and fulfilled passion, they fell asleep in each other's arms....

In the morning she stirred first; he lay curled against her back, happily exhausted. She turned, sleepily, and brushed her lips along his shoulder.

"Oh God, I hope I'll be able to walk today without having it show. I think we set a few records last night—and I can feel it."

"I was about to suggest that I give you a wake-up call—"

"Not that kind of room service, thanks, I'd conk right out and never get to work." She sat up suddenly. "Do you really have to leave so soon? Can't you stretch your trip for another day of research in Rome? Everything's here—socialists and, reading from left to right, communists and fascists. Even a few Christians. Every shade of opinion that a good delegate needs to know—"

"Dammit, I wish I could—"

"You can research me. Oh God, sorry to be so corny but—"

He leaned over to kiss her and said that he already was a day overdue.

"Well, I'm going to hide your clothes so you'll have to stay over. You'll cause a riot walking naked down the Spanish Steps and get arrested and I'll bail you out on my recognizance and lock you up in this room."

"Make it my room—I've got a double bed and two pieces of chocolate."

"I hope you weren't cramped here...we seemed to have fitted—"

"In every way, Jennie."

She shook out her tousled hair and snuggled into the crook of his arm.

"Do you want to know my favorite part of you, Sam?" She half-opened one eye and turned toward him. "And it's not what you think."

He put his arms around her.

"Right here, right where I am now, my head on your chest..." He could feel her heart beating. "You know the trouble with the Pepsi generation? They're always trying to discover new orifices, and in the process most of them overlook the other really good parts."

"You're the really good parts, Jennie. All of you."

He turned her over on her stomach. Below her left shoulder blade there was a cruel scar. Long ago, before they had met at the newspaper, she had been engaged to a violent young man. Once, in a fit of jealousy, he had picked up a piece of tin Mexican sculpture and with its sharp edge had slashed a deep wound in her skin. She had told Sam the story—how lucky she felt to have broken their engagement after discovering the sick young man's true nature— when he had once touched the scar as they were making love at her place in Gramercy Park. Now he lowered his head and brushed his lips along the length of the welt in her flesh.

He heard her catch her breath and cry softly, and hearing her, his own eyes teared.

"Your kissing it always makes me feel better," she said.

"It's my way of sending you a message."

"I know, and I love the message."

"Shall we talk, Jennie?"

She shook her head. "No, Sam, let's leave it this way...it's been perfect."

He got out of bed and checked his watch.

"Dammit, now comes that bad time—the leaving time."

"It's been so different in Rome, far away from everything, being alone together..."

His eyes brightened. "I have a crazy notion—why doesn't National Public Radio send a correspondent to report on the Algiers meeting?"

She laughed. "God, wouldn't that be great. But with all those budget cuts for public broadcasting they'd probably send me there by rowboat."

"It's a real story, I think, the kind we would have covered in the news analysis section. It's got all the elements—satellites, censorship, newspapers, television—stuff that's hidden behind the vague theme of international information."

"I wouldn't get my hopes up. If they wanted it covered, it would have been assigned by now from Washington."

They showered together, soaping each other and embracing...

Linkum dressed quickly. Jennie offered to see him off at Leonardo Da Vinci Airport but he said it wouldn't be necessary because she needed her rest before going to RAI and he could doze on the plane.

"I don't want to drag you out there and then have you return alone. Anyway, I'd rather we said good-by in private, right here in your room."

She reached for his hand, and their fingers locked.

"Please fly carefully."

In the past they had always said that before going off on assignments for the newspaper.

"Would you have time to call me when you get to Kennedy? Just to let me know you're there?"

He promised to signal her when he landed, in New York or Washington.

"No matter how late," she said. "I'd love to wake up and hear your voice as I come out of sleep."

"I'll be able to listen to *your* voice from Rome over WNYC," he said. "Don't start any revolutions."

They held each other, savoring the time as long as they could, until she lowered her face from his lips into his shoulder, and he kissed her closed eyelids.

152

He moved to the doorway. "Semicolon?"

"Comma," Jennie replied, smiling.

"Thank you," Sam said. "Progress."

Airborne, the canned musical program on Alitalia inevitably began with "Arrivederci, Roma," and when the 747 landed at JFK the passengers applauded the captain and their good fortune. Linkum understood the fatalism of the gesture; no one ever clapped after a crash landing.

As he stepped up to the passport desk a voice behind him quietly called his name. It belonged to one of Hap Chorley's aides dressed in J. C. Penney mufti. The colonel found his luggage, flashed credentials and mumbled a few words. Linkum was moved along through customs without having his bags touched. At the far end of the airfield a jet trainer with no markings on its fuselage waited for him. Hap only boasted about two privileges that came with his intelligence post: his Havana cigar connection and his private air fleet. In less than an hour the jet landed at Andrews Air Force Base in Maryland. There, he stepped into a Huey chopper that fluttered and rose above the Capital Beltway, then flew westward to the enclosed landing circle on the grounds of the Pentagon. The sun was just beginning to go down over the Virginia hills when Linkum entered Room 3224-AF on the outer ring facing Arlington.

"Greetings," Chorley said, giving him a bear hug.

Linkum dug into his handbag and presented Chorley with a box of Montecruz natural leaf Cuban cigars that he had picked up at the last minute at Leonardo Da Vinci Airport.

"Okay, you can leave now," Chorley said. "That's all I wanted— mission accomplished."

"I've got something else for you, Hap," he said, "but don't light it with a match."

Linkum took a half-hollow tube of shaving cream from his toilet kit and from its concealed bottom shook out the roll of film that he had shot at the *fondazione* in Dongo. He placed the roll on Chorley's desk.

"Can you get this developed?"

"Anything urgent?"

"You can see for yourself."

Chorley ordered the leaf-colonel in his outside office, who was just preparing to make his nightly raid on the PX, to have the film developed right away. "And don't send it out to Kodak, colonel. You stand over the laboratory people until they finish." The colonel saluted. "One print only and return the negatives to me personally."

As if aware that Linkum was startled to see him turn the chunky colonel into a messenger boy, Chorley smiled and said in self-mockery, "Break me to civilian."

The civilian director of USAFSS opened the seal on the Montecruz box, carefully snipped off the ends of two cigars with his special *zigarrenabschneider* and lit them with a long wood match. "Slightly dry," he said, emptying the remainder of the cigars into his own cedar humidor, "but not bad, chum."

They leaned back. Linkum wondered why he had been rushed here, still groggy, air express.

Chorley asked him, "Any pain develop from that crash landing you made, wheels up, at Bellagio?"

Linkum shook his head. "No. But what the hell gives? What's the story, Hap?"

"I've got an acquaintance of yours here who can tell you all about it."

He tapped a square button on his desk controls. "Send him in."

A moment later, a familiar round figure came into Chorley's office.

Tweed Jerome stood there, still attired in his trademark rugby shirt, this one with bold red stripes. A holster bulged through his seersucker jacket, which barely closed at the bottom button. His toothy grin gave him the look of a startled rabbit.

"Sorry the bastard got away in his confederate's truck. I could have given him a good bashing."

"Was he after me?"

"Doubt it, old boy. This looked like the second act of an old mountain family feud. Ancient roots, like deflowering your maiden cousin. Don't know where your friend is from, but his arse could be in danger. Depends which side of the bed those chaps get out

154

of in the morning. Those were Algerians warning one of their brothers."

Tweed Jerome knew only so much. In any case, the Moose wasn't
his concern. *He* was.

"You did okay, Tweed," Chorley said. "I trust you'll be on the
scene in Algiers too."

"It's part of our arrangement. A boring town, and I have a low
boring point. Two weeks and that's it. How long is that meeting
supposed to last?"

Chorley shrugged, turned to Linkum, who said that the agenda
and voting added up to less than ten working days, according to the
documents he was given by the U.N. agency.

"I suppose you'll find a way to carry that shooting iron with you,"
Hap said, pointing at Jerome's bulging jacket.

"Not on your life," Jerome said. "These are my best weapons."
He clenched and unclenched his thick fists, then unwound a wire
from a device that looked like a pocket tape measure and watched
it snap back with a cutting hiss. "Works quietly, no need for a
silencer. No, gentlemen, I only carry my little convincer in your
lovely country because it makes muggers in Washington and New
York think twice. It's a Walther P38 that once belonged to a de-
ceased officer in the Hermann Goering Division. I traded it for a
Donald Duck watch with a Russkie general in Vienna. Never carry
it loaded—it's the visibility that matters."

Linkum listened, almost hearing the echo of footsteps and the
fleeting figure in the shadows of the Romanesque church behind
the Dongo dock.

"Were you there when my Algerian friend and I were in Dongo
that night?"

"I was," Jerome said. "So was one of them."

"I sensed that sombody was out there in the dark—"

"The other chap had been hanging about town, watching who
came through the gates of the *fondazione*. I saw Berber written all
over his face, and the Sahara in the way he loped along. It was my
footsteps, not his, that you heard. I wanted the chap to know that
he was being watched and not to try any funny stuff. Might have
scared him off—"

"I guess I ought to thank you."

Tweed Jerome shrugged. "All in a night's work, so to speak."

"I'll look for you in Algiers."

"You probably won't see me, Mr. Linkum. If you do, by chance, I won't acknowledge you. Never saw you before. Just out looking for a little amateur football match."

"Okay, Tweed, we'll settle our accounts in the usual way through the usual channel," Chorley told him.

Jerome nodded. "Well, keep your pecker up," he said, and walked out of Chorley's office.

"A strange one," Linkum said. "He doesn't seem for real, including those two names."

"That's the most real thing about him. His family past checks out. I could use a few more like him. Remember the war dogs that used to be trained to attack and then had to be retrained? Well, Tweed Jerome was never retrained after his stint with MI–5. Didn't want to be, it got into his blood. In a way I feel sorry for him. In wartime he got medals for the things that would put him behind bars in a half-dozen countries today."

"Yes, but you still use him—"

"I'm not running a reform school, Sam. I'd rather have him under my control than working for one of the private firms that have their own intelligence operatives tied to the dictatorships. You remember how the CIA destabilized the elected government in Chile after getting carte blanche from Nixon and Kissinger? I could name a few more places in the Middle East that are in the pockets of conglomerates. First they build their pipelines or oil rigs or dams, then they have a foot in the door of their palaces. They need to know who's up and who's down in the ministries and who's for sale, same as I do."

The leaf-colonel came in and after placing the negatives and a contact sheet on Chorley's desk, saluted and got his goodnight.

"I told him prints, not contacts," Chorley mumbled. He placed the contacts under a magnifying glass, studying them closely, then looked up.

"Interesting painting," Chorley said.

"Uninteresting bug."

"Mediterranean-American?"

"Right in my bedroom. Behind the painting and the wallpaper."

Chorley thought for a moment. "You didn't call from there, did you?" Linkum shook his head. "Or mention my name to the Moose?" Linkum said that he refused to speak to the Moose anywhere inside the *fondazione;* that he was sure every room was wired.

"Sorry I couldn't clue you in better about Mediterranean-American's shenanigans."

"I thought you'd want to know something about them but I didn't expect to run into that kind of scene. Not exactly cultural . . . That's why I brought back some evidence about the so-called scholarly work they're up to. It's run by a weirdo of a director, name of Woodrow Wilson Condon."

"I never put the two together. He's the guy who used to work for Kissinger in the Nixon White House. No wonder he knew about bugging."

Linkum smiled. "He also now knows that I knew he was snooping. I ripped the microphone out of the wall and gave it to him when I was leaving—"

"Was that smart?"

"Probably not, but it was awfully satisfying. I'm sorry I indulged myself—"

"Maybe better to have an ace in the hole and play it when you need a bargaining chip."

"But that wasn't the only game they played, Hap. I was offered nearly fifty thousand dollars in gold coins as bribe money."

"By Mediterranean-American?"

"By one of the so-called scholars at the conference working for them as a consultant. Read that: *bagman.* Some professorial type I never met before, Elwood Normie. Struck me as a real academic hustler."

"I thought your pockets looked a little weighted down, Sam. What were you supposed to do with the gold?"

"Pass it around among the delegates for votes, make friends and influence people for Mediterranean-American, and keep a little for myself. I'm pretty sure Woody Condon and Professor Normie were in cahoots. The professor was mad as hell when I told him to stick his krugerrands up his keester."

"What did I say about a nice little junket on Lake Como? Well, I couldn't predict a bribe, at least not at the foundation. I know the top management at Mediterranean-American has influence, especially among the Arabists in the State Department. And I know they wink and deliver the baksheesh and the broads. But this is the first time I've met up with a direct approach to an American delegate. The bastards are so powerful and wealthy they've gotten shameless, think everyone and everything has a price. You and I represent one government, but they think they do, too, only theirs is called Mediterranean-American."

Linkum paused for a moment before asking, "Am I supposed to report the fifty-thousand-dollar understanding to anyone at State or in the New York mission?" He looked directly at Chorley, puffing away. "I think I know your answer in advance."

"You guessed right. As the old Venetian saying goes..."

Before you speak, silence. Anyway, I'm steering clear of the U.N. mission people. I don't want to get my head filled with their diplomatic lingo that would interfere with my journalistic lingo."

"Makes sense." Chorley stood up. "Now let's get down to cases. The Moose—is he with us?"

"Personally, he couldn't be friendlier. Officially, he's going to have to sing another tune—even told me so. Don't forget, he has to dance around Algerian censorship himself."

"What are their rules for reporting?"

"All summed up in the line he gave me: *Don't draw a mustache on the ruler's face in print.* Otherwise, you can get away with a little satire, a few needles disguised as parables and even some straight reporting. As long as you kiss the ruler's ring and blame everything on the King of Morocco."

"What about licensing Western journalists and shortstopping the satellite ground stations?"

"He's against the licensing resolution but his vote may have to be for it—that's been his country's position all along. But it isn't hopeless. If the language is changed and we put in a few lines about peace, mankind and brotherhood we might be able to mitigate the terms. He could help us there and convince some of the others—"

"Good. Ground stations?"

"Your information is on-target—television by satellite that reaches directly into these countries from the Western skies is the real enemy. Newspapers and wire services require a literacy that television doesn't. He thinks the same group that is fanatically opposed to foreign TV stations is the one that winged him."

"Tweed Jerome is putting together some intelligence on them for me. What did you say was the name of the group, Sam?"

"I didn't say, Hap."

"Hey, you're talking to your friend, Sam."

"I know that, Hap. So next time don't pull the old third-degree tricks when we talk. Just ask me straight out."

"Sorry about that—force of habit."

"Right. I'm touchy myself. Long flight home and no shut-eye." He hesitated for a moment. "It's the Independent Moslem Brotherhood..."

"Sounds like a crock."

The dynamiter who called himself Batna had just received his orders from the Brotherhood's central command in the garage adjacent to the automobile tire shop on the Boulevard Frantz Fanon, three blocks north of the Bibliothèque National in Algiers: Proceed with the strike plan against the main French satellite ground station at Pleumeur-Bodou. Nothing was put in writing; all instructions were conveyed by couriers. Each man on a mission carried a single piece of information in his head; a captured anarchist could only implicate the handful of brothers in his own cell, if in fact he did speak. Ever since the radical Moslem group had been formed in the aftermath of independence, only one Brother had been persuaded to talk while in the custody of the ruler's secret police. He was released by a police van in full view of his comrades in their hangout on the Boulevard Che Guevara. Unfortunately for him, the Brother had provided a few names. The secret police had learned their lessons well from the *colons* when Algeria was a French Department;

they knew that life could be worse than a death sentence. The Brotherhood cut out his tongue.

One courier provided Batna with a new identification on his passport; another a handful of genuine tickets on Air Algérie with open dates to and from Marseilles; still another, with baggage checks. Everything had to be done swiftly: in and out of France in less than two and a half days. At the last moment, without passing under the X-rays and metal detectors at the Dar El Beida Airport off the motorway east of Algiers, two cheap cardboard satchels bound with leather straps and covered with bright stickers from soccer football clubs were slipped into the baggage compartment by a handler in the pay of the Brotherhood. As Batna stepped into the cabin of the Air Algérie flight to Marseilles, he conspicuously carried a couple of Inspector Maigret detective stories, like any ordinary traveler.

But the Simenon stories were more than a diversion; the paperbacks identified Batna to the two students from Algeria who had been planted by the Brotherhood in the Sorbonne. They followed him into the men's room at the Marseilles airport. He handed them the baggage checks. The three separated and then rejoined in the parking lot. The satchels were placed on either side of the floor on the back seat of the old Peugeot, under blankets and newspapers, with Batna sitting in between them. They started out along the coastal road toward Toulouse, avoiding the town centers. Batna had refused to put the satchels in the trunk because of the heat and gasoline fumes; he knew their volatile properties only too well after the disaster at the ground station outside Oran. The satchel to his left contained the detonating cord, safety-fuse igniters and galvanometer, the other held the half-pound blocks of Tovex dynamite and the Du Pont electric blasting caps. Batna told the driver to slow down, they could not take a chance on being questioned; and he did not want their explosive cargo shaken up on the highway.

Darkness began to descend as the Peugeot headed along the coast and then turned inland toward Nantes. They would not stop except to refill the tank and take turns at the wheel. In the middle of the night, they risked speeding to make time on the approaches to Brest on the Brittany coast. But when the young men boastfully told him that they had made a reservation in advance at the Continental Hotel on the Place de la Tour-d'Auvergne in the center of the city, Batna screamed at them. Dead tired, they continued onward to a less conspicuous location where no one could possibly know they were expected. After studying the road map Batna took the wheel himself and followed the N.12 to Morlaix, only a few miles from the earth station. Knowing that few questions would be asked by an inexperienced or an ancient concierge stuck with the night shift, he pulled up to a small inn without a name on the Rue Gambetta. They devoured a salami, cheese and wine that the Sorbonne men had brought along for the journey. Two rooms were available, cash in advance, no register. Three o'clock in the morning. That would give them two hours of sleep before the rendezvous with the second team of Algerians coming from the Belleville *quartier* in the 20ᵉ Arrondissement of Paris.

Before dawn, the dynamiter called Batna and his youthful companions from the Brotherhood were on their way. Avoiding the national highway, they circled among the back roads that rose and fell between the granite cliffs of the Brittany coast. The rich loam of clay and decaying grass in the fields filled their nostrils with the pungent odors of the morning earth. In the distance the masts of fishing trawlers bobbed in the inlets; and the foaming surf curled and crashed against gorges that harbored the tidal waters before breaking out into the flannel-gray Atlantic.

Five miles from the satellite station at Pleumeur-Bodou, through an opening in the hedgerows they spotted the great white dome housing the horn antenna. Fanning out from the command complex, five antennae that resembled giant erector sets spiraled to pluck signals from the heavens. At the rendezvous point on the crossroads a mile north of the earth station they slowly passed a battered Renault with a lone occupant that was parked inside a lay-by. The Peugeot backed up behind the other car. Batna's companions introduced him to the Renault driver. He, too, was an overage student at the Sorbonne. Quickly, they transferred the two satchels to the rear seat of the sacrificial Renault.

Working alone, Batna attached the silver chloride cell in the galvanometer to the detonating cord, inserted a spring over the blasting cap, and armed the eight-inch-long sticks of Tovex 220 dynamite. He signaled to the driver. Both cars crawled toward the Pleumeur-Bodou station. Fifteen minutes past six. Only a few lights were on in the command building; most of the technicians arrived after eight. Not a guard was in sight; after all, this was considered a commercial communications facility—no secrets. The small Renault was positioned just below the steel stilts of the dish antenna that stood silhouetted against the skyline. The Peugeot was parked a hundred yards away, its motor purring. Batna motioned the driver to leave and join the others in the Peugeot. Once again, he was alone. Now he looked at his watch and set the mechanism. At this point it was up to him; no one would know the difference in Algiers. Advance the timer by a half hour and give themselves a little longer to make their getaway, or cause a few faceless deaths among the French technicians by having the explosives go off fifteen minutes sooner.

Batna's instincts told him to kill—even if it increased the risk of his own capture. The French police knew how to execute an Algerian in custody. The report would simply read: died while attempting to escape. Batna disagreed with the more cautious Tlemcen about the Brotherhood's homicidal tactics. His mind was made up for him by the sight of the headlights approaching the command building. The sooner, the better. The way to deliver a message to these foreign broadcasters from the Continent and the United States was to stamp it with their blood.

Batna set the explosives to blow soon after their getaway. With luck, the blast would turn the Renault into a thousand pieces of flying shrapnel that would kill or maim anyone standing outside the complex buildings. A few seconds later, he ran toward the waiting Peugeot and his nervous companions from Belleville. He slid into the front seat and slammed the passenger door shut, told the two men in the back to bend down out of sight and ordered the driver to proceed slowly for the next five minutes. Nothing to suspect: just a couple of technicians from the night shift. Several miles away, through a break in the hedgerows, they peered from a cliff toward the dome and antennae.

Batna tapped his watch and held up his index finger. One minute to go. The others tensed and held their breaths. Just as the second hand swept to twelve, they heard a rumble that grew into a series of explosions. And then they saw a bolt of flame climbing the steel stilts of the satellite antenna.

Pleumeur-Bodou's southern antenna was ablaze.

For the first time since crossing the Mediterranean, Batna relaxed.

Avoiding the heavily patrolled N.12 and its roadblocks, they drove south along the Canal de Brest and then swung eastward toward the environs of Paris. At Marly-le-Roi, a Renault was waiting for them behind the churchyard. The men from the Moslem Brotherhood separated. Batna was driven by an Algerian wine merchant into the warrens of Belleville. He remained overnight in Paris. Early in the morning, before boarding the train for Marseilles, he stopped to buy the newspapers. Nothing in *Le Figaro*. Nothing in *Le Monde*. On the back page of *Le Parisien Libéré* he found:

BREST (AGENCE FRANCE-PRESSE)—A TECHNICAL FAILURE OCCURRED YESTERDAY MORNING IN THE TELECOMMUNICATIONS FACILITY AT PLEUMEUR-BODOU, TEMPORARILY BLACKING OUT SATELLITE TRANSMISSIONS TO GROUND STATIONS IN MOROCCO, ALGERIA AND TUNISIA. THREE ENGINEERS WERE REPORTED TO BE INJURED IN THE COURSE OF MAKING REPAIRS. THE AUTHORITIES FROM THE MINISTRY OF POSTS AND TELECOMMUNICATIONS DECLARED THAT THE SOUTHERN ANTENNA IS EXPECTED TO BE IN OPERATION AGAIN WITHIN FORTY-EIGHT HOURS.

Nothing more. The lying French news agency, Batna said to himself; as always in collusion with the "authorities." So officially it was simply a "technical" matter.

At least he had put three Frenchmen into the hospital, with injuries serious enough to be reported in the cover-up news account. Did they think it was possible to conceal an explosion that could be heard and seen for miles around? Those in charge at Pleumeur-Bodou would know what had really happened. He glanced sideways to see if the police were on the lookout in the railway station. Two of them stood together, flirting with a group of bare-legged college girls wearing T-shirts that read "University of California" across their unbrassiered chests.

Batna boarded the train to Marseilles unnoticed, then caught the afternoon flight on Air Algérie and landed an hour later at Dar El

Beida. Tlemcen was waiting for him in the garage on the Boulevard Frantz Fanon. Batna showed him the newspaper version of what had happened at Pleumeur-Bodou.

Tlemcen nodded. "Paris and the other delegations already in Algiers know that our Brotherhood was responsible for blowing up the antenna. We made sure of that. *Now* they can proceed with their International Information Agency meeting."

They kissed each other's unshaven cheeks.

At the Pentagon, Hap Chorley was saying to Sam Linkum, "You're a quick study, all right. For a dumb journalist you're doing pretty good as a diplomat. You picked up some useful stuff in Dongo."

"Only job I've got at the moment."

"And don't get me wrong—I didn't mind so much your telling off that shithead running the foundation who bugged your room. He behaved more Mediterranean than American. So did that Levantine rug peddler from Bronx University with the pot of gold who calls himself a professor. Only thing is, don't forget to let me know the moment anyone from the conglomerate approaches you again. I don't think it'll happen once you're sitting in place as the delegate. But they're nervy operators...and you're my personal responsibility. Anything I can do for you—"

"There's one small matter, Hap."

"Jennie Ives?"

"Her assignment in Rome is winding down. You yourself told me her reporting for National Public Radio was first-rate. I was wondering if she could swing over to Algiers to cover the U.N. meeting on the way home—"

"And cover the American delegate personally?" Chorley puffed on his Montecristo. "I don't know anyone over there. They're independent, aren't they?"

"Yes, until someone in the White House discovers how independent they really are and blows the whistle on them."

"Where does their funding come from?"

"Mainly from the Corporation for Public Broadcasting."

"That's better. Meaning Congress. I've got some people on the

Communications subcommittee who owe me one. Let me give it a whirl."

"Thanks, Hap."

"Don't thank me yet. Incidentally, I think she could do a real job there for National Public Radio. These sessions have usually been covered as hit-and-run affairs, them against us, the clashes instead of the areas of agreement. She could give the Algiers story some dimension."

"You're playing my song."

"I'm rehearsing my lines for an approach. Now, let's get the show on the road. Helen's waiting for us with dinner."

Chorley walked down the moving steps and then the long corridor toward the parking lot at the Pentagon. He drove the Bentley along the River Road into Maryland, then on the rutted country lane up to the farmhouse. Helen stood in the doorway waiting for them. She kissed Hap and embraced Linkum like an old friend.

"I hope you had a pleasant journey, Sam."

"The best part was running into an old colleague who happened to be in Rome."

"Oh yes...we listened to her broadcasts on the Vatican. Hap mentioned that she was a friend of yours."

"One day I hope you can both meet her."

Hap broke out one of his bottles of Margaux to go with the lamb stew Helen had prepared. When Sam complimented her, she smiled and described her dinner as "leftovers."

"She means it, too," Hap said. "I've finally found a woman who never wastes anything, even stale bread gets to be bread pudding. She also tolerates my Havana heaters."

"I like their smell," Helen said.

"I hope you're a tea drinker, Sam," Chorley said. "An old pueblo recipe."

"You either like it or you don't," Helen said. "I grew up with the stuff because we couldn't afford the real thing. But I've got some teabags in reserve so please feel free to say it tastes awful." She poured hot water over two spoonsful of herbs and let the pueblo tea steep for a few minutes. Linkum inhaled the tea and sipped it. "Incredible—it tastes like...the juice of flowers." Helen said,

"You've got it. It's made of chamomile and hibiscus flowers, rose blossoms and cinnamon, peppermint and spearmint leaves. No artificial coloring or flavoring, as the phrase goes on the store-bought package... What's your friend Jennie like?"

"Like your tea. All natural, no artificial anything."

Helen smiled. "Do you mind if I ask you something personal? Hap told me about Elena..."

Linkum glanced toward Chorley, who excused himself, saying that he had to check the overnight cables with USAFSS at the Pentagon.

When they were alone Sam asked Helen, "What did you want to know?"

"Are Elena and Jennie very different?"

"No one has ever asked me that before—not even Jennie."

"I'm sorry..."

"No, don't be. I just haven't thought about it that way."

"May I tell you why I've asked? Because of you, and also because of me and that big hulk of a man I love."

"He also loves you, Helen. You've created a new person."

"That's what interests me as a woman, Sam. You're his oldest friend, and I know that neither of you gives your friendship lightly. Wartime was a special time for both of you. You got married then, Hap never did."

"He was never in love before."

"Were you—or was it just—?"

"I loved Elena."

"Can someone come along in midlife and make it happen all over again? I'm obviously talking about Hap and me..."

"I think so, Helen. In my case, maybe in Hap's, too, there wasn't just a life, there are *lives*. The time before the war, that was one I hardly think about. The second life burned the deepest mark—that's what war does. Those were days with twenty-four hours. Then the third life came along, the uninvited one without the same fun and games, the reality life where we put ourselves in the hands of companies and sometimes governments, the getting-ahead time and the unnecessary-war time. If you were lucky you kept your independence and could stand to look at yourself in the mirror. If you were luckier you didn't lose anyone you cared about. And if you had real dumb luck, someone new came along to love you, that you could love..."

"Thank you, Sam. That's what I wanted to hear."

"It's different, Helen, and it's the same." She stood up and walked over to his chair and hugged him.

Chorley came back, carrying a slip of paper. "I leave you alone, you try and steal my girl, *capitano,* up to your old Sicilian tricks again."

Helen winked at Sam.

"See you later, after we get rid of this guy." She kissed them both goodnight, sensing it was their time, and went up to the master bedroom.

Chorley handed Sam the slip of paper. All it said was: *Pleumeur-Bodou.*

"They've blown one of the big antennae at the French earth station. ELINT picked it up first and relayed it to me. Just got confirmation from one of my sources in the *Deuxième Bureau* in Paris. Dynamiters from the Independent Moslem Brotherhood in Algiers. Claimed credit, and no reason not to believe they pulled it off. A damn professional job. Three engineers died in the hospital. The *Deuxième Bureau* has put out the word that it was a technical failure in the circuitry. Accidental blackout is the official story. They don't want to give them more publicity."

"When do you think I should leave for Algiers, Hap?"

"Tomorrow. Get yourself a pro forma briefing from the international organizations desk at State first thing in the morning. Don't tell them you know about Pleumeur-Bodou. Let's see how long it takes them to find out for themselves. They've got your tickets and reservations at the Aletti Hotel plus the briefing books. You're working for them now, it says here, right?"

Linkum nodded.

"If I can do anything about Jennie and National Public Radio, I'll signal you there. If it works, act surprised and let her tell you."

As they walked up the steps to their bedrooms, Chorley said, "That Brotherhood gang isn't exactly playing games. Don't be a hero."

CHAPTER SIX

Showdown in Algiers

THIS IS JENNIE IVES REPORTING FOR NATIONAL PUBLIC RA-
DIO . . . FROM ALGIERS. THE U.N. INTERNATIONAL INFORMATION AGENCY
OPENED ITS TENTH ANNUAL SESSION HERE TODAY IN AN ATMOSPHERE
OF CORDIALITY THAT SOON TURNED INTO ACRIMONY.

DELEGATES FROM OVER ONE HUNDRED COUNTRIES ASSEMBLED IN
THE CONFERENCE HALL OF THE LUXURIOUS AURASSI HOTEL, A MODERN
SAND-COLORED BOX THAT OVERLOOKS THE SLUMS OF THE CASBAH AND
THE SPRAWLING PORT OF THIS MARITIME CAPITAL.

THE DELEGATES REPRESENT THE WORLD'S CONTINENTS—AND ALL
THE POLITICAL SHADINGS: THE NORTH ATLANTIC TREATY ORGANIZA-
TION NATIONS, THE EASTERN EUROPEAN BLOC LINKED TO THE SOVIET
UNION, THE WEALTHY AS WELL AS THE DEVELOPING NATIONS OF ASIA,
AFRICA AND LATIN AMERICA.

IN FACT, THAT WORD "DEVELOPING" IGNITED THE FIRST FLASH OF
ANGER HERE. THE DELEGATE FROM LIBERIA, WHICH IS RULED BY A

FORMER MASTER SERGEANT WHO OVERTHREW THE PRESIDENT, OB-
JECTED TO A REFERENCE MADE BY THE DELEGATE FROM CANADA TO
THE "UNDERDEVELOPED" STATES BELOW THE SAHARA. THE MASTER
SERGEANT'S MAN SAID THAT THE WORD "UNDERDEVELOPED" SMACKED
OF RACISM AND MENTAL RETARDATION. "YOU SEE, SIR," SAID THE LI-
BERIAN, "I AM NOT BAREFOOT, I AM NOT WEARING A RING THROUGH
MY NOSE, AND MY SUIT WAS TAILORED ON SAVILE ROW." AFTER SAYING
HE MEANT NO OFFENSE AND THAT IT WAS MERELY A MATTER OF SE-
MANTICS, THE CANADIAN ASKED THE LIBERIAN FOR THE NAME OF HIS
LONDON TAILOR.

AND SO, IN WHAT THIS REPORTER OBSERVED AS A MIXTURE OF WHITE
LAUGHTER AND BLACK PIQUE, BEGAN THE OPENING SESSION OF THE
INTERNATIONAL INFORMATION AGENCY.

MORE TO COME. JENNIE IVES REPORTING FOR NATIONAL PUBLIC RA-
DIO . . . FROM ALGIERS.

Instead of banging his wooden gavel, the director-general of the
U.N. agency, a former minister of tourism in Uganda, rattled a
baby rhinoceros horn filled with pebbles below his nose and thick
black-rimmed glasses. The director-general had made a small fortune running his father's business: smuggling rhinoceros horns, el-
ephant tusks and the furs of what westerners called "endangered
species" out of Africa. Only 25 percent of the family's illegal income
had to be kicked back to his country's military government.

Now the Ugandan greeted the delegates:

"Communications must serve the social, economic and cultural
lives of all peoples. In this respect, it is essential to include the new
technologies opening up for mankind in the heavens above us—the
international communications satellites that send programs and news
to people through ground stations in our own countries. The mass
media send us information from which none can escape. We have
seen wars from distant jungles in Southeast Asia and cities in the
Middle East in our living rooms. And yet, must we not be free to
preserve our own cultures and national identities?"

Robin Jenkins, the British delegate from the Independent Broadcasting Authority representing Her Majesty's Government cupped
the microphone in front of him to avoid being heard. Leaning toward

Sam Linkum, seated behind the UNITED STATES desk plate, he whispered: "Ready or not, Sam, he's about to drop the other shoe."

The director-general from Uganda said: "Communications means power for those who possess it. The hopes of the third world are being raised here in Algiers. If we have little else, at least we are willing to share our anxieties with our friends. The concentration of the media has caused many professionals among us to examine their consciences. And so I must say frankly: the expressed desire for a New World Information Order is a direct response to the changed world of print, satellites and other technologies beyond our wildest imagination."

Jenkins winked at Linkum.

Linkum nodded, not wanting to show any public face in his strange new role as delegate instead of reporter.

A dozen hands shot up to be recognized. Linkum decided to hold back until after speaking to Moussi Ali privately to see where the third worlders really stood. They had the numbers. But he had covered enough international meetings to realize what was lip service for the press and television and what could be done behind the scenes by tradeoffs, bargaining and bribes.

The director-general called on the delegate from India.

"Alphonse and Gaston," said Jenkins to Linkum. "Want a brandy? I've heard this act before."

Linkum said he'd stick it out for a while.

"Put in your earplugs," said Jenkins, retreating to the lounge.

The Indian delegate walked to the floor microphone next to the director-general. Although French was the working language, he spoke stuffily in Oxonian English with a subcontinent lilt:

"Fellow delegates, India does not consider itself a so-called developing nation, but we are in total sympathy with a New World Information Order. Instead of free exchange, there is cultural imperialism. Foreign agencies from Great Britain, the United States and France dominate our news, vestiges of a discredited colonial past. To the outside world, India is a land of floods, beggars and untouchables. Our daily flow of life is ignored. And now there is television. The cameras are turned upon us and what do our people see? What British, American and French cameras tell them about *themselves!* In an instant, these foreign cameras transmit satellite pictures while official news from our own government is considered unreliable. The press laws of our nation are ignored—"

"You call those laws?" the Canadian delegate broke in. "We call them censorship."

The director-general shook his rhinoceros horn. Voices demanded to be heard. Finally the Indian continued:

"The press law in my country is not censorship. It is designed to protect public officials and journalists themselves from breaches of security and abuses of language. The law is directed against character assassins who cause social discord through untruth. Why should journalists be exempt from our national goals? Are they not citizens of their countries first? The reasonable press limitations under our constitution should not prevent any *responsible* journalist from functioning."

The director-general said, "The chair recognizes the delegate from the United Kingdom."

Jenkins had returned to his seat, carrying a paper water cup half-filled with brandy. He took a sip, as if to clear instead of warm his throat, and bowed toward the delegate from India.

"As a cultural as well as colonial imperialist," Jenkins said, "I should like to note that when Great Britain ruled India, no such law existed." He took another swig from the paper cup, priming his Cambridge double negatives. "We are not unfamiliar with the Indian censorship law and we are not unaware of the existence of amateurs with typewriters, there as elsewhere. Nonetheless, I, for one, deplore the key word 'scurrilous' in this obnoxious Indian law. It is defined as anything likely to be injurious to morality. A noble gesture. But one that handcuffs any responsible reporter—print or broadcasting. Sir, my concept of responsibility differs from yours. To me, a journalist is responsible when he dares to inform his audience regardless of the consequences."

So be it, Linkum thought to himself; for the moment he's said it for me. Then he glanced across the long conference table toward Moussi Ali and the Algerian delegation. But the Moose, like the other third world journalists in the hall, was poker-faced . . . publicly.

THIS IS JENNIE IVES REPORTING FOR NATIONAL PUBLIC RADIO. DATE-
LINE ALGIERS: THE TENTH ANNUAL SESSION OF THE INTERNATIONAL
INFORMATION AGENCY.

CLASHING VIEWPOINTS HAVE SURFACED HERE ABOUT WHAT CON-
STITUTES NEWS COVERAGE AND WHEN CENSORSHIP CAN BE IMPOSED
BY LAW IN WHAT SOME GOVERNMENTS CONSIDER THE HIGHER NA-
TIONAL INTEREST. THE WORD CENSORSHIP ITSELF IS SELDOM USED BY
DELEGATES AT THE U.N. AGENCY MEETING IN THIS CITY ON THE NORTH
AFRICAN COAST, WHERE ONCE BARBARY PIRATES PREYED. NOW—AT
LEAST IN THE VIEW OF ANGLO-AMERICAN JOURNALISTS—THE CUT-
LASSES OF SUPPRESSION ARE BEING WIELDED BY GOVERNMENT OFFI-
CIALS IN BUSINESS SUITS. THEIR NEW BOOTY IS NOTHING LESS THAN
THE NEWSPAPERS AND TELEVISION AND RADIO STATIONS IN THEIR OWN
COUNTRIES.

THE MAJORITY OF THE DELEGATES HERE COME FROM MINISTRIES OF
CULTURE OR TOURISM. SOME BELIEVE THAT UNPLEASANT NEWS WOULD
DISCOURAGE VISITORS BEARING HARD CURRENCIES, WHILE THE MORE
SOPHISTICATED DELEGATES WITH GOVERNMENT-OWNED PRESSES ARE
AWARE THAT LOANS FROM THE UNITED STATES COME MORE HANDILY
WHERE OVERT CENSORSHIP AND THE DENIAL OF CIVIL LIBERTIES ARE
CONCEALED.

BECAUSE OF THE IMPORTANCE OF TELEVISION AND RADIO, THE CA-
NADIAN, AUSTRALIAN AND BRITISH DELEGATIONS ARE HEADED BY
BROADCASTERS. THE UNITED STATES DELEGATE, SAMUEL LINKUM, IS A
NEW YORK JOURNALIST WHOSE NEWSPAPER WAS RECENTLY CLOSED
DOWN BY ITS WHOLLY-OWNED COMMERCIAL NETWORK. THUS FAR, THE
AMERICAN DELEGATE HAS NOT ADDRESSED THE SESSION BUT, ACCORD-
ING TO A WELL-INFORMED SOURCE, HE IS PERSONALLY OPPOSED TO
GOVERNMENT CENSORSHIP IN WHATEVER GUISE.

JENNIE IVES, REPORTING FOR NATIONAL PUBLIC RADIO . . . FROM AL-
GIERS.

At the next morning session, Robin Jenkins slipped into his seat
and whispered to Sam Linkum:

"This little drama takes three acts. In the first, the director-general
jerks around his phallic rhino horn and lets the third worlders tell

us what monsters we are in the free world. In the second, the Soviet delegate—that's Madame Gorokov over there, she's deputy director of *Pravda*—plays the role of friend and protector of the small countries. She's damn smart, but everybody knows she's got a dirty little secret: the Russians don't want a New World Information Order. They like their *old* Order. *Pravda,* as you know, means Truth. What was it you bloody Yanks used to say about Nixon— would you buy a used car from him? Well, would you buy a story that ran in a newspaper called *Truth?* Another thing, the Russians don't want any Direct Broadcast Satellite going straight to their people. Don't blame them, not after watching the programs on your telly. No offense."

Linkum smiled and Jenkins sipped from his disguised water cup. "I think the Ugandan smuggler is getting ready to recognize her— right after that Chilean delegate. He's the brother-in-law of the general who stole the last election there. A strong advocate of press freedom, Latin American style, from jail."

Linkum turned on his simultaneous translation switch to hear the Chilean, then cut him off in mid-sentence. "He's an asshole," Linkum said.

"But he's *your* asshole," Jenkins replied. "Every time his brother-in-law sees Red and sends a new batch of political prisoners to the dungeons, Washington blinks and delivers a new shipment of arms to his palace guard."

Linkum covered his desk microphone. "And when does the third act begin?"

"In the last day or two of the session," said Jenkins. "That's when the authoritarians join the totalitarians and try to put across some of their high-minded resolutions on press responsibility."

"How do we stop them?"

"Every theater has its backstage, even the Theater of the Absurd and the International Information Agency, which resemble each other. We work behind the scenes. The third worlders aren't monolithic, especially their journalists. Not even in Algeria. You know that chap from *El Moudjahid* sitting across from us—get a chance to speak to him at the Mediterranean-American *fondazione?*"

Linkum admitted that he and Moussi Ali had talked in Dongo but didn't reveal that they knew each other.

"Well, I'm told by my people in the embassy who read his column that he's a moderate. He could help tone down the more outrageous resolutions in the closing hours."

The Ugandan director-general, whose government had just been given a squadron of Mig fighter planes for "purposes of self-defense" by the Soviets, now recognized Madame Gorokov. The delegates wandered back to their places to watch the *Pravda* deputy director's performance.

Madame Gorokov walked up to the floor microphone. She was a slim woman in her mid-forties with shocks of closely cropped gray hair that gave her a deceptive *gamin* look. In her wanderings abroad she had acquired good copies of a Chanel wardrobe. Her chic suit helped to accent her authority. In a voice that was surprisingly deep, a trained voice, Madame Gorokov said:

"We in the field of communications speak the common language of information for all our peoples."

Linkum, listening intently, thought, Why do the Russians always talk of "peoples" instead of people? Was it something real—because of their different republics and languages? "We, the people," seemed enough in colonial America. Or was it deeply ideological?

"I have found that since our last two meetings in Belgium and Ecuador the new communications technology has not brought us closer together. This is a great irony." Madame Gorokov bowed modestly, acknowledging the applause of the majority of the delegates. "There is an inequality in information resources. Almost 80 percent of the world news flow emanates from the western agencies. However, these devote only 20 percent of news coverage to developing countries. Yet these countries make up three-quarters of mankind. The developing countries cannot protect themselves against foreign broadcasts. They are relegated to the status of *consumers of information* sold like dry goods." Now Madame Gorokov played to the balcony. "The present-day information system enshrines a form of political, economic and cultural *colonialism*. The fact cannot be blinked away that the present international information order is based on a quasi-monopoly of concentrated ownership. I would like in particular to emphasize the disorder in telecommunications caused by the use of satellites. My distinguished friend from Libya has labeled it plainly: a violation of national territories and private homes, a form of mental rape!"

The Arab bloc, normally splintered, applauded her words. Madame Gorokov, encouraged, raised her voice a decibel. "The new earth stations being put in place all over the globe by private and government interests perpetuate the stranglehold of the rich countries on the flow of information. The western carriers obtain bargain rates because of greater use of facilities while the developing countries are burdened with higher rates. So the imbalance in telecommunications constantly worsens."

Linkum turned to Jenkins. "She's done her homework—it's not all propaganda." Jenkins replied, "A mixture of the two—she's smart."

"Thus, my fellow delegates," she continued, "we come to the New World Information Order. We in the Soviet Union tell you: *Information is not a mere commodity but a social need.* The New World Information Order must prevent abusive use of the right of access. Appropriate criteria must be devised to govern truly objective news selection. The social function attains its objective only if the information transmitted is truthful. If a journalist gives information that is false or tendentious, he betrays his mission. The state should have the absolute right to rectify improper information. No nation should be permitted to impose its own Direct Broadcast programs upon the peoples of another nation without the consent of the government."

Madame Gorokov began to roll up her documents. The Ugandan director-general smiled approval.

In an aside Jenkins said, "If I remember her script correctly, Sam, she ends her song and dance with a heartbreaking plea to license journalists..."

Madame Gorokov wound up from memory:

"My dear colleagues, journalistic responsibility is essential to uphold the fundamental doctrines of the International Information

Agency. Sovereign states must be responsible for the activities of all mass media. Only governmental monitoring and regulation of a state's own writers in every field as well as foreign journalists can combat racialism and apartheid, defeat war propaganda and create peace."

As most of the delegates applauded, Linkum thought: Don't they know what she's advocating? Suddenly he was aware that eyes in the hall were turning toward the UNITED STATES desk plate...toward *him*.

The U.S. and U.S.S.R. Even between journalists.

"You're going to have to say *something*, old boy," Jenkins whispered behind his hand.

The director-general stared at him.

Short and sweet, he told himself; or short and *not* so sweet.

Madame Gorokov had returned to her place. Linkum decided to skip the public microphone and speak from his chair. But before he could begin another voice cut through the tense silence of the hall. It belonged to the deputy delegate representing Algeria. Moussi Ali.

For a moment he stared directly at Sam across the long table and their eyes locked. Then, without formal recognition, the Moose spoke up.

"I have listened to the eloquent delegate from the Soviet Union speaking about the grand aspirations of the International Information Agency. I, for one, and no doubt other delegates, are in agreement about the need to discourage war and racism in the press, on television and in all international forums."

Linkum wondered if he and the Moose were in the same ballpark.

"However, speaking as a charter member of the *Union Algérienne des Journalistes,* I would respectfully like to advance the views of professional journalists of my acquaintance here, in Europe and North America. It is this...truthful reporting can exist only in an atmosphere where freedom is permitted *all* correspondents, foreign and domestic, by all governments. Thank you."

Moussi Ali leaned back in his chair. But nobody in his own delegation looked his way; nobody in the hall showed any response in their faces. Madame Gorokov seemed to busy herself in her briefcase. In a few sentences the Moose had picked up her high-flown words and flung them down to earth.

The Ugandan rattled his rhinoceros horn.

"The chair regrets the interruption and now recognizes the delegate from the United States."

Prima di parlar, tasi.

Or however the hell you say it in five working languages. It was too late to be quiet; not too soon to cool it. At this moment I wish I was with Jennie Ives, up there in the press-radio booth, instead of down here on the floor, covering the news instead of maybe making it.

Jenkins leaned toward him. "Good luck, Sam."

Linkum spoke from his seat. No major statement, no big deal . . .

"I thank the chair for the chance to make a few informal remarks. I happen to live only a few blocks from the U.N. headquarters complex in New York, facing that famous soft-drink sign across the East River. As I walk past the entranceway almost every morning, with its inspiring Barbara Hepworth sculpture and the familiar outlines of the Secretariat and Assembly I am still moved. But I am also saddened because the U.N. stands like some great medieval castle, little more than a site for tourists. Nevertheless, it is a forum. We are here because it is there. Only fools would prefer to see that forum destroyed and the nations retreat behind their castles again.

"In the field of communications there is little that I have heard here in the past few days that I find unexpected or even unpleasant. The aims of combating war and racism through an open and dedicated press are not the exclusive property of any country or bloc of nations—neither West nor East, neither the Soviet Union nor the United States.

"Fundamentally, the dispute is between the traditional Western idea of a free flow of information, independent of government constraints, and the desire of the developing nations for an information flow of their own, without outside scrutiny. But just as the search for peace belongs to all of us, so too information cannot be anyone's private property. The notion of a free press was not invented by the founding fathers in the United States or even by the British barons

178

at Runnymede. History tells us that China actually conceived the forerunner of the modern news agency during the Han Dynasty two thousand years ago when provincial reports were sent to Peking. But I won't blame the Han Dynasty for the shortcomings of the press today. It's an old story but we can't kill the bearer of bad tidings. Nor, in a larger sense, should we permit one form of communications—television—to kill another—magazines and newspapers. Freedom comes with access, meaning domination neither by government *nor* commercial companies. Here is where the advanced countries can help the others—with training, with exchange of news articles, with newsprint and broadcasting facilities. Then comes the ultimate freedom: to read a newspaper *or* ignore it, to watch *or* to switch the television dial to *off*."

Linkum wondered if the delegates recognized that the man behind the UNITED STATES desk plate was talking to them as a journalist. He was almost finished; but something urged him to a final comment. . . .

"I'd like to compliment the delegate from Algeria who spoke before me about the universal need for foreign and domestic correspondents everywhere to function freely. I sympathize with those journalists who work for publications or stations that are subject to government control. I'm aware that conglomerate control exists as well. But no matter where, I believe the journalist's role is to be skeptical of governmental authority and to maintain his personal independence."

He pushed the microphone away from him. Jenkins leaned over and shook his hand. There was no applause for him. Unlike Madame Gorokov, an ominous silence followed.

THIS IS JENNIE IVES REPORTING FOR NATIONAL PUBLIC RADIO. DATELINE: ALGIERS. THE PLACE: THE HOTEL AURASSI, A FOUR-STAR CARAVANSERAI ON THE AVENUE FRANTZ FANON WHERE CAMELS FOR TOURISTS ARE PARKED NEXT TO MERCEDES FOR DELEGATES, AND THE ROOM SERVICE DOES NOT EXERT THE NO-STAR STAFF. THE EVENT: THE PENULTIMATE MEETING OF THE INTERNATIONAL INFORMATION AGENCY.

THE OBLIGATORY SCENES ARE FINALLY BEING PLAYED OUT IN THE CONFERENCE HALL. THE SOVIET AND AMERICAN DELEGATES HAVE HAD

THEIR SAY, AND ASSORTED BIT PLAYERS FROM THE THIRD WORLD HAVE ALSO SPOKEN UP. INTERESTINGLY, THE SMALLER NATIONS HOLD THE CARDS BECAUSE OF THEIR NUMBERS—THEY CAN OUTVOTE BOTH THE SOVIET AND ANGLO-AMERICAN BLOCS. VOTING IS EXPECTED NEXT MONDAY ON THE MOST SENSITIVE SECTIONS OF THE NEW WORLD INFORMATION ORDER. IN BRIEF, THIS NEW ORDER WOULD REDUCE THE DEPENDENCE OF DEVELOPING COUNTRIES ON WESTERN NEWS AGENCIES, PRINT AND TELEVISION, INCREASE FACILITIES FOR COMMUNICATIONS WITHIN THE THIRD WORLD, AND CURB THE RIGHT OF ACCESS BY WESTERN JOURNALISTS THROUGH CODES OF CONDUCT—A EUPHEMISM FOR LICENSING.

THE DIRTY WORD *LICENSING* ITSELF WAS NOT MENTIONED EITHER BY THE SOVIET DELEGATE, THE WELL-TAILORED MADAME GOROKOV, WHO HOLDS ONE OF THE HIGHEST POSTS IN MOSCOW, DEPUTY DIRECTOR OF *PRAVDA,* THE OFFICIAL COMMUNIST PARTY PAPER, OR THE AMERICAN DELEGATE, THE INFORMALLY ATTIRED SAMUEL LINKUM, A NEW YORK JOURNALIST NOT AFFILIATED WITH ANY PUBLICATION AT PRESENT. BUT IT WAS CLEARLY HOVERING IN THE BACKGROUND.

THE SOVIET DELEGATE USED PHRASES SUCH AS *JOURNALISTIC RESPONSIBILITY* BUT SHE MADE IT CLEAR THAT THE STATE WOULD BE THE JUDGE OF WHAT THAT MEANT AND SHOULD CONTROL THE FLOW OF NEWS. THE AMERICAN DELEGATE EMPHASIZED THAT NEWS DEPENDS ON FREE ACCESS—MEANING, IN HIS WORDS, "DOMINATION NEITHER BY GOVERNMENT NOR COMMERCIAL COMPANIES." HE NOTED THAT HE WAS SPEAKING AS A JOURNALIST, THEREBY UNDERSCORING THE DIFFERENCE BETWEEN HIMSELF AND THE SOVIET SPOKESPERSON WHO IS, OF COURSE, A PARTY OFFICIAL.

THE DELEGATES, OBSERVERS AND REPRESENTATIVES OF THE INTERNATIONAL PRESS NOW ADJOURN FOR THE WEEKEND OR, AS WE SAY IN FRANCO-AMERICAN, *LE WEEKEND,* SOME TO PONDER RESOLUTIONS, SOME TO RELAX—INCLUDING YOURS TRULY, JENNIE IVES, REPORTING FOR NATIONAL PUBLIC RADIO, FROM UPTOWN ALGIERS.

They woke up at dawn, their arms entwined just as they had fallen asleep after lovemaking, to the chanting, tape-recorded sound of the *muezzin* amplified through the speakers mounted on the minaret of the *Mosque de la Pêcherie* above the sea front. As she opened

180

one eye mischievously and turned into the spoon of his body, he kissed her on the nape of her neck. The undulating call to prayer penetrated the shuttered wooden blinds of his high-ceilinged room with a patio at the old Hotel Aletti on the Rue Asselah Hocine overlooking the quays and jetties of the harbor. *Allahu Akbar, Allahu Akbar. God is Great, God is Great...I testify that Mohammed brought the message of God...*

He slipped out of her arms and quietly stepped onto the patio, unable to sleep. His Mediterranean engines were running. The smells of the morning city came to him, a mixture of cooking oil, warm bread and curling smoke from the charcoal braziers in the alleyways. Below the red-tiled roofs and along the windows the night's sheets and undergarments flapped in the wind, exposing the private lives of the residents. He had ventured alone into the streets below on his first morning in Algiers, trying to find some of the old haunts, but the familiar names were gone: no Boulevard Baudin, no Rue Michelet, no Rue d'Isly, not even the Place du Gouvernement. A new set of revolutionary heroes had replaced the Parisian and co-lonial names, erasing over a century of ruling history with forgettable streets: Boulevard Salah Bouakouir, Rue Didouche Mourad, Avenue des Frères Oughlis Mouradia.

He had stopped off at the United States Embassy to see if anyone had a map with both the Arabic and the old French names. The political officer—Linkum assumed he was the station man for the CIA—gave him a hand-drawn map with the French names penciled in and cautioned him against flaunting it. It would be an offense against the ruler of the state if such a vestige of colonialism was discovered; only maps with the names of the ruler's relatives and military friends were allowed. Using the forbidden map, he found the headquarters building of the *Sixième Régiment, Spahis Algérien,* on the Place now called Dar-Es-Salaam near the botanical gardens. It had become another security police headquarters. He decided to skip the nostalgic look at the offices where he had served as liaison in counterintelligence. Instead, he walked through the gardens; the state had not yet renamed the flowers and shrubs....

Hap Chorley had come through all right: Jennie Ives was sleeping next to him at the Aletti, sharing his pillow. She had called him excitedly from Rome only a week earlier. "Sam, I've got the assignment!" He shared her enthusiasm, acted surprised. "They're letting me cover the whole meeting. I promised them it would last ten days or less—so don't go making any long speeches." On the pretext that he did not want her to run up a bill for an international call to his apartment in New York, he told her to hang up and that he'd call her right back. "The State Department can afford it better than National Public Radio," he said. Chorley had told him to avoid calls to or from his home since his appointment as delegate. He called her from the lobby of a nearby hotel in Murray Hill. They both decided that separate places in Algiers would be best. He suggested the Hotel Albert on the Avenue Pasteur, remembering it as a fairly quiet place. The Algerian Revolutionary Government had even allowed Pasteur to retain its street name, at least until the next colonel seized power.

The embassy had provided him with a car and driver, and he had met her Alitalia flight from Rome at Dar El Beida. The International Information Agency session was to begin the next morning. They dined on the day's catch of crayfish at the Chez Madeleine along the waterfront at Les Deux Moulins a few miles west of the city. Afterward, in her room at the Albert, they talked about their separation for the week in Algiers.

"No sleeping with news sources, right?" she said.

"No sleeping with journalists by delegate-types, right?" he said. "I don't want to influence your broadcasts."

"I don't know the radio game—just read what I write."

"It seems to be working, from what I've heard. I'd love to listen to you while the session is on."

"Not a chance, Sam. The Algerians won't let me be heard in their country, can't even use the facilities of Radiodiffusion-Télévision Algérienne... whew, what a mouthful... for my broadcasts to the States. They're touchy as hell about foreigners speaking directly to their citizens, as if you didn't know. I have to call in my stuff directly over the transatlantic phone lines. But they tell me in Washington that I come through loud and clear via satellite."

"National Public Radio leases time on the birds?"

"Yes, and I'm told they pay a pretty penny to the commercial

182

companies who own the transponders. That's why I'm limited to three minutes or under for my broadcasts."

"I won't even ask to see your transcripts—"

"Don't, Mister Delegate. But I'll show them to you anyway, if you really want to read them—after they've been aired in the States."

"No prior restraint, right? Well, fair enough. As a matter of fact I think I'd better not even *read* them. We can both do our thing independently. I'll wait till I get to New York and read them all at once."

Jennie nodded, then moved from the sofa to the edge of her bed.

He sat down beside her. They embraced, kissing deeply, rediscovering their bodies, but this time they undressed slowly, savoring the precious moments of intimacy before coming together.

Afterward, she again snuggled her head into the crook of his arm. "My favorite spot," she said.

"I can hear a heart beating but I don't know if it's yours or mine," he said.

"It's ours," she said quietly.

At midnight, he dressed and she put on her robe with the split in its seam and saw him to the door, and he kissed her closed eyelids goodnight.

In the corridors of the Aurassi the next morning they nodded and spoke for a few moments about the International Information Agency as delegate and reporter. They played it that way until the Friday session before the weekend adjournment, she at the Albert, he at the Aletti, keeping up appearances in front of the other delegations and correspondents.

"What the hell, no work for a couple of days," he told Jennie when they found themselves alone near the end of the session.

"You were good," she told him.

"I was afraid that I was wandering."

"No, you sounded natural, personal. The others delivered the usual boiler plate, except for your wartime friend Moussi Ali. He pulled a surprise, didn't he? You could tell he was on the mark because they were afraid to applaud him. He's got guts."

"The Moose has invited us to his family place in Biskra for the weekend. It's down on the edge of the desert, an oasis town with a million date trees, only a half hour or so by Air Algérie."

"Am I really included?"

"Definitely. I told him we were good friends and once worked on the same paper and he insisted that you come along. Just the four of us—he's bringing along his friend Ibrahim Nuri."

"Because I wouldn't want to break in on your work, Sam. Especially if you have to talk delegate business with him. You could probably use some breathing space—"

"*You're* my breathing space, Jennie. You know that. Besides, he's anxious to meet a woman in journalism—there are hardly any in this part of the world. And he's also curious for another reason— he thinks we're more than just friends. I wouldn't want to disillusion him."

"Okay, I'd really love to visit an oasis town instead of seeing Algeria only from the inside of the conference hall. When do we leave?"

"Crack of dawn—right after the *muezzin* sounds. Stay with me overnight at the Aletti."

"Do you think it's all right?"

"It is, by now. We've behaved, gone through the motions of separate hotels. The session's almost over anyway, everybody's leaving for *Le Weekend.*"

He looked around to see if any of the delegates were around and then bent down and brushed his lips across her hand.

That evening Sam and Jennie decided to walk along the ramp overlooking the harbor. They saw the white hem of waves flapping against the jetties and cargo ships berthed in the artificial ports; turning away from the sea, their eyes traveled up the labyrinthine streets and the whitened bones of the hills rising to form the great amphitheater of Algiers. Sam glanced at his hand-drawn map to orient himself on the renamed streets. They circled up the Boulevard Baudin and followed the twisting Rue Michelet until they came to the unchanged Rue Lafayette. Moussi Ali lived with Ibrahim Nuri in a corner apartment house a few blocks from the university.

"Greetings, my friends," Moussi Ali said. "Sam promised on his sacred word that he would come to my home, but I could not imagine when we were in Dongo that I would also have the pleasure of your company, Miss Ives."

"Please—Jennie."

"And I am delighted that you will join us in my ancestral home. Biskra will give you a different view of Algeria. It is real country where the palm trees are not eaten by pollution."

"The gateway to the desert," Ibrahim Nuri said.

They dined on the patio of the apartment and watched the running lights of the ships in the distance entering the great harbor.

Nuri's English was even better than his roommate's. He told them that he had redesigned his course in the classics at the university to include Melville and Hawthorne, his two favorite American writers. "In my opinion," he said, *The Scarlet Letter* is one of the finest novels ever written about sexual hypocrisy. A subject, as you might imagine, that concerns me."

Sam asked him if the authorities had to approve changes in courses that included western literature.

"They have much bigger concerns than the teachings of a university professor who plays around with comparative literature."

"I'm not so sure you are right," Moussi Ali said. "The authorities are interested in anything unusual—in a classroom or in a public meeting."

Moussi Ali explained that he had warned his friend about the dangers of teaching foreign subjects that had not been approved in advance.

Jennie turned to Moussi. "I want to compliment you on your remarks at the U.N. session."

"Even when I said that *most* journalists felt the way I did about freedom to write and report? I took a chance—"

"That's what I had in mind. Don't you agree, Sam?"

He frowned and stood up before an imaginary microphone. "Speaking as a journalist, yes. Speaking as a delegate, I refuse to agree with anything said by this underdeveloped individual from the developing third world who just served us dinner."

"Spoken like a true member of the old *Sixième*," Moussi said, and threw a handful of pistachio nuts at Sam.

Nuri refilled their silver cups with tangerine brandy. Linkum and Moussi began to mimic the Russian, Indian, Chilean and Canadian delegates. Pouring the remainder of the pistachio nuts into a milk bottle, the Moose called for order, rattled the bottle and waved it over his head as if it was the director-general's rhinoceros horn.

"Now's the time to break up this party," Linkum said. "One more tangerine brandy and I'll never hear that *muezzin* from the *Mosque de la Pêcherie* in the morning."

"I'll finish his," Jennie said, her eyelids drooping. "This stuff is marvelous, Moussi."

"Only with friends does brandy achieve its full effect."

Linkum looked at his watch. The evening had stretched past midnight. In the harbor, the lights twinkled along the quays where containers and contraband were being unloaded from South Korea and Taiwan and Marseilles. From this height on the terrace of the spectacular city, concerns about licensing journalists and protecting U.S. intelligence sources dissolved in the warm wind of the sirocco and the sea.

They promised to meet for a cup of chicory coffee a half hour before takeoff at Dar El Beida for the milk run to Biskra.

Walking down the aisle of the Air Algérie Caravelle, Linkum spotted the striped green rugby shirt first and then the man: Tweed Jerome. He was reading the back sports page of *Al Shaab,* the Arab-language daily, and talking with a young passenger seated next to him about the exploits of Mustafa M'Hida, the famous goalie from the team in Oran. Linkum could not understand what they were saying but he recognized the goalie's picture from the story he had read in that morning's French edition of *El Moudjahid,* where Moussi Ali's column appeared.

Just as Linkum started to greet him, Jerome looked up from *Al Shaab* and caught his eye, signaling silence and nonrecognition...

The Caravelle flew southward, over the mountains and then across the desert's useless if irreplaceable beauty. Moussi and Nuri pointed out the landmarks to Jennie, naming the djebels and wadis visible in the folds of the sand dunes. From the air, the hills and dry riverbeds ranged from delicately shaded hues of ochre to deep violet. A necklace of oases was strung above the Grand Erg, and as the Caravelle banked under the morning glare its shadow flew below them, racing along the barren ground. Then the earth suddenly turned green as the plane passed between the shoulders of a gorge in the Aures and entered an archipelago of oases. The crushed-rock landing strip stretched almost to the horizon and the Caravelle touched down at great speed, barely having to reverse its motors, until it described a lazy circle at the end of the long runway and taxied toward the terminal. The sign in Arabic and French proclaimed that Biskra was an "international" airport too.

"This way, my friends," Moussi Ali said.

He had laid on a Land-Rover with a driver from the town to take them to his house in the old section of Biskra.

Linkum looked at Tweed Jerome out of the corner of his eye. He was standing nearby but something about him appeared different; if he hadn't been forewarned of his presence in Algeria during their encounter in Hap Chorley's office, he would not have recognized him. The telltale gap between his front teeth had been closed up so that he now had a plastic overbite, and his reddish-blond hair was tinted a funereal black. Moussi Ali did not recognize the man who had taken him to the doctor in Bellagio.

As the Land-Rover headed for the old quarter Linkum turned around several times and saw that Jerome was following them in an ancient taxi. What he failed to notice was a third vehicle, a small Renault, carrying someone he did not know: Batna, the boldest dynamiter in the Independent Moslem Brotherhood. With a confederate, a printer on *Al Shaab,* he had flown on the same Caravelle from Algiers. Batna had received new orders . . .

In the afternoon, while Biskra dozed, Moussi took Sam and Jennie on a carriage ride around the oasis. Nuri stayed at the dazzling sand-and-white domed house with its tiled rooms off a serene inner courtyard, preparing dinner. They drove through twisting lanes and hamlets scattered among palm trees and along the mud-brick walls to the souk in the medina. Pyramids of dates and baskets of fried locusts rose on oily newspapers. Veiled old women sold matches and Gauloises and Marlboros in packs or one at a time. They stopped for a few minutes at the desert gambling casino that had served as headquarters of the bomber wing of Flying Fortresses during the Tunisian campaign, and Linkum discovered that it was now used for the national lottery to support the personal charities of the head of state. Returning to Moussi Ali's house, the carriage passed through the narrow Rue Bou Saada where unveiled, tattooed women from the Ouled Naïl tribe leaned over the wooden balconies and jangled their silver bracelets and gave them the universal fingers of scorn when they failed to stop. Moussi explained that the women performed their *danse du ventre,* belly dance, after dark, and provided more fundamental human services in the daytime.

In the courtyard of the house Ibrahim Nuri served them couscous and lamb charred on spits, and they drank a white wine from a vineyard near the Chott El Hodna that Moussi said was mixed into certain famous French chateaux brands. At sunset they strolled under an arcade of palm trees to the Landon Gardens. Along its winding pathways a thin vapor covered the baked earth. The rich scent of cypress mingled with mimosa, oleander and climbing wisteria under a transparent sky of almost pure blue that fought back the night...

It did not sound like gunfire. At this close range it sounded more like a series of corks popping during the acronical moments between dusk and darkness in the oasis garden. From behind the bougainvillaea to his left, Linkum caught the reflected gleam of the Chasseur semiautomatic, smoke curling slowly from the lip of its barrel.

Jennie was screaming Sam's name. He covered her body with his own and pitched her to the ground just as a second volley of shots coming from the right stitched the shrubbery and splintered in human flesh.

The figure of Tweed Jerome charged past them, his own Walther P38 firing.

"Got you this time, you bahstard." Jerome stood over the fallen body of the dynamiter called Batna and kicked him in the groin. The body was lifeless. Jerome quickly bent low and crouched in front of Jennie and Sam, covering them with his circling German military weapon. His eyes pierced the darkness, searching for Batna's confederate...but this looked like a one-man job.

Jerome detached the Chasseur from Batna's crumpled fingers and jammed it into his shoulder holster. He looked around, listened another minute and without a word to Sam or Jennie disappeared into the night as suddenly as he had appeared.

They stood up, shaken. Sam caught a glimpse of the Chasseur and remembered one like it that day on Lake Como.

Now searchlights illuminated Landon Gardens and footsteps raced along the flower-bordered pathways. They heard the whine of approaching sirens. The pathways began to fill with security police and curious villagers who had come running at the sound of the alien gunfire that broke the stillness of the desert evening.

Ibrahim Nuri came up to them, unable to speak. Linkum asked him: "Where's Moussi?"

"There..." He pointed to a stretcher carried by hospital attendants.

Moussi Ali's face was covered with a cotton sheet stained with spreading blood.

A second stretcher was brought into the garden for Batna.

The police searched Batna's body for identification. He had none.

Both stretchers were placed in the same ambulance: the killer, the victim.

Jennie placed her hand in Nuri's. They followed the ambulance to the small hospital.

Onlookers murmured, *"Inch'Allah."*

Morning came. They had finally slept fitfully in Moussi's house, guarding their private thoughts, consoling each other by their presence and silence. Sam and Jennie joined Nuri as he made the funeral arrangements for Monday. The weekly holiday was still observed on Sunday in Biskra, a relic of French colonial rule; Moussi could not be buried immediately as Moslem custom decreed. From the oasis town and surrounding villages, friends and cousins arrived to pay their respects and join in common prayer for the dead: *Gratitude to God, peace be upon the Messenger, forgive us and forgive him . . .*

Sam and Jennie could not stay for the burial service; the final session of the International Information Agency was scheduled for the next morning in Algiers. They delayed their return flight as long as possible to be with Nuri. He insisted on driving them in the hired Land-Rover to the airport. Just before the Air Algérie Caravelle took off, Linkum turned to Nuri, looking for the answer to the unasked question.

"They finally did it," Nuri said bitterly.

Linkum nodded, waiting for him to continue, to have his own suspicions confirmed.

"The Moslem Brotherhood, those fanatics who did not like what he wrote or said—"

"Did it have anything to do with the speech he made before mine defending freedom and access for everybody?"

"Oh, Moussi had been warned by them before."

"Is it anything that *I* said or did? I praised what he had to say publicly—"

Jennie interrupted. "If this is private, Sam, something I shouldn't know—"

"No, Jennie," Nuri said, "I'm talking to you both as *his* friends . . . It began before the meeting—they even suspended him for a year. He was lucky to remain under house arrest here in Biskra instead of going to jail in Algiers. He truly believed in what he said and wrote."

The last flight to Algiers was called over the loudspeaker.

Nuri suddenly said, "We loved each other, Jennie," as if a woman would especially understand what his love for Moussi meant.

"I know," she said. "I'm sorry . . ."

Linkum reached into his pocket and took out the emblem of the *Sixième Régiment, Spahis Algérien.* He put it in Nuri's palm.

"This belonged to Moussi. A talisman saved a long time. I want you to have it."

"Thank you, Sam."

They all said they would see each other again, somewhere.

Moussi's friend was still waving at them, a lone figure behind the departure gate, as the Caravelle sped down the runway.

190

A few moments before they saw the white harbor lights of Algiers in the distance and then the green lights on the dark runway at Dar El Beida, Jennie asked, "Who killed him, Sam?"

He acted puzzled, trying not to lie or tell too much.

"What do you mean? You heard—"

"I also heard someone, a strange voice, saying something in English when our heads were down. And then gunfire . . . and then two people dead. I don't get it. The police in Biskra blamed it all very quickly on local politics, rival factions bumping each other off, but there are missing pieces . . ."

And it would have to remain that way for a while, Linkum said to himself. So far as she was concerned, there was no Tweed Jerome, no Hap Chorley, no United States Air Force Security Services.

"I don't know all the answers," Sam said. "For now, all I can think of is that I've lost an old friend who lived during an important part of my life."

Jennie touched his hand, and their fingers stayed locked until the Caravelle landed in the darkness.

"Tomorrow's session is going to be the one that counts," she said. "One more broadcast for me and the coach turns back into a pumpkin."

"Will you have to go back to New York?"

"Or Washington. I promised them it would be ten days of their money, at the most, and it'll be just about that. I don't want to overstay my welcome at National Public Radio in case they invite me to do more work for them."

The taxicab pulled up in front of her hotel. She looked at him for a moment as he started to tell the driver that the next stop was the Aletti.

"Sam, I'm a little shaky after what happened . . . I'd like to hold onto a best friend during the night . . ."

Linkum hesitated, then decided they owed it to each other.

"You've got yourself a date, Miss Jennie."

She was still asleep at dawn when he untangled her arms from his waist. The concierge at the Hotel Albert glanced at him with a mixture of suspicion and sullenness as he walked past the desk. The taxicab going to the Aletti took the long way through the narrow streets, running up the bill and turning into the Avenue Franklin Roosevelt, as if the driver recognized his American-accented French and wanted to impress him. Linkum overtipped the canny old man behind the wheel. He was pleased to see any street name that had survived war and the so-called people's revolution.

Linkum's key box at the Aletti contained a single message. It had been delivered in a sealed envelope from the United States Embassy. Dumb of them not to call him to come over and pick it up; probably some third-string vice-counsel had drawn the weekend duty. But it must have been sent in the open—nothing to be de-coded—because it sounded like an ordinary message from someone unofficial:

HEARD ABOUT WHAT HAPPENED TO OUR OLD FRIEND. SORRY ABOUT THAT. BUT GLAD YOU ARE IN BEST OF HEALTH. GOOD LUCK TODAY. CALL WHEN TIME IS RIGHT. CHEERS. MARYLANDER.

Once again Hap Chorley proved USAFSS had its long reach, courtesy of Tweed, right into a bloodied garden in a desert oasis town.

The session was scheduled to begin at two, meaning three, in the afternoon, allowing the delegates enough time to return from their long weekends, take their long lunch hours and assume their positions behind the national nameplates. Diplomats, awash in vague resolve and duty-free whiskey.

Linkum suddenly felt alone. He could not rely on the embassy people for information; they had their personal agendas and he was a stranger on their turf. Anyway, their loyalty ran to the ambassador, a Palm Springs Mercedes dealer who had been given the embassy after contributing a half-million dollars to the President's television campaign. And he did not figure he ought to call Chorley. He ordered a pot of coffee and dozed off while reading *El Moudjahid*.

At noon the phone woke him. "Hello, darling," he said instinc-tively.

"Why, I didn't know you cared." Robin Jenkins laughed. "How about lunch on the roof of the Aletti?"

"Give me a half hour—glad you called, Robin."

The rooftop restaurant was almost empty at half-past twelve, and they chose a table overlooking the harbor.

"How does it look for the voting this afternoon?"

Jenkins ordered a second brandy. He sipped it slowly. "I don't anticipate any problems."

Linkum looked puzzled. "Just like that—"

"Well, you and I will have to team up. *You* can emerge as the hero diplomatically this year. Your country holds the cards or, rather, Mediterranean-American does, because I took the cake two years ago. Won the medal for most delaying tactic against licensing journalists from the wicked west."

"What the hell does that mean?"

"No confrontation. Face-saving for all concerned. At worst, a Pyrrhic victory for them, at best, a real one for us—and business as usual."

"But how are we expected to offset their numbers?"

"By the formula that has worked around the oil-stained, wine-dark sea since Homer, the wind-powered galleons, the splintered oars of chained galleys and the rest of your cradle of civilization and commerce stuff: slaveys and silver. Or, if I may bring it up to the twentieth century, fair-haired women and gold krugerrands from South Africa. Did you ever hear of Imperial House?"

Linkum shook his head.

"It was once owned by the Imperial Oil Company when the Empire was still alive and well. Right in the heart of Cairo, on a small island in the Nile, where one of your Sheratons or Hiltons now stands and has introduced the latest in haute cuisine to the wogs—the sheepburger. It used to be known as Imperial Laundry Services, staffed by women from all over the Empire, every color and race, for the benefit of the old sheiks. It was very useful for gaining oil concessions from the United Arab Emirates. A girl could retire after a few years on those hundred-pound tips the sheiks gave them. The Mediterranean-American Development people took it over when they gained control of the Arabian Peninsula. Now the sons of the sheiks go there to get dry-cleaned by the ladies in the Age of OPEC. Mediterranean-American runs the fanciest call-girl service in the Middle East. They flew in a dozen of the girls to Algiers over the weekend. And a few of the boys, too, for the third world delegates who have mixed preferences."

"Robin, are you saying that for a night of screwing the delegates are going to vote right?"

"Could be . . . and I find it rather honest—in a dishonest, Mediterranean sort of way. Something like the barter system. We each have something the other wants and strike a bargain without too much hypocritical foreplay. Don't make the mistake of applying your puritanical standard of behavior to theirs. Once a man has slept with a woman you've provided and accepted your money, he's beholden to you."

"Krugerrands, too?"

"Oh yes, Mediterranean-American has been rather busy over the weekend. A couple of its emissaries were greasing palms with apartheid currency—it's the most popular baksheesh in the Arabian Peninsula today."

"Which delegates have been bought?"

"My sources tell me that the safe ones from our viewpoint are Bahrain, Kuwait, Oman, Saudi Arabia, Iraq, the Yemen Arab Republic and United Arab Emirates. Then, too, there are at least five more from the former French black colonies who come under the influence of the OPEC Arabs because they need their oil."

Suddenly Jenkins began to choke back laughter. Linkum filled his water tumbler with bottled San Pellegrino and asked him what the hell was so funny.

"Don't count on the gentleman from Qatar, now or in the future," Jenkins said.

"I never count on gentlemen from Qatar. I couldn't even find it on the map."

"It's one of those tiny oil sheikdoms on the Arabian Peninsula. Rich as Croesus. A Rolls parked next to every tent, color television sets, Atari video games and the biggest library of porno films in that corner of the world, all smuggled in diplomatic pouches. Well, the Mediterranean-American laundry fixed him up with the services of a professional from Corsica, a voluptuous tart with a little Moor in her blood, and the Qatar delegate refused to give her up after midnight, as agreed, to the delegate from Oman. In the early morning hours, when Qatar was drugged with sex and who knows what else, Oman stole into his room at the Aurassi Hotel and squeezed out a whole tube of something called Krazy-Glue over Qatar's cock. It's the strongest adhesive made—I've seen it advertised on your telly. Can sustain a two-thousand pound weight and once applied cannot be separated. Oman then took the Corsican call girl for a session at his own hotel. When Qatar woke up his cock was stuck solid at half-mast. He couldn't pee and he couldn't get it up *or* down. A medical first."

"Come on, Robin, you'd better reveal your source, and I don't mean Mediterranean-American's Corsican woman, or I won't believe a word—"

"Cross my heart...I heard it from the British surgeon at our own embassy. Qatar was rushed to the hospital, but they're puzzled about what to do with his dingus. The alternatives are either to heat the glue to a burning temperature and melt the sorry cock off or try to skin it surgically with high-energy lasers. Whichever, I don't think he'll have much need to be aroused by those porno films in his diplomatic pouch for a very long time, if ever."

The tale of the Krazy-Glued delegate from Qatar helped to relieve their worry about the final session, the payoff to a week of maneuvering and violence and sudden death.

"Poor chap," Jenkins added, "he may well end up as a eunuch in the royal palace."

Linkum looked at his watch. It was nearly three o'clock, time to get going for the meeting hall. He recognized several delegates in the rooftop restaurant who were beginning to leave. Jenkins asked for a refill of his brandy glass; Linkum asked for his check.

"All right, Robin, you forgot to tell me how to win that medal you mentioned."

Jenkins downed his brandy quickly, then cleared his throat. "For the things which are seen are temporal, but the things which are not seen are eternal..."

"And what does *that* mean?"

"That, Sam, is from *Corinthians*. I am saying that the obvious will not necessarily achieve one's temporal aims. The choice is not between the angels and the devils. They're both too hard to distinguish at these international meetings. Truth to tell, the good Lord is not necessarily on the side we represent. The blokes on the other side, though somewhat more obvious and less articulate, do have some right too. On Judgment Day our government leaders, and theirs as well, may have to knock rather loudly to enter the Kingdom of Heaven. The behavior of Mediterranean-American this weekend..." He hesitated. "But then it isn't cricket diplomatically for me to comment about the conduct of an esteemed ally or one of its respected multinational corporations—"

"Come off it, Robin, you're not talking to my country's nameplate, you're talking to me."

Jenkins smiled. "Oh well, I suppose the call girls and the krugerrands *are* tax deductible... I have no secret formula, Sam. Except perhaps this: why not speak this afternoon as if you were speaking for *yourself?*"

The director-general of the International Information Agency, puffed up with self-esteem, rattled his rhinoceros gavel.

"Your chairman wishes to thank the delegates for the frank and honest discussion heard here today and for the thoughtful resolutions you have introduced..."

Jenkins leaned over to Linkum, covered the open microphone with his hand. "It's now or never, Sam. Don't let them win it by default."

He had been thinking about this moment ever since taking his place behind the nameplate little more than a week ago, thinking about it for most of his professional career...

Linkum's hand went up at the same time that a half-dozen other delegates in the hall waved theirs to gain the little Ugandan's attention. Something about Linkum's insistent manner for the first time in the session caused the director-general to recognize him.

Linkum left his place at the long table and walked to the floor microphone. He looked toward the press booth on the far side of the hall, unable to see Jennie behind the glass but wanting to let her know that she was in his mind. This was the one that counted.

"Fellow delegates, before I speak for myself I would like to pay tribute to one of the delegates who is no longer here..."

Linkum stared at the swarthy lawyer who led the Algerian delegation. He and the others from Algeria shifted in their seats. No one had mentioned their dead deputy delegate. Someone else now occupied Moussi's chair. It was as if he had never existed, and they were playing it as "an internal affair," as silently as they had listened to his words.

"Moussi Ali, the deputy delegate from Algeria, died under violent circumstances in Biskra two days ago. How or why his death occurred is a matter for the authorities of his own country to pursue. I offer no comment in this forum. I do regret, however, that no news of his death has been reported in the press, including in his own newspaper, *El Moudjahid,* up to now. I say this because many voices have been raised here during the past week about the need for developing nations to have their own independent presses without the presence or influence of news agencies from the west."

Linkum glanced around the conference room and noticed that the surprised delegates were staring at the Algerian delegation, whose faces were masked.

"I am sorry to be the one who must break this sad news. I trust that eventually Moussi Ali's death will become known to his compatriots. Because I do agree that the presses of all nations, developed and developing, should be free to roll so that the news can be reported—fully. The Algerian deputy delegate had the courage to stand up in front of this meeting and say as a charter member of the *Union Algérienne des Journalistes* that fair reporting can thrive only where freedom is permitted for *all* correspondents, domestic and foreign, by *all* governments. I pay my respects to the memory of Moussi Ali."

Linkum was about to go on when he was interrupted by a smattering of applause. He looked up in surprise from his handful of notes as the applause began to spread among several of the delegations.

Somehow, by personalizing the news of Moussi's death, and the failure of the Algerians to reveal anything about it, he had apparently touched a common nerve among the journalists in the delegations.

The director-general looked blank, obviously fearing that the applause would insult the Algerians.

Linkum, following Jenkins' advice, now spoke as if he was sitting around with some of his friends at Mannie's Place after their paper had been permanently put to bed.

"Fellow delegates, although this is called the International Information Agency, we lack information ourselves. I don't know enough about why so many newspapers in my own country are gone or going. I don't know much about the papers in the Soviet Union except that they are official organs of the government and can't veer off the acceptable course. Maybe Madame Gorokov, with her knowledge of the inside workings of *Pravda,* can enlighten us, if she will. I know even less about the permissible bounds of reporting on the heads of state who govern most of the developing nations represented in this meeting room today. I've read no studies in the past ten years put out by this U.N. agency that can enlighten me. And so I ask the International Information Agency for nothing less than information itself. Before we can tell each other how to behave professionally or ethically, we first need to inform ourselves.

"For example, I would like to know the effect of television—national, international, via satellite or by direct broadcasting—on the traditional means of communication. I'd like to know how televised pictures of violence, including violence in the streets as well as on the battlefields, affect viewers and the outcome of events. The Vietnam War, brought to the public in living color between commercials, lasted longer than any in American history. I would like to know the effects of multinational companies on news coverage of their activities and their advertised products. I would especially like to have information on which multinationals hold interests in television networks and newspapers—who their true owners are beneath the layers of public relations misinformation and disinformation. And, finally, can we learn more about the pioneering efforts undertaken by a number of newspapers in western Europe to bring democracy to their newsrooms? Amazing as it seems, reporters have elected their own editors and working journalists sit on the boards of directors of their newspapers. They share responsibility for news policy instead of having it dictated by remote managements. Naturally I'd like to find out how that process can be spread to newspapers and networks in other countries, including my own..." Linkum paused to catch his breath, noticed that the delegates were listening and some were even scribbling notes. Okay, now for the touchy resolution... "Fellow delegates, I propose that we table voting on the difficult provisions of the New World Information Order, with its imposed licensing and limitations on news coverage, and instead undertake factual studies on the matters that I've proposed. We have nothing to gain by confrontation and head-on collisions. So I offer these ideas on the way to justify the International Information Agency. Thank you."

Again, mild applause broke out as Linkum returned to his place at the long conference table. Again, he was surprised...

One of the most vociferous advocates of licensing, the delegate from Libya, spoke by rote about the need to restrict foreign journalists in his country to avoid "insults" to the head of state.

Then Madame Gorokov stood up:

"Why should a government which is doing what it believes right be criticized by the press of its own country and by outsiders who are hostile to peace-loving peoples? My government would not allow opposition by lethal weapons. Alien ideas can be more damaging than guns. Why should individuals be allowed to disseminate personal opinions that go against the state? That is not the way to progress."

The director-general looked around the hall. He recognized two other speakers from the third world, the delegate from the United Arab Emirates and the delegate from Oman. Both spoke approvingly of the need for further studies similar to those mentioned by the United States delegate so everybody could meet again in greater harmony two years later in Saudi Arabia.

Jenkins turned toward Linkum and confided with a smile, "Never underestimate the power of Mediterranean-American or of Krazy-Glue."

The Ugandan director-general saw which way the wind was blowing. He was up for reelection.

"It is the consensus of this meeting that committees will be appointed representing various nations to undertake further studies of mutual interest," he announced abruptly, shortstopping any licensing resolution and suddenly discovering his own consensus. "I now declare the conclusion by unanimous consent of this session of the International Information Agency to be the most successful in history. I thank all the delegates, pray for the leaders of their respective nations and trust that you will join me and come together in the Aurassi reception room for refreshments in friendship."

With a look of triumph, the Ugandan rattled his rhinoceros horn overhead. The delegates applauded him—and congratulated themselves.

THIS IS JENNIE IVES REPORTING FOR THE LAST TIME FOR NATIONAL PUBLIC RADIO FROM THE DEMOCRATIC AND POPULAR REPUBLIC OF ALGERIA. DATELINE: ALGIERS.

WHEN YOUR INTREPID CORRESPONDENT WAS LAST HEARD FROM, THE INTERNATIONAL INFORMATION AGENCY SOUNDED AS IF IT HAD ASSUMED ALL THE HURTS AND BURDENS OF THE WORLD. THE SOVIET DELEGATE, MADAME GOROKOV, LECTURED THE OTHER DELEGATIONS ABOUT JOURNALISTIC RESPONSIBILITY, BY WHICH SHE MEANT RESPONSIBILITY TO THE STATE. THE AMERICAN DELEGATE, SAMUEL LINKUM, TALKED ABOUT THE NEED FOR FREE ACCESS WITHOUT DOMINATION BY GOVERNMENTS OR CONGLOMERATES. AND THE DEVELOPING NATIONS SAID THAT THE FOREIGN—MEANING, WESTERN—NEWS AGENCIES ONLY REPORTED THEIR DISASTERS INSTEAD OF THEIR ACHIEVEMENTS.

HOVERING IN THE BACKGROUND WAS A THREAT OF LICENSING OF JOURNALISTS THAT WOULD, IN EFFECT, CAUSE CENSORSHIP OR SELF-CENSORSHIP.

THERE WAS A SURPRISING TURN OF EVENTS IN THE FINAL MEETING. THE AMERICAN DELEGATE CALLED FOR A SERIES OF STUDIES ON MULTINATIONAL OWNERSHIP OF NEWSPAPERS AND NETWORKS, ON THE EFFECTS OF REPORTING WARS AND VIOLENCE ON THE TUBE, AND ON BRINGING DEMOCRACY INTO THE NEWSROOMS OF THE WORLD. HIS REMARKS, WHICH HE SAID APPLIED TO HIS OWN COUNTRY AS WELL AS TO THEIRS, WERE RECEIVED WITH UNEXPECTED ENTHUSIASM.

THE UGANDAN DIRECTOR-GENERAL, WHO IS ASSURED REELECTION TO ANOTHER TERM BECAUSE OF HIS UNCANNY ABILITY TO AGREE WITH EVERYONE AND ANTAGONIZE NO ONE, DECLARED IT TO BE THE CONSENSUS OF THE MEETING THAT FURTHER STUDIES WOULD BE REQUIRED. THE LICENSING RESOLUTION WAS TABLED WITH DELIBERATE SPEED. THEN, WITH A RUSH OF SELF-CONGRATULATIONS, THE TENTH SESSION OF THE INTERNATIONAL INFORMATION AGENCY CONCLUDED.

THOMAS JEFFERSON ONCE WROTE: "WHERE THE PRESS IS FREE AND EVERY MAN ABLE TO READ, ALL IS SAFE."

AFTER OBSERVING THE PROCEEDINGS HERE FOR A WEEK, ONE VENTURES TO SAY ALL IS FAR FROM SAFE. YET THERE ARE STILL A FEW VOICES OF FREEDOM TO BE HEARD, VOICES WHICH SPEAK FOR THE SURVIVAL OF US ALL."

JENNIE IVES, REPORTING.

PART III

CHAPTER SEVEN

The London Connection

AFTER they were airborne and the Air France Airbus banked and described a farewell arc over the disappearing harbor and hills of Algiers and then began to climb across the mother-of-pearl Mediterranean, Robin Jenkins signaled the hostess, ordered three splits of champagne, reserved three for later and asked Sam Linkum if he noticed who was seated four rows behind them.

Linkum started to turn and look over his shoulder when Jenkins poked him and whispered, "It's Herself—Madame Gorokov."

"Oh no... I've already done my bit for God and country. If she wants the microphone she can have it. All I want to do now is carry on the cold war by cooled champagne."

"Sam, the honor of the Western World is at stake. You're going to send her one of these splits and we'll raise a plastic cup to her. In defeat, resolution. In victory, magnanimity—or however the hell

Churchill put it. And say something clever on this piece of note-block."

"I can't think of anything clever—and I wouldn't want to be *too* clever."

"Then say something amusing—you're the writer, I'm only a bloody broadcaster."

"Come on, Robin, I'll play along but help me out."

Jenkins leaned back, took a long sip. "How about something like: 'Greetings, socialist swine, Cordially, capitalist pig?' That has a pleasant relevancy to it."

Linkum laughed. "I don't know how much of a sense of humor she has. You know her from past meetings. Does she ever let her hair down?"

"Not in front of me though I confess that I've often wondered, while listening to one of her homilies, how Madame Gorokov would perform between the sheets. Probably by the textbook. Quite frankly, I've always been put off by women who are too clever by half—"

"Catch up with the times, Robin. Among other things, it helps overcome post-coital *tristesse* to be with someone who's also got a brain."

"Oh, I don't really mind intelligence in a woman—I just don't like it to *show*."

"Are you married—"

"Was. And *both* were terribly clever."

Jenkins emptied his pocket of the crumpled Algerian dinars and paid the hostess for the champagne. "Paper play money," he said, "and not from one of my favorite colonelcies."

Linkum suggested that it would be best to keep the message short and let the champagne speak for them.

He ripped a piece of blank paper out of the back of his pocket diary and wrote one word on it:

Tovarich.

Which more or less exhausted his Russian vocabulary.

Jenkins said, "Not bad," they both signed their names and called for the hostess to deliver the comradely note with the split of champagne to the woman with the closely cropped gray hair seated four rows back. They both stood up in their seats and raised their glasses in her direction. She looked up, startled, and then allowed a faint smile to play around the corners of her mouth.

A moment later two miniatures of vodka were placed before them by the hostess. And with the bottles came a note:

O virtuous fight! When right with right wars who shall be most right?

—Troilus and Cressida
(*And Oriana Gorokov*)

Once again Linkum and Jenkins turned in her direction and toasted the Russian woman. This time, she actually laughed and lifted her glass in return.

"Well, we lost that exchange," Linkum said. "By the way, do vodka and champagne go together?"

"Thirty thousand feet over France anything goes with champagne," Jenkins said. "I told you that I've always had problems with clever women. As you just saw they don't come any smarter than Madame Gorokov."

"Topped us with Shakespeare—*your* man. Do you think we should answer with something out of Chairman Mao's Little Red Book? All I know is the one about political power growing out of the barrel of a gun..."

Jenkins chased his vodka with champagne. "No. I know when I've lost."

The Air France Airbus touched down at Orly. At the terminal Linkum strolled over to one of the duty-free shops just as he saw Oriana Gorokov walking away with a package from the perfume counter. A chauffeur from the Soviet embassy in Paris saluted, took her luggage and she disappeared through the exit doors into a limousine. Linkum thought he'd have enjoyed getting to know her outside the diplomatic atmosphere of the Aurassi conference hall, where everyone had to follow the steps of a familiar state minuet. He must remember to ask Jennie for her impressions of the Soviet delegate from *Pravda*.

Madame Gorokov's purchase reminded him to pick up some perfume and bring it back to Jennie in New York. He walked up to the counter and asked the salesgirl for the same brand as the bottle she had just sold to the gray-haired woman. He realized that he didn't know Jennie's. The salesgirl said "Shalimar" and gave him a whiff. He felt almost airsick for the first time and asked the salesgirl, "Have you got one that's a little more...subtle?" She leaned over and raised the hair behind her ears and asked him to smell. It was a lot more subtle than the salesgirl's charming technique. He bought a vial with his remaining Algerian dinars, and then some. The label said, "Calèche," by Hermès.

For Benjamin Oliver Sassoon, his old friend and overnight host in London, Linkum picked up a bottle of Martell cognac. Then, instead of buying a whole box of Romeo y Julietas, he suddenly decided to settle for a small package of five less expensive Havana cigars. He wondered why himself; maybe it was a measure of his doubts about the mission he had undertaken for Hap Chorley and USAFSS...and its intertwined relationship with Mediterranean-American, *amen*.

Linkum and Jenkins took the bus that ran from Orly to Charles De Gaulle Airport in time to catch a British Airways Trident flight to Heathrow. Jenkins offered him a lift to his hotel in London but Linkum said he was staying with a newspaper friend in Thurloe Square, across the Cromwell Road from the Victoria and Albert Museum.

"Could that be Ben Sassoon?" Jenkins said.

Linkum explained that he and Sassoon had covered stories together for their papers when he was based in London for his newspaper and that they had kept in touch, staying at each other's places on both sides of the Atlantic.

"I know Ben, of course. Part of the great old Persian-English Sassoon family. One of the most respected editors in the City, writes a little poetry on the side, like his famous forebear. Poor chap, I hear his newspaper is pretty shaky ever since it was acquired by the Whipley Group. Give him my best regards, in case I don't see him when we land at Heathrow."

"How close do you think it is for his newspaper?"

"I don't know, Sam, been away and out of it for a while, but I do know that without his paper our broadcasters will have a tough time of it. We steal most of our stuff, especially the long-range reports and analyses, from the press. Nothing to hide or be ashamed of, it's just the way it is—ours is more of a feature service."

"Yeah, I've heard that's the way it is—and not only in London."

The seatbelts–no smoking sign was turned on and the Trident began its descent.

"In the unlikely event that we don't run into each other again, Sam, I do want to tell you that I thought you made a real contribution in Algiers. I hope some of those studies you proposed happen. Damn good idea, if only to hold off that damn licensing resolution that would make us all kaput."

"I'm glad you told me to do my own thing there, Robin."

Jenkins hesitated for a moment. "I trust that you didn't cause any difficulty for yourself with your people..."

Linkum shrugged. "That remains to be seen," he said.

The Independent Moslem Brotherhood along the littoral of North Africa had moved its planning base of operations from the garage on the Boulevard Frantz Fanon in Algiers back to the private residence above Mers el Kebir west of Oran after the death of the dynamiter Batna in the Biskra garden. The ruler's security police, who usually looked the other way, had been forced to make a superficial roundup of suspects because of the attention given in the press to the killing of Moussi Ali.

After Linkum had spoken out in front of the International Information Agency delegates, the news about Moussi Ali had been published. From members of the Brotherhood in Biskra and the oasis region, the leaders had learned that a professional gunman had stalked Batna. The gunman had spoken English as well as Arabic and French, but they did not know his name or if he came from the United States or Great Britain.

"Our brave brother's death must be avenged," said Tlemcen, the organization's leader, "to wipe out the shame of having one of our men killed in our own country. We must show the world that we are still a force to be reckoned with. I am willing to undertake a mission personally against a satellite station to set an example for the brothers."

His two closest lieutenants, Arzew and Tebessa, immediately said that the honor of revenge should be theirs.

"We are better trained in handling explosives," they said, "and we are not as recognizable at the airports. It is safer for us, and we do not intend to die."

"Nor do I," Tlemcen said. "To the fainthearted, I say that by killing the traitorous journalist Moussi Ali we have sent a message to the leaders of all Moslem states along the Mediterranean that foreigners should not be given license to capture the minds of our people with their broadcasts. His speech was practically an invitation to intervention in our lives."

The other regional representatives of the Brotherhood nodded their approval.

"Next we shall strike in two places," Tlemcen said. "Arzew and Tebessa together will lead one group of students living in Britain against their earth station in Goonhilly Downs, Cornwall, and I, myself, will lead another group against the American station in Andover, in the state of Maine. For the American operation our students will come from colleges in Boston and New York and be joined by our students from colleges in French Canada. For the British operation the best-trained students will cross over and join them from the Sorbonne—the same ones who assisted our brother Batna in his successful mission that destroyed the southern antenna at Pleumeur-Bodou."

The scraggly-bearded representative from Oran asked if the French station was back in operation. Tlemcen said that it had taken them a week to restore service there and then only on half the channels.

"The chief aim of our mission was accomplished," he said. "We prevented the Mediterranean-American consortium from going ahead with its plan to erect new satellite receiving antennae in Constantine and Carthage. Our Arab workmen will not take jobs with the foreign companies once they are informed that what they are building is a new colonialism."

The expert dynamiters received instructions that they were told to memorize: checkpoints and communications telephone numbers for emergencies, recognition signals, detailed maps of the areas around Goonhilly Downs and Andover and the back-road escape routes.

The dynamiter Arzew asked Tlemcen to explain to the newcomers among them the purpose of these missions so far from Algeria. He told them in grandiloquent fashion:

"We must magnify the name of the Independent Moslem Brotherhood to show the foreigners that we are not afraid to strike at their very roots, and we must show our own people that when necessary for the cause we can send our message by dynamite."

One by one, the dynamiters embraced Tlemcen and kissed each other. For reasons of security, the exact timetable was not disclosed; but Tlemcen declared that the attack groups against Andover and Goonhilly Downs were already on the move . . .

Standing just outside the customs ring at Heathrow Airport, dark-eyed Ruth Sassoon waved at Sam Linkum. They embraced, and in that moment with their arms around each other Linkum remembered that Elena and Ruth had been such good friends, when they were all young marrieds, during their exchange visits in New York and London.

"Your chum's still at the paper—latest in a series of crises," she said, "so I was given the honor of meeting you. I hope you won't mind being nuzzled by Siegfried—we've just come from the veterinarian and I didn't get a chance to drop him off at home." The spaniel jumped across the back seat of the family Rover and licked Linkum's cheeks in recognition.

"You're still the fastest driver in London—don't mind me if I close my eyes and pray."

She laughed and continued to weave in and out on the A4, passing taxicabs, a daring, different person behind the wheel.

As they approached the familiar red-brick row houses of Hammersmith and then the stucco facades and plane trees of South Kensington, she overtook the Number thirty bus and turned into Thurloe Street.

"Drop me off at Daquise and you go ahead and find your parking space," Linkum said. "I know my way to the house from here. I'm going to pick up a few loaves of that great crusty bread and some of the sinful strawberry and apple tarts." It was almost a tradition, he stopping at the Polish restaurant-bakery a few doors down from the South Kensington station and bringing the dessert for dinner at the Sassoons.

Ben Sassoon was home when Sam Linkum came through the entrance of their house on Thurloe Square. He looked drawn and worried.

"I read in the *Telegraph* that you and Robin Jenkins managed to stop the licensing resolution. Good work, old boy."

"Only temporarily, Ben. It's a hardy perennial and someone else will have to fight it at the next session of the International Information Agency. But that's yesterday's news. What's this Ruth tells me about a new crisis at your paper?"

Sassoon smiled, as if to avoid worrying his wife. "Oh, it's not all over yet. We'll know more when Walt Whipley himself gives the word at a staff meeting in the newsroom tonight. Want to come along? It might be part of your education as a veteran of newspaper burial ceremonies—"

"That education I could do without—for your sake. Actually, I wouldn't mind if *he* wouldn't mind having an outsider present."

"Oh, there'll be a crowd there, everybody's showing up to find out whether we go to the work camp or to the ovens with a wave of one man's swagger stick. You'll be lost in the crowd."

Linkum handed them the bottle of Martell brandy that he had picked up at Orly.

"Thanks, friend, we may need this before the night's over," Sassoon said.

"Okay, but I hope you don't have to crack it open for a long time." He looked at his watch and subtracted five hours. "If you both will excuse me I've got a couple of overseas calls to make. My international credit card is still good for a few days. I can go outside—"

"Use the phone upstairs in your bedroom. It's private, unless Siegfried comes in and starts licking and listening."

212

In the bedroom Linkum kicked off his shoes and stretched out with the phone cradled in his shoulder.

He dialed Hap Chorley first. Owed him one for the last few days...

The director of USAFSS was on another line but as soon as Linkum's name was mentioned he was told to hold and not hang up—"we've been trying to reach you everywhere," said one of the front-office colonels in a chilly voice.

Hap Chorley got on. "The wandering delegate—nice of you to find time to call." He was polite; but Linkum knew when he was mad.

"My pleasure," Linkum said. "It's your nickel. This is the first chance—"

"Where you calling from? Somewhere on the Riviera? Paris? That's where you were sighted last..."

So Hap still has his operatives out, keeping track of me. Changing airports in Paris must have thrown off the scent; or maybe they were busy keeping an eye on Madame Gorokov.

"I'm in London."

"At the embassy?"

"At a friend's place—don't worry, it's secure."

"How do you know?"

"Because they don't bug private residences here."

"Do you mind if I have the phone number of where you're staying?" Linkum said it wasn't a secret and gave it to him. "You're a day late—when can I expect you?"

"I'm not *late,* Hap. I finished my assignment and decided to come back by way of London. One day of R and R. I'll be back in New York tomorrow afternoon. Unless you want to stake me to a ride on the Concorde—what's the hurry?"

"Your lady friend managed to find her way to New York without any delay."

"She had to get back for some panel program National Public Radio is preparing about the International Information Agency. But that, if I may say so, is not your business."

For a moment, neither spoke. Linkum wondered what was eating

Chorley. And he didn't like the "lady friend" crack.

"You and I have a few things to discuss—about the way you handled your mission, and something even more urgent—"

"Sure, Hap." He wasn't going to fish for a compliment or ask him what could be *that* urgent.

"Don't report to the State Department people until you've spoken to me."

"That's okay with me—you got me into the job in the first place—"

"Remember that, Sam... And, yes, there's a reservation in your name on the early Concorde. I'll have one of my planes waiting for you at JFK for the flight down here. You'll be spotted. Good-by."

Linkum leaned back on the bolster, the dead phone line in his hand. Instead of a kind word, there had been an unspoken reprimand: was it for failing to report sooner or for something more fundamental, something he had said for all the world to hear in Algiers? He got up and looked out the window toward the leafy treetops at his eye level in Thurloe Square. The wooden sign in front of the pub on Old Brompton Road floated into his reverie. *Take Courage*... it was an inviting command to enter and a cheering observation in general.

He picked up the phone again and dialed the number of National Public Radio's news department in Washington. Yes, Jennie Ives was there; no, she was in a meeting; don't want to interrupt, just slip her a note saying her friend from the Scalinata di Spagna in Rome was on the line, she'll know who it is...

"Sam! Where are you calling from?"

"The Sassoons in London—you've heard me talk about them. I decided to lay over one night here. Get some fresh perspective in a civilized place I happen to love with some close friends. Decompression chamber before facing up to reality. How are things going for you?"

"They liked my sliders and sinkers in between the hard news— so they've told me, anyway."

"Don't forget to save me your scripts or better still a cassette of your Algiers broadcasts. How can I know what *I* said unless I hear what *you* said?"

Jennie promised that he would hear them.

"Algiers was stifling after you left. I was glad to get another wartime city out of my system. Especially after what happened in Biskra...Look, I know I've pulled you out of a meeting—don't want to hold you up, just wanted to touch base and say it was great."

"Especially in Rome, Sam." He heard other voices on her end of the line. "I'm sort of in Macy's window here and I'm being called to lunch. I'd better run. Fly carefully..."

He smiled to himself as they said their good-bys.

Ruth Sassoon set out a dinner of Hungarian goulash, which she confessed had been prepared by a friendly chef at the Gay Hussar on Greek Street. "I thought you'd enjoy a typical un-British dinner and I'd hold the roast beef of Olde England for another time," she said.

Linkum laughed. "And thanks for skipping the couscous from Algeria, too, but I insist on my kippers for breakfast or I won't know where I've spent the night."

Ben Sassoon slipped into his jacket and lit his pipe. "Are you really still game to come with me, Sam?"

"Sure, if it really won't be an embarrassment."

"Not to me it won't."

Ruth told them to go along and that she would save the strawberry tarts for later in the evening.

"They go with cognac," Linkum said.

"We may have to crack open that bottle after all," Sassoon said as they stepped into the Rover and he drove along the edge of Hyde Park and turned toward the newspaper offices in the shuttered City.

The sprawling newsroom was already crowded with reporters and editors, clerks and secretaries when Sassoon and Linkum arrived. They stood around in small knots, section by section, some knowing each other only by recognizable bylines and as elevator faces. The only time everybody assembled was during crises, and their paper had lived through several in the last five years.

The managements kept changing: there had been the family of old shareholders, ownership passed down by inheritance, and this somewhat casual arrangement had worked for decades until some of the disinterested young heirs discovered that there were far more profitable investments than newspapers and sold off their stock; then came an interregnum when a combination of Scotch distillers and baronial landholders, with personal wealth in Bahamian trusts, acquired controlling interest for legitimacy and prestige, failed to shut down the unprofitable Sunday edition because of indirect pressure from Her Majesty's Ministry for Inland Revenue, and were struck by a series of labor disputes; finally, the paper was acquired by an aggressive press and television mogul from the Commonwealth: the Walt Whipley Group.

"Quite a turnout," Linkum said, looking around the room. "When is Whipley due?"

"Whipley or one of his top editors, Roger Malvine, who was imported to jazz up the news and editorials and carry out orders. He usually does his dirty work—"

Suddenly there was a parting in the crowd and a lowering of voices. Linkum moved to the side and looked between the heads of two of Sassoon's section editors.

"Here they come," Sassoon said. "The little king and his equerry."

Linkum spotted the loud green sports jacket first, then Whipley himself. "That's Malvine with him," Sassoon whispered. "The short chap with the potbelly—Whipley never hires editors who are taller than he is."

With a boost from his aides, Whipley stepped on top of one of the desks and stood head and shoulders above the crowd.

"Ladies and gentlemen, I have asked the staff to attend this important meeting in order to put an end to the rumors that have been launched in the left-wing periodicals about our newspaper. They would like to see us buried. Let me be forthright and say that I have no intention of losing circulation to our opposition. We have all made major investments in this fine newspaper and I intend it to continue with—"

Applause interrupted him. He held up his hand for silence.

"Do not mistake generosity for acquiescence. I do intend for this newspaper to be published, but only with your willing cooperation. If the Whipley Group is to continue its investment, certain econ-

216

omies will immediately need to be put into effect. As I have said from the start, there are redundancies. The investors in the Whipley Group have instructed me to reduce expenses by approximately one-third. This means, ladies and gentlemen, that one-third of the editorial staff will no longer have employment in this building—"

Shouts of "No, no," resounded in the newsroom.

"I have not finished. Every opportunity will be given for those deemed redundant to be placed on our newspapers or television stations elsewhere in the Commonwealth."

Whipley ignored the boos and mutterings. He was expert at facing up to reduced staffs all over his publishing empire.

"I have one more announcement. My associate, Roger Malvine, will be available with more specific details. Henceforth the Sunday edition of the newspaper will be suspended, as such, in its old-fashioned traditional full-size format and become a convenient tabloid specifically redesigned for television viewers. In addition to the regular channel listings for BBC and ITV stations, it will include features about prominent programs and their personalities, advertising and listings for satellite shows, direct broadcasts, videotex and the latest video games."

That announcement was greeted with shocked silence.

Suddenly, a pastepot was flung to the ground, its glass shards flying. Heads turned in the direction of where Linkum stood next to Sassoon and his Sunday section writers and editors.

Walt Whipley peered toward the commotion at the far end of the newsroom. His eyes and Linkum's met. A startled look and then a flash of anger crossed Whipley's face. He leaned down and whispered to Malvine. Standing erect, he pointed his finger at Linkum.

"I regret to say that there is an American journalist in this room who has not been invited. This is not a press conference but a staff meeting for members of this newspaper only. I shall have to insist—"

"Don't bother, Mr. Whipley," Linkum spoke up. "I'm not here as a reporter and I'm leaving right now."

Someone in the crowd shouted, "Let him stay, let's not cover up our *own* news."

Linkum shook his head. "Thanks, but I'm not wanted here."

Linkum walked to the exit, not looking back, afraid to identify Sassoon as the one who had invited him. Sassoon, and the Sunday staff, had enough problems.

Outside, he hailed a cab. The driver of the high-backed Austin asked him where to, and he told him Thurloe Square. But as the taxi proceeded along Piccadilly Linkum decided to have a drink and told the driver to drop him off in front of his favorite pub in Mayfair, the Audley. He needed one after the embarrassing confrontation with Whipley on his newspaper turf. Curiosity had bested reason; he realized that it had not been very wise to be an onlooker at the meeting affecting the working lives of other journalists, in another country. Misery was a private matter. In the gilt and velvet bar he quickly downed a mug of Guinness, avoided conversation and stepped through the jeweled cut-glass doors back into Mount Street.

Some instinct made him walk a few blocks north to Grosvenor Square. He cut across the grass and stood in front of the memorial to President Roosevelt. For a few moments he stared at the caped figure illuminated by the moon in the shadowed square, emptying his mind and stopping time. Then, turning away, he strolled along the familiar streets of W.1 and caught another cab on Park Lane that took him to Thurloe Square.

Ben Sassoon drove up and parked just as Sam alighted from the cab.

"Sorry about that," Sassoon said, but Linkum quickly put an arm on his shoulder. "Don't worry—I heard more than enough by the time I left. The script is pretty much the same, in the States or over here."

As they plopped down in the wicker chairs in the front room facing the square Ruth Sassoon opened the bottle of cognac and, without a word, filled all their glasses.

"How did you know?" Ben said.

"I saw the outcome in your face *before* you went to the City," his wife said. "Let's drink to . . ."

"To old friends and old newspapers?" Linkum volunteered.

They clinked their glasses without touching.

Ben told her what had happened at the meeting. Whipley had little more to add to what Linkum had heard while he was there, except that there were plans to start a new magazine featuring the life stories of television and sports personalities—a monthly that might be developed into a weekly.

After a few minutes Ruth went to bed and the two men talked alone.

"Do you think there's any way that the Sunday paper can be stopped from turning into a TV listing sheet?"

"Not so long as Whipley's in charge, Sam. His whole record on every paper he's touched is down-marketing. Anyway, he and his partners in Mediterranean-American Development are primarily interested in television by satellite and direct broadcasting."

"What do you mean, Ben? Is the Whipley Group involved in Mediterranean-American too?"

Sassoon sighed. "It came out during a parliamentary commission hearing on cross-ownership. There are all sorts of layers beneath layers—combinations of natural resources, tax havens, investments by the Saudi Arabians, satellite facilities and program software provided by the network you once worked for. They've got deep pockets."

Linkum said, "I knew about the network's interest in selling its news programs and made-in-Los Angeles series to stations all over the world. Software—don't you hate that word?—what writers create. The word always makes me think of soft in the head. I didn't know that the network had a piece of Mediterranean-American . . ."

"I didn't mean to disillusion you."

"Oh, I had no illusions in the first place. It's just that no agency in Washington has exposed the links between the networks and the petrodollars and the rest of it . . . including the military and its intelligence satellites."

"Well, Sam, it's not the kind of story that the broadcasters are encouraged to go after, in your country or mine, but bits and pieces of it have come out here and there . . ."

Linkum shook his head. "Trouble is, it mixes up the white hats and the black hats."

"Translation, please, Sam."

"You remember in the Westerns the heroes wore the white hats and the villains the black hats—at least they did in the silents."

"I get it, friend." Sassoon refilled their brandy glasses with the last few drops in the bottle. "What do you call people like us who have to work for the black hats or not at all?"

"Well, what's in between black and white? Mud color?" He raised his glass. "Here's mud in your eye."

The two friends looked at each other and were able to laugh.

"Strangely, there's only one hope for continuing our operation," Ben Sassoon said. "Walt Whipley knows he'll never get his knighthood if he fools with the traditions of the paper too radically. It all comes down to how much he's willing to pay for the honor of being called Lord Whipley."

"Are you serious? A knighthood would do it?"

"Or slightly higher on the Honors' List. Yes, that's the way the parsnips are buttered."

"In that case, arise Sir Walter," Linkum said. "And God save the Queen."

CHAPTER EIGHT

An Iron Nightingale

THE snouts of the tactical fighter wing of Phantoms at Andrews Air Force Base in Maryland were raised in their revetments, looking like prehistoric beasts sniffing the air for signs of danger, when Sam Linkum landed in the unmarked F-16 jet trainer at the far end of the field after the swift Concorde flight from Heathrow to JFK. Another plane from Hap Chorley's private fleet, a stretched Huey helicopter, already had its rotors whirling. He ducked instinctively and clambered aboard for the ten-minute hop that ended in the circular landing pad at the Pentagon.

The two front-office colonels had already cleared out after battling their nine-to-five office wars in Room 3224-AF when Linkum turned the door handle to Hap Chorley's private office.

The civilian director of USAFSS was leaning back in his deep chair, puffing his Montecristo. He pushed the cedar humidor across the desk to Linkum, who declined. Instead Linkum placed the small pack of Havanas that he had bought at Orly on the desk. Chorley nodded his thanks. Linkum broke the ice.

"What the hell was the big hurry, Hap?"

"You'll see."

Neither had bothered to say hello.

"I wanted you to compare notes with an acquaintance of yours from Biskra, in my presence."

Chorley snapped his fingers twice, impatiently.

Tweed Jerome entered from the small room behind Chorley's office.

Linkum said, *"Déjà vu.* You were a little slow on the draw this time."

Jerome looked surprised. "What do you mean by that? That Arab gunman was plugged at least three times by my P38. He was dead as a doorpost. If you have any doubts, here's his Chasseur." Jerome pulled it out of his shoulder holster. "Took it out of his hand as a souvenir for my collection."

"No, I didn't mean the gunman—I meant the Algerian delegate Moussi Ali. My host and friend. You didn't save *his* life."

Hap Chorley jumped out of his chair and waved his finger at Linkum.

"You've got it all wrong, Sam. Instead of showing gratitude, you're putting blame in the wrong place. Tweed was there to protect *you,* not the Moose. He did his job."

"True, Mr. Linkum . . . you and the woman with you, the American radio person. I didn't know how many of them were waiting in the bloody garden. You're not too bloody popular there, you know."

Linkum said, "Well, thanks, but apparently I wasn't the target, neither was she—"

Chorley broke in, face flushed. "Look, we're not here to conduct a wake for the Moose. All right, the Moose was killed. Too bad, nice guy. But one of his own countrymen pulled the trigger. Now, let's move our agenda forward. Tweed Jerome has another assignment in Central America and he's got to get at it tonight. What I want to know is, have either of you picked up anything more about the Brotherhood's next target?"

Linkum shook his head. "If I met one of them, I wouldn't know it. Anyway, I didn't think they were on my plate—"

"Saving my intelligence network is on everybody's plate," Chorley said. "And don't be so sure. What about you, Tweed?"

"The Brotherhood went still deeper underground after the Moose was shot. You know the rest. The Algerians tried to cover it up—including in his own newspaper—but Mr. Linkum here blew the story open. That's when the rest of the Arab press picked it up. Had to—the French papers ran it. So the Brotherhood isn't claiming credit publicly for the Moose's death, but privately they're saying they knocked him off because he betrayed their cause."

"Any rumors about who they might use to hit one of our ground stations? You heard about Pleumeur-Bodou, didn't you?"

Linkum said, "The news was all over the Aurassi Hotel. That one the Brotherhood bragged about."

"Ground stations are going up on both sides of the Mediterranean," Jerome said. "Could be anywhere."

Chorley nodded. "I mean in the States." If he knew more himself—and Linkum was sure that he did—he was not letting it out.

"Okay, Tweed, you can get your show on the road," Chorley said, dismissing him.

Tweed Jerome stuck out his hand.

"Nice running into you again, Mr. Linkum. Which newspaper can I read your stuff in?"

"None at the moment," Linkum answered. "It seems I'm between assignments. But thanks for asking."

After Jerome had left by the back office door Linkum turned to Chorley. "Well, Hap, what's bugging you?"

"Two things—first Algiers, then Andover. The A-rabs in the Brotherhood are targeting it tomorrow. You and I are going to be on a plane tonight for Maine. Last part of the mission—them against *us,* whether you like it or not. One for you, one for me, remember?"

"You're stretching our deal, Hap. I'm not operational."

"Can't be helped. You'll see why in a moment. Let's talk Algiers first. Want a drink?"

"I'll pass."

But Chorley reached into his liquor cabinet and filled two water tumblers halfway with Jack Daniel's black label over ice.

"You exceeded your authority, Sam, and I've heard about it from the same people at State I convinced to appoint you American delegate."

"Are you serious? The people at State didn't give me a damn thing except a bunch of transcripts of old sessions of the International Information Agency."

"They sent me copies, too, but you didn't follow their scenario— you've got to admit it. All you were to do was talk against licensing of correspondents based on your own experience and knowledge."

"And that's what I did. In my own way. If you happened to notice, the licensing resolution got shortstopped this time—didn't even come to a face-saving vote. That didn't happen during the last few annual sessions—"

"Come on, Sam, you know what I mean. You didn't just stop there. Instead, you went into your own song and dance and did a number on the American press too."

Linkum reached for the Jack Daniel's and rattled the ice cubes.

"Well, that's one way of looking at what I said—a damn narrow way. I'd interpret it as a *defense,* not an attack, a way for the press to survive without losing its guts. I didn't mention a single paper in either of my two speeches. Or a network, for that matter. Didn't give any names—to protect the innocent, or guilty. I was being even-handed—"

"They didn't think so—"

"Who's *they?* The Neanderthals at the U.N. mission in New York or the knuckleheads at State? What the *hell* do they know about how newspapers, or television stations for that matter, work? What do they know or care about what makes them live or die?"

"Not as much as you do, but they took a lot of heat from Farron and Whipley. They felt *I* had let them down by getting you appointed—"

"Hold it right there, Hap. I'm not interested in them. What about *you?* Do you think I let you down?"

Chorley hesitated a moment. Then, smiling for the first time, said, "No, hell no. You did real good."

"Thank you. What did I do to get them so mad?"

"You can guess, Sam, can't you? It was your call for studies of multinational ownership of the newspapers and networks and, on top of that, the stuff about participation by journalists in management decisions."

"Democracy in the newsroom? It isn't even my phrase, I didn't invent it, I was repeating something that's spreading all over western Europe. Reporters and editors on boards of directors, even voting for their own managing editors. That's why what I had to say struck a responsive chord with the journalist-delegates in Algiers."

"Well, it didn't go over too big back here. The State people got a lot of feedback from the associations representing the big chains and networks. They considered it an intrusion into domestic affairs and an implied criticism of their operations. You sort of tore up the peapatch—what you said made headlines—at least in some of the independent opinion weeklies and on National Public Radio."

"I guess they prefer to have Mediterranean-American pull their chestnuts out of the fire. I mean with baksheesh and broads—the traditional way of making deals. I don't have to tell you that some of the Arab delegates were lined up beforehand—"

"No, you don't. Mediterranean-American's laundry services are known from Gibraltar to the Bosporus. Certain intelligence agencies have even been known to avail themselves of the services and wire some of the ladies."

Linkum took another swig of Jack Daniel's.

"Hap, you know it runs much deeper than getting the sheiks laid regularly when they're carrying contracts and representing their oil kingdoms. I learned something that I should have guessed long before I got to Algiers and did what you call my number. The Mediterranean-American Development Corporation has a piece of the action all over the place and they're not very particular about who their partners are—and the partners themselves know how to look the other way. The whole thing is interlocked—the oil and mineral resources, the underwriting bankers and the legitimatizing lawyers, the communications satellites put up by the government and then sold and leased for private gain, Robert Farron's transponders on the big bird and Walt Whipley's down-market papers..."

Chorley smiled. "You're polite enough not to mention the United States Air Force Security Service. But *we* interact with some of these characters too—we know how to look the other way when we have to."

"I wasn't putting you in their class, Hap..."

"I hope I'm not, but I've got a different obligation. I'm trying to protect my USAFSS resources. You've helped me pinpoint the infrastructure of the Brotherhood in Algeria and how they're linked to other fanatical groups where I have intelligence facilities. I told you it's more than the Russkies I'm worried about. That's why I wanted you to throw a monkey wrench into the New World Information Order—"

"But what about the New World *Economic* Order, Hap? Run by multinational pirates like Mediterranean-American? They're a clear threat—"

"Sam, in an imperfect world, I have to live with the reality of one and the fear of the other. Between us, I'd say that *both* of these orders are blood brothers—*bad* blood brothers."

Chorley looked at his chronometer and snapped his fingers nervously.

"I wish to hell I didn't have to involve you in the Andover thing but we've got to play this out to the finish."

"But I *did* my number—"

"Not quite—I still need your help. Does the name Tlemcen mean anything to you?"

Linkum looked puzzled. "A town in Algeria?"

"No, someone called Tlemcen. Did the Moose ever mention him?"

"Nope."

Chorley reached into his desk drawer and placed a grainy blowup in front of Linkum. There were three figures in the photograph. "Recognize the guy in the center?"

"Sure—I'd know that five o'clock shadow anywhere. He's Abdul

Fahd, the chief of the Algerian delegation at the meeting last week. The Moose served as his deputy."

Chorley nodded. "Abdul Fahd, also known by the *nom de guerre* Tlemcen. Also known as the leader of the Independent Moslem Brotherhood."

"The Moose crossed him in Algiers," Linkum said. "No wonder..."

"Fahd or Tlemcen is holed up in a small town in Quebec at this moment while we're sitting and talking here. Down in a place called Lac Megantic, only about ten miles across the border from Maine. Now why would he want to be freezing his ass off when there's nothing to do there except throw snowballs?"

"How far is Lac Megantic from the earth station in Andover?"

Chorley nodded in acknowledgment. "Sixty miles as the crow flies, maybe a hundred by the scenic route heading down past Rangeley Lake and Beaver Mountain. A drive of under three hours. I figure he'll have to cross the border at Moosehorn—only place where the road's always open unless you're wearing snowshoes. He picked up the car at the airport in Quebec City and stayed overnight in the old town below. The car was rented in the name of one of the A-rab students at McGill, a Ph.D. candidate, majoring in dynamite."

"Are you going to nail him at the border crossing?"

"No reason to do it there—we want to catch him in the act, or just before. Find out who his partners and confederates are, serve as a warning to foreign students trying to meddle in this country."

"So you were able to keep track of his movements that closely in Canada?"

"There's an inspector in the Mounties who owed me a big one—at *least* one. The Royal Mounted have had their little problems with security—the Separatist movement in Quebec gets violent now and then. My ELINT people gave them a piece of information they found useful so my inspector friend gave me the signal as soon as he picked up Tlemcen's scent. By the way, that's between us."

"U.S. Secret Equals Canadian Most Secret."

"You asked me, I told you," Chorley said seriously.

Linkum nodded. "Do you think Tlemcen and company are really

going to try and pull off a Pleumeur-Bodou in the States?"

"I'm putting two and two together. Tlemcen arrives in Quebec for no real reason, a group of A-rab students from Montreal and Boston check into a ski lodge south of Andover, but none of them are carrying skis, twenty pounds of dynamite are reported missing by the Rumford Timber Company. You know, some of the logging companies place blocks of TNT inside the tree trunks to save manpower and cutting time. So what is the Moslem Brotherhood up to? No good, I'd say, but we'll find out for sure soon enough. Here— this is for you."

Chorley handed Linkum a coverall flak suit that fit over his clothing, then zipped one on himself. He said that they were warm and protective...

"Are you telling me that we're going to be in the line of fire?"

"You're not scared, are you, Sam?"

"I'm out of the hero business. That was two lives ago—"

"There could be a need to identify Tlemcen, in case he's put on a different face."

"You haven't answered my question..."

Chorley poked Linkum. "Let's get airborne, chum."

At Andrews, they stepped into a converted F-101 Voodoo fighter-bomber rebuilt for reconnaissance. The pilot saluted Chorley. Two large men were already seated in the plush chairs behind them. At their feet were Thompson submachine guns with fifty-round drums. Inside their flak suits they packed .45-caliber Colt automatics.

Chorley introduced them as federal marshals. "Mr. Smith and Mr. Jones," he said without bothering to mention Linkum's name.

The stripped fighter-bomber tore a hole in the sky, followed the lights of the coastal towns heading north by northeast, then turned and banked over the islets and bays of Maine. Linkum peered through the plexiglass window where the cannon had been removed and saw the yellow-orange flame of the afterburner pods glowing below the fuselage. The Voodoo began its descent a little more than a half-hour after takeoff. In the dying light at dusk, the snow glistened in shades of violet and smoke. Giant machines harvested the snowflakes and blew them in clouds off the grated metal runway as the unmarked plane skidded to a stop at the Air National Guard side of the field northwest of Augusta.

As he stepped outside, the cold made Linkum catch his breath and exhale frosty streams of air from his heaving chest. He sank his bare hands inside the roomy pockets of the flak suit and buried his head in the cape.

Chorley looked at his huddled figure. "Take a leak here, Sam, you make an icicle by the time it hits the ground. Let's move inside."

Two more federal marshals were waiting for them in a private room in the Air National Guard hangar. Both appeared to be six-and-a-half footers like Mr. Smith and Mr. Jones. Both carried long guns with sights slung from their shoulders.

Hap Chorley looked at his watch, gave them all his time.

"Gentlemen, you've been picked because we've worked together in the past and because there may well be federal crimes involved in this operation. I say *may be* since the Andover earth station is open to visitors at certain hours. It could be an easy out for the people we suspect to say that they're only tourists interested in American television—unless we catch them red-handed. You've all got pictures of the man we expect to cross the border tonight. His confederates are already in place at the ski lodge on this side of the border a few miles south of the big horn antenna. They're being watched by a couple of marshals at the lodge who are dressed as skiers. But the big fish we're after is Tlemcen..."

"Who's your friend?" asked one of the marshals.

"No mystery—say hello to Sam Linkum."

The marshals waved with their hands or weapons. Linkum nodded in return.

"Sam just came back from Algiers, where he served as American delegate at a meeting. Sat across the table from Tlemcen. That's why he's here—if necessary he ought to be able to spot him through a disguise. We also worked together during the war. Any more questions?"

Chorley handed them detailed maps of the roads in and out of Andover. The marshals gathered around him.

"Now, after crossing he's got to come down Highway 17 past

Byron and Frye—only way to go. At this point he has two options. He cuts west on Highway 120 and proceeds for a mile past Ellis Pond to the station. Or he continues a little farther south to Rumford, then swings sharply north for a mile on Highway 5 past Whitecap Mountain to the station. We'll be positioned at both crosspoints. Linkum and I will be in one car with two marshals, and two marshals will be in the other car. Divide yourselves up anyway you want to, but I think there ought to be one submachine gun and one long gun in each car."

"Who's carrying the dynamite?" asked one of the marshals.

"Probably one of the phony A-rab skiers. I don't see Tlemcen risking it across the border—too easy to detect unless he's playing with *plastique*. In the past they've favored dynamite. In this attack it figures to be the TNT stolen from one of the timber companies working the woods right near the earth station. So Tlemcen has to rendezvous with his students at either of the two crosspoints. Whoever spots them first radios the other car to circle and serve as a backup. Is that clear?"

The marshals nodded. The one called Smith said he had brought along a couple of extra .45's, loaded with clips, in shoulder holsters and offered them to Chorley and Linkum.

Chorley placed the .45 inside his flak suit. Linkum made no move. Chorley took the second automatic from the marshal.

"This one's for you, Sam."

"I'm too old to play with guns. Probably shoot myself—"

"Unless they shoot you first. I can't account for their crazy behavior. Here—"

He held out the weapon again. Linkum shook his head. Chorley started to say something, then held back.

The marshals looked at them, puzzled. Smith broke the ice. "The front end has the hole—nothing to it."

His joke fell flat.

For an instant Chorley and Linkum stared at each other.

This time the marshals looked away. Without a word, Chorley placed the second weapon in his briefcase.

At midnight both cars took off from the hangar and separated.

Chorley and Linkum were in the Oldsmobile with Smith and Jones. They drove in silence over the lonely road and parked on a hidden rise behind fir trees overlooking the crosspoint on Highway 5, between the ski lodge and Andover earth station.

One o'clock. Chorley ordered them to sleep in two-hour shifts. A great stillness descended over the woods. No one spoke. At first Linkum could not close his eyes. He loosened his belt and untied his shoelaces, trying to recall the last time outside a plane he had slept in his clothes. A blast of cold air penetrated the car at three o'clock when one of the marshals stepped outside to relieve himself. Linkum did not know when he finally fell asleep.

Five o'clock. Chorley poked him awake in the back seat. They checked their watches and passed around a thermos bottle filled with black coffee. Linkum stared into the shadows, trying to distinguish the outlines of the fir and hemlock and tamarack trees that stood like sentinels in disciplined formation guarding the unlighted crossroads.

At five minutes before six o'clock an alien sound broke the stillness of the matutinal hour: the surprising, deep-throated sound of church bells, rising and falling across the echoing hills of the radio-quiet enclave of Earth Station One, as if yanked by a joyful carillonneur in some ancient monastery in Tuscany. They listened in wonder to the chromatic tone of the bells, the irregular notes played almost defiantly against the elements.

"What the hell's going on?" whispered one of the marshals. He switched on a flashlight below the dashboard of the Oldsmobile and studied the area map. A few hundred yards outside the satellite tracking complex stood a small church, marked by a cross.

"Roman Catholic—run by one of those worker-priests," Chorley explained. "Sorry, my briefing line on him didn't say he had a set of bells in his log church. The only thing I've got on Father Shannon is that he's big with the woodcutters' union and was reprimanded by his bishop for defying the papal directive against wearing dungarees in the confessional booth."

"Jesus," said the marshal called Smith, shaking his head.

"Not exactly," said Chorley, "I'd call him harmless."

Nobody laughed.

Night began to fold back on itself. The skies above the distant mountains blushed faintly, heralding the morning.

Five minutes past six o'clock. They saw the lights first, yellow fog lamps inscribing a bumpy signature across the barks of the roadside trees, coming closer, and then they heard the coughing of an engine and the clanking of snow chains. A small car came into view, illuminated in the lights of a larger car behind it. One man was at the wheel of the first car; four or five men trailed in the second. Both cars crawled along the road...

The marshals slid back the bolt of the Thompson submachine gun and clicked the safety on the Armalite long gun.

Chorley told them to freeze.

The four men in the Oldsmobile lowered their heads into their shoulders, motionless, only their eyes roving.

Now the secondary roads became visible in the gray dawn, and from their hidden rise Chorley and Linkum saw the complex of Earth Station One stretched out in front of them: the huge horn antenna rising like an artificial sun on the horizon, the control tower in the center, the command and telemetry antennae tracking the signals from the iron nightingales in synchronous orbit far overhead in the mindless heavens.

The two cars on the crosspoint of the highway stopped.

Tlemcen stepped out of the first car. He was joined by four students in ski jackets; a fifth remained behind the wheel of the second car. Linkum thought of a shark and its sucker fish. Tlemcen motioned the driver to turn the heavier car with the chains around, facing away from the complex. The getaway car's fog lamps shone for an instant toward the copse where the Oldsmobile stood, then the lights lowered onto the bending road of Highway 5.

Quickly two satchels of explosives were transferred to the back seat of the small car. Tlemcen and the students waved their arms, arguing about something. One of them attempted to join him in the small car but Tlemcen pushed the student aside.

"Radio our location to the other marshals," Chorley whispered to Smith and Jones, then turned to Linkum. "Is that the delegate from the Moslem Brotherhood?"

232

Linkum nodded. "It's Abdul Fahd, all right."

"Tlemcen..."

The marshals spoke to Chorley. "Our people are on the way. They'll cut off the students if they try to make it down the highway. What's our next move?"

"The moment they're separated and Tlemcen starts going toward the earth station, you gun the Oldsmobile between them. Take advantage of the surprise. Let them know we're here with a few welcoming shots, see if they're carrying any heavy stuff. Doubt it—probably only concealed weapons. You know the rest of the plan. It looks like they're using the same scenario as the one at Pleumeur-Bodou. Except that we try to stop them beforehand. If they try to rescue Tlemcen, do whatever you think the situation calls for. Tlemcen has information I need—spare him. But the phony students are expendable..."

Linkum looked at Chorley, surprised by his tough command.

Twenty-two minutes past six. Tlemcen returned to the small car, turned on the ignition, slowly began to drive toward the searching quad-helix antenna that rotated in the sky barely a hundred yards away.

"Go," Chorley ordered, tapping Smith's shoulder.

The Oldsmobile leaped forward, chewing up dry pine needles and slush beneath its churning wheels.

The startled Arab "students" in the second rental turned at the noise behind them. One of them pulled out a revolver and fired at the charging Oldsmobile. The marshal called Jones pumped a round from his Armalite at the back window, shattering the glass. The revolver flew out of the Arab's hand onto the roadway. The others in the back seat screamed in pain, bleeding from the shards implanted in their ripped cheeks and matted hair. The driver tried to take off just as the federal marshals arrived from the other crosspoint, blocking the getaway car. The wounded Arabs in ski jackets faced the barrels of four long guns and stumbled out of the car, their bloodied hands clasped overhead in surrender.

Now the Oldsmobile with Chorley and Linkum in the back seat veered sharply to the left, going after Tlemcen and his small car, knowing it was loaded with two satchels of TNT. The leader of the

Brotherhood saw them coming in his mirror and sped toward the quad-helix antenna...

"Stop the bastard," Chorley ordered. "Don't let that car hit the pylon..."

Again Jones leaned out the window and took aim with the Armalite, but Smith pushed the long gun aside, handed him the Thompson submachine gun. "The tires, not the gas tank."

Jones sighted down the barrel. A burst of Tommy-gun bullets tore into the rubber of the back wheels. The car screeched and fell smoking into a ditch twenty yards from the pylon.

Tlemcen jumped out of the shot car, tried to open the jammed back door to reach the explosives, looked behind. The Oldsmobile was bearing down on him.

Directly across the road stood Father Shannon's log church, topped by a simple wooden cross. Tlemcen kicked open the door and ran down the center aisle. He entered the priest's study behind the altar, a Chasseur automatic in his hand.

Outside, Smith and Jones doused the burning rubber with an extinguisher. Two other federal marshals quickly removed the satchels of TNT from the ditched car.

Chorley took the .45 out of his shoulder holster and clicked it into the firing position. He reached into his briefcase for the second automatic and pushed it into Linkum's hand.

"This one's yours, Sam. We're covering each other."

Linkum's fingers curled around the grip. It felt cold. Chorley hadn't given him the holster. He blew breath on the knuckles of his hand, warming his fingers. The .45 was the first weapon he had held since the war.

"We're going inside after him," Chorley said.

Cautiously they entered the log church, their eyes circling the primitive pews and the foot-high altar.

At the far end, Tlemcen stood with the priest in front of him acting as a human shield.

Father Shannon, whose dossier included antiwar marches and spilling animal blood on draft-board files and months behind bars for disturbing the peace, held up his hand. He was dressed in dungarees, looking more like a carpenter than a priest.

234

"Gentlemen, no guns in here please—"

Chorley waved his automatic. "What about the one sticking in your ribs, Father?"

"I don't know what this dispute is about but none of your guns is going to settle anything. This man has taken refuge in my church."

"He's no refugee, Father. He has just committed a number of serious federal crimes. I'm going to bring him in—"

"Let me try to talk to him. The only way to settle this thing before someone gets killed is for you to put your guns away." He looked over his shoulder at Tlemcen. "Including you."

Tlemcen still showed the steel of his Chasseur.

No one in the church would walk forward or change positions. All were in accurate automatic range. They had reached a stalemate.

After a minute had passed, Linkum whispered to Chorley, "Okay, I'll try to talk that gun out of his hand. Otherwise he'll kill the priest and maybe one of us too..."

Linkum slowly lowered his hand to the ground. Tlemcen stood watching him, newly alert. Linkum tossed the .45 halfway down the aisle of the church. The gun lay between them.

"For crissakes," Chorley said angrily, "have you gone out of your skull?"

Linkum held up his now empty palms...as if to signal Tlemcen to do the same. Still no move by the Algerian leader. They could hear him breathing, hard.

"Abdul Fahd," Linkum called out. "We know each other. Only a few days ago we sat across the same table in Algiers. Whether we agreed or disagreed we at least managed without weapons. I'm unarmed. Give yourself up. Otherwise—"

Tlemcen spat in Linkum's direction. He waved his Chasseur in front of Father Shannon, thereby telling Linkum not to come closer.

For an instant Linkum thought to himself, This is the fanatic who ordered Moussi gunned down in Biskra. I wish the hell I had that .45 in my hand again...except if I did I'd be no different from him, I'd be like one of *them,* everything I believed in would go up in smoke—

Abruptly a voice behind the cornered Algerian and his hostage: "Drop it, Tlemcen."

Tlemcen turned at the sound of his *nom de guerre* and got off a shot in the direction of the marshal's voice. Chorley's .45 kept Tlemcen off guard, half-turning, exposed.

Smith squeezed the trigger of his automatic. Tlemcen's body seemed to lift into the air, then fell to the ground, a bullet in his heart.

"Dammit," Chorley said to the marshal, "I wanted to take the bastard alive."

"Saves the government a million dollars in paperwork and trial time," Smith said.

Chorley shrugged. "Well, no use crying over spilled A-rab blood." He turned and touched Linkum's shoulder. "Nice college try, chum. At least you distracted the bastard long enough for Smith to let him have it before he got one of us."

Father Shannon knelt in front of the altar, then leaned over the body of the Algerian leader of the Moslem Brotherhood.

A trickle of blood began to flow from his wound down the aisle of the roughhewn church.

Seven o'clock.

A good morning's work for survivors.

Departing, Chorley and Linkum started to drive toward the remote USAF hangar near Augusta, where the upholstered Voodoo was parked.

In the distance, on a rise above Andover, they heard the tolling notes of the renegade church bells echoing over the shrouded woods and satellite hills of Earth Station One ...

In Room 3224-AF later in the day at the Pentagon, Linkum drained his coffee mug and checked his watch. He stood up. They had talked themselves out.

"And that's why this is the last assignment I'll ever take for you or anyone else around here. We play on different ball fields, Hap. You're in the government, I'm an outsider—and that's where I have to live. At least where I always want to be, even if it means I'm flat on my ass."

Chorley shook his head. "Sorry to hear you say that, Sam. Worse, that you feel that way. I said from the beginning that we'd both get something out of this. I learned a lot more and maybe kept my intelligence lines open a while longer around the Mediterranean. You scored some points against licensing and for the other hobby horses you rode at the U.N. meeting."

"Yeah, and Mediterranean-American picks up the pieces and goes on with business as usual."

Chorley unwound from his chair. "No hard feelings, Sam?"

"Not toward you personally . . ."

Chorley looked relieved to hear it. "Where do you go from here?"

"Right now all I want to do is catch up on my jet lag and think about what happened this morning and climb into my sack in New York."

"I'll have my pilot fly you to La Guardia."

Linkum hesitated for a moment, then turned the doorknob of 3224-AF.

"Hap, no offense, but I'd rather take the civilian shuttle home."

CHAPTER NINE

The Lordly Air

LATE in the morning of the next day Sam Linkum was awakened by the super's son tapping on his apartment door. The youngster handed him a sealed envelope without a stamp on it and said it had just been delivered by a chauffeur. He gave the boy the only coins in his pocket, a couple of Her Majesty's shillings, and told him to thank his father for holding the mail all this time and that he would pick it up later.

He slit open the envelope, which had nothing on it to identify the sender. On top of the engraved notecard was a neat duplicate of the gold-on-black sign at the entrance to the estate:

FARRON FIELDS

The message below was written by hand in italics script.

Dear Sam (mind?):
Welcome back to the States. Heard you did fine. Would like to hear

about it in person. Would you have the time to come by here for lunch today around two? Promise no one but ourselves. Call if possible, otherwise just show up.
Cordially, Robert.

Linkum looked at his watch. He had a couple hours to dress, rent one of the compacts on Second Avenue and drive to the network chairman's estate on Long Island. But did he want to go? The note was cordial enough—"*Cordially*, Robert." Even with a sly touch of humor—"Promise no one but ourselves." Meaning no Walt Whipley this time. The man did fascinate him, admit it. He had a large presence and a certain directness that charmed. Once more into the breach: Farron Fields. What was it the Army Air Corps sign used to say in the intelligence school when he was studying the silhouettes of the Luftwaffe fighters? *Know Your Enemy.*

Okay, Robert *(mind?)*, I'll play out a final hand with you...

Linkum took him at his word in the invitation and decided to show up without calling in advance. What the hell, it was too late for Farron, so far as he was concerned, to take no prisoners.

He had a choice in midweek and selected a low-slung Toyota. In less than an hour with so little traffic going eastward he came to the fading denim-colored fence, and the tradesman's entrance, and then the rows of foreshortened iron jockeys with their black faces whitewashed on the long sweeping lawn.

"Greetings, Sam. Glad you could find time to visit with me all the way out here in the country."

Linkum was glad that he was five minutes early. Farron apparently had been out on the lawn waiting for him.

"Hello, Mr. Farron. It's a nice drive, no trouble doing a reverse-commute from the city."

"You must be hungry. Let's sit right down to lunch."

One of the silver trays was filled with smoked fish and oysters and mussels and a casserole of sole Florentine, the other with cold meats and Cornish hens. The chateaux wines wore the right labels and years.

No mention of what had happened in Maine. Farron didn't know—
yet. He wouldn't tell him.

Farron's face creased with good humor. "I heard that you showed
up at Whipley's newspaper and he kicked you off the premises."

"Your intelligence is right but your facts are wrong. He didn't
kick me out—I left voluntarily."

"Yes... well, Whipley isn't a very subtle fellow. Probably couldn't
make it as a reporter on his own newspaper."

"If there's a newspaper to report for—he may be taking a leaf
from your book and closing it, or what's probably worse turning it
into one of his down-market sheets."

Farron's jaw suddenly tightened, then just as quickly he buried
his flash of anger.

"Well, Sam, I don't think it is very constructive to mourn too
long. Even in my mature years I look to the future, and the old
paper didn't have one. It shut down but I'm not saying it's dead
forever—I've still retained the right to the title. Let someone come
along and show how it can *communicate* to large numbers of people
and advertisers and I'll be the first one to give it the go-ahead again."

He invited me here, Linkum told himself. All I've got to lose is
a glass or two more of that Bordeaux from the right region and the
right side of the hill... "You've got a wrong view of the paper,
Mr. Farron—"

"Robert."

"*Okay,* Robert. Your basis of comparison is television and everything that goes with it—the Nielsen ratings and head counts of
all the children and dogs and cats watching the shows in the family
living room, the bid for the highest numbers that leads to the least
common denominator thinking behind the programs, the fate of the
news and documentaries depending on the drop of a point or two,
and the rest of that bullshit."

Farron leaned back and lit up a Romeo y Julieta. He offered one
to his guest. He had heard it all before, not from a stranger this
bluntly but from his own sons who had decided not to follow their
father in the business of broadcasting. "I'm still listening," Farron
said.

"The only thing I have to add is that newspapers don't work the same way. You don't go out and ask the reader what to print—you let the news and events make that decision with the help of good reporters and editors."

"And who is supposed to underwrite these papers when they can't make it in the marketplace? We're not charitable foundations, you know, we're responsible to our shareholders—"

"The reason some of these papers don't make it is that their managements panic and start chasing the television style of news. Class and professionalism still count—in ponies, people and papers. End of speech."

Robert Farron looked directly at Sam Linkum for a moment, neither saying anything. Then he applauded. The sound of his hands clapping slowly struck Linkum as a sarcastic statement. Well, screw it. At least he'd had his say.

"Sam," the chairman of the network finally said, "if you were as outspoken in Algiers as you are in my house, I can understand why you scored your points there. I don't agree with you—let's say that we have a difference of opinions—but, believe it or not, I respect your sincerity. Even when you refer to our tested methods of bringing entertainment, news and advertising to tens of millions of people in their homes as bullshit."

Linkum was sorry he'd given Farron that opening.

"Now, Sam, let's move on to what you achieved in Algiers. I hope that some of the background material that I provided was of some use to you..."

Even network chairmen, Linkum thought at that moment, have to fish for compliments.

"It was, Mr. Farron. I heard a lot about transponders and direct broadcasting by satellites to ground stations—especially from some of the third world delegates."

Almost too casually Farron got to the point; and Linkum realized that he had not been invited here for his wonderful personality.

"Did any of the delegates happen to mention my network's interests in the big bird?"

"Not specifically."

"Much discussion about Mediterranean-American?"

"Not openly during the sessions..."

He decided to let his response about Mediterranean-American, and its links to the network and the Whipley Group, twist in the wind. It was clear that Farron had more than a casual interest in the multinational. He wished there were a newspaper around that could unravel the connections and print the whole story... without *neutral* words. He didn't hope to get the answers at Farron Fields.

Farron stood up, signaling that Linkum's time was up. Nothing had been said about exceeding his mandate, nothing about the death of the Moose, nothing about what they both knew—that some of the ground stations around the world in which Hap Chorley and Robert Farron shared different interests could be struck, that others faced the risk of anarchic human lightning... even in the States.

Farron walked him to his small car and started to wave him good-by, when suddenly he motioned Linkum to stop. He disappeared for a minute in the toolshed next to the converted stables, then emerged carrying a brilliantly painted silk box kite and an elaborately carved wooden spool in the form of a dragon's head.

"We're all grateful to you for stopping that licensing resolution," Farron said, smiling. "I'd like you to have one of my small kites and a spool—antiques from prewar China. Don't fly it in too high a wind."

Before Linkum could protest, Farron placed the kite and spool on the back seat of the Toyota. Linkum thanked him and drove down the lane until Farron was out of sight and he'd reached the tradesman's exit.

At a fork in the road he almost instinctively turned east, to continue along the tree-lined highway toward the military cemetery at Farmingdale and then onward to the residence for the emotionally disabled near Riverhead, as he had done so often to visit Antonio's grave and to see Elena on those silent Sundays, but both of them were now interred in the soil of Italy and buried, deeper still, in his memory.

Instead, Linkum turned westward. He was in no hurry. Jennie would not be back in the city until tomorrow.

Going toward Manhattan he decided to avoid the expressway and drove along Northern Boulevard, steering around the potholes until he came to a stoplight just before the Queensboro Bridge.

A couple of ten-year-old boys, one white and the other black, attacked his windshield with chamois cloths and then held out their hands. He gave them a few British coppers, the only coins in his pocket, and felt a little guilty.

"You guys fly kites?" he suddenly asked.

"Sure."

He handed one the kite and the other the antique spool, feeling like a big shot.

"Don't put it up when it's too windy," Sam Linkum said, laughing.

CHAPTER TEN

Punctuation Marks

THE autumn winds were tangled in the pollarded branches of the sycamores and ginkgos growing bravely out of the city's concrete earth. Walking alongside the perimeter of Union Square Sam stooped to pick up a few of the curling leaves streaked with yellow gold between their dying green stems. The magic of Manhattan worked its afternoon charm.

Alone, with a little time before Jennie arrived at her place, he continued past the street hawkers and hustlers until he found himself in front of the old newspaper plant. The windows had been boarded up and the prize-winning bronze plaques removed, leaving rusting holes in the brick facade. Graffiti were scrawled in crazy defiance across the ground-floor walls. Only the ornate tower clock high above the entranceway remained in place, beyond the reach of vandals, but the luminous pale green glass was now cracked on one side and the intricately designed hour and minute hands no longer moved. They were stopped at fifteen minutes before noon or midnight, interrupted newspaper time.

Linkum looked at his own watch. He still had time for a beer; not working in the afternoon had its advantages. Heading north, he turned into Irving Place and stopped off at Pete's Tavern and stood against the dark mahogany bar with the serious drinkers and nursed a Carlsberg from the tap. Staring at the distorted reflection of himself in the smoky mirror behind the lineup of for-show bottles of unopened brandy, he discovered to his own surprise that his face was relaxed and faintly smiling. The last time he had wandered down to the newspaper block and stood in the shadows, watching the final edition being put to bed, he felt despair turning into anger. But now, he realized, there was nothing left to mourn, the past was a monument of ashes, covered with graffiti. Encountering those who were responsible for the demise of the newspaper, he found that the ogres had human faces and ordinary goals. They were, in fact, merchants of the ordinary.

He walked outside and dialed her number and she asked him where he was calling from and he said from a phone booth near Pete's Tavern and she said he'd better stop hanging around street corners alone or he would find himself in bad company.

"What's taken you so long, Sam? I've been home for at least five minutes waiting for your call..."

He took giant strides from Irving Place across the short streets and then around Gramercy Park to her apartment and punched the buzzer next to J. IVES in short bursts. She clicked open the doorway to the building, no check of the caller's name. Instead of waiting for the elevator he bounded up the four flights, thinking of when he had stood on the outside looking in after their cool walk back from Mannie's Place.

The door was half-open. As he entered, she surprised him from behind and slammed it shut. She fell into his arms and kissed his throat and he brushed his lips across her forehead as she buried herself against his chest. She was wearing the familiar crimson housecoat and he slid his fingers through the open seam.

"I still haven't had the chance to sew it up, you bum."

"Don't bother—I was only checking to see if I was in the right place. Yes, it still feels like you."

"You seem to be in a good mood. Is it me, the beer I smell on your breath or the state of the union?"

"All, or some of the above—especially you."

"I've missed you so. It seems ages ago . . . Rome, our reunion at the Scalinata di Spagna, Algiers when you were wearing your delegate's name tag and I was getting all those secrets while you were talking in your sleep."

Sam laughed. "Don't forget, you promised to let me hear your broadcasts."

"They're making a cassette for me at the Public Radio office in Washington."

"How did it go for you there?"

"Pretty well—they told me they'd be receptive to other roving assignments."

"Great . . . Jennie, I've been meaning to tell you something. About why I happened to be there as the American delegate . . . and why you were there covering the International Information Agency."

"Me?"

"Yes, *both* of us. What I'm about to say doesn't cancel one line of anything I said on my own as delegate and you said on your own as reporter. Those words hold up without temporizing or backtracking, they're part of the record. Remember that, will you?"

"You're sounding very mysterious."

Linkum explained how his old friend Hap Chorley headed Air Force intelligence and had engineered his appointment with State, that Hap's interest was to keep his sources free and clear of assaults by licensing resolutions or fanatical groups, and Hap's feeling prevailed that a professional journalist could be more convincing than a diplomat in Algiers.

"And what about *my* appointment, did Hap Chorley have a hand in that too?"

Linkum said that had been his idea—for her professional career and because of his personal desire that they be together.

247

"I'm disappointed," Jennie said softly. "Not that I didn't love every minute of it but because of the side-door auspices."

"I know you, Jennie. If I told you beforehand that Chorley of the Pentagon had put in a good word for you, you would have refused the assignment."

"You know me all right, Sam."

"And that's why I *didn't* let you know."

She nodded. "Tell me, Sam, and this will help me...did you make up all that stuff yourself about investigating multinational ownership of the media and democracy in the newsrooms?"

"Yes."

"And what did the powers-that-be think of what you said?"

"They didn't much like it, in fact they're pretty pissed at me."

"Well, that's good," she said, "because I reported exactly what you proposed to be studied so they're bound to be pissed at me too."

"I'm sorry that I couldn't tell you before, Jennie, but I was honor bound not to reveal the USAFSS sponsorship."

"Once a spook, always a spook, Sam?"

"You really know how to hurt a guy..."

"Just kidding...well, *half*-kidding."

"If it matters to you—"

"Everything you say and do matters to me, Sam."

"I was about to say that I told Hap Chorley that he couldn't count on me for another assignment. That a journalist just can't hook up with the government. The two don't go together."

She reached across the couch, entwined his fingers in hers and lowered them to her lap.

Punctuation mark...

In recent months their relationship had gone from long affair to full stop to doubtful semicolon to what it had become in the last few days, a promising comma...

"Okay, Jennie, let's talk. Really talk."

"I'm listening." Silence. "Okay...me first. Even while we were making love, neither of us said the word. We never did. Don't pretend you don't know what I'm talking about."

"I know...but do you know why I held back? Because while Elena was alive I couldn't abandon her. I couldn't make good on the words that meant commitment until now."

"I needed to hear you say it, Sam. Say you loved me. I'm pretty old-fashioned for a news dame."

He drew her against him and kissed her parting lips.

A tear rolled down her cheek. He kissed the wetness.

"Don't," he said.

She smiled. "You can't love without tears. Anybody knows that."

"When Elena died I decided to give you space," he said. "I was confused myself. I loved you but I wanted you to have a chance to free yourself if you wanted to. That's why I saw less and less of you—"

"I thought you didn't feel the same way about me, and I didn't want to force it. Right up to the moment when I left you standing in front of the door downstairs, I was waiting for some sort of signal..."

"Maybe I should have broken your door down that night."

"I probably would have helped you do it. I was half-mad coming up here alone."

"We were both acting out something..."

"Yeah, at our age." She smiled and said, "So I went out and sold my hair and you went out and bought me a beautiful comb."

"Well, this is O. Henry's old neighborhood."

"The characters in his story had a happy ending, if I remember. How about ours?"

Afterward, when they had showered and dressed again, Sam announced that they were going out to one of their favorite places to celebrate.

"I'm game and hungry," Jennie said, "but what are we celebrating?"

"Us," he said, "and you'd better put on your dashing Panama hat."

"First disagreement," she said. "It only works when in Rome. I haven't got the courage to wear it in New York."

"We're not going to eat in town. Until midnight, Hap Chorley's United States Air Force Security Service is paying for the chariot I've got parked on Irving Place. If you promise to skip dessert I'll be able to get it back in time to the Budget Rent-A-Car office. No, we're not dining in the back room of Mannie's Place. We're heading for the River Barge in Brooklyn."

"That's a lovely idea, Sam. The last time we ate there was for my birthday when you gave me the Victorian pin with my birthstone. I'll stick it on my jacket again but, if you don't mind, I'd better skip the Bogart look in Brooklyn."

"Up to you—I just wanted to be reminded of a beautiful woman I saw wearing it on the terrace of the Casina Valadier overlooking the Tiber."

They drove along Second Avenue and through the downtown streets leading to the approaches of the Brooklyn Bridge and crossed beneath the delicate steel strands that seemed to glisten like finely spun spider webs floating above the river. He parked the Toyota on the pier where the River Barge stood facing the cityscape of Manhattan.

The Brooklyn headwaiter vaguely remembered that they were newspaper people from the terra incognita across the East River, and he gave them a reserved table with a one-hundred-and-eighty-degree view. Looking downriver they saw containers and crates stacked from ports all over the world and, farther below where the filled land curved, the jagged profile of presumptuous lofts—daring survivors living beyond their time. Upriver, in the shadow of the bridge, they could see a small park with a marker in front of it noting that General Washington's ragtag riflemen had crossed the river at this point, when salmon swam here and deer hid in the woods of Manhattan, over two centuries ago.

They dined on baked salmon that had swum elsewhere and drank a white table wine called Segesta, from vineyards on the slopes of western Sicily, that would never make it to the selective cellar of Farron Fields.

"Sam, I haven't had a chance to tell you until now but I was damn glad for your final message to the delegates. Even more important than delaying that political effort to license journalists where the truth hurts."

"Well, maybe I planted a seed or two."

"What do you think is going to happen here—including to those of us who'd like to go on writing?"

"Strange, but I'm not that worried. I was before I went to Algiers but not now. I passed the old newspaper plant and I didn't feel even a twinge. What for? *They* don't. They've been exposed for what they are. I hope we've grown a little wiser. You know, and I should have known since I'm usually a minute behind that practical mind of yours... *a company isn't family*. You never heard of a father firing a child, have you?"

Jennie said she hadn't, that it was conglomerates these days that threw you out in the snowstorm and told you, never darken my door again, daughter.

"So I figure we'll make it, Jennie. There are still papers around that need pros to put them out, on the fringes of the city if not in the city itself, and pieces to write for the weeklies and monthlies that cut across the spectrum of special subjects and opinions— without having to lease time on the commercial transponders from the Farrons and Whipleys. If you really have something to say you might even get some unsuspecting publisher to put your stuff between covers. And since you've proved that words can still count in any forum, there are stints on Public Radio and some of the other independent stations."

They watched a barge go past pushed by a tugboat that sounded its foghorn directly in front of the river restaurant.

"Sam, you make the prospects sound possible... even likely."

"I hope so, I mean it."

He directed his gaze straight ahead, across the river, toward the twinkling lights of lower Manhattan, and he turned his head slightly to the left.

His lips began to move silently.

"You're talking to yourself," Jennie said, nudging him. "Do you mind sharing your thoughts with a friend?"

251

"Sorry, I just had a . . . look there . . ."

He pointed toward the World Trade Center's twin towers, standing below the nighttime clouds like illuminated tombstones, honoring dead giants of another civilization.

The towers were crowned with transmitting antennae for most of the television networks and stations.

"You know, that north tower with all the antennae wouldn't be an impossible shot for a good mortarman."

He took a pen out of his pocket and began to make calculations on a paper napkin.

"Let's see, the azimuth multiplied by—"

Jennie broke in. "I'm glad that I brought along the big butterfly net for you."

"Too small probably for an 81-millimeter mortar unless you got within two miles . . . hard to judge distance across water . . . but a 105-millimeter mortar, muzzle-loading, would do it nicely from this spot . . . with a fin-stabilized projectile . . . throwing a thirty-three-pound high-explosive shell . . . wouldn't need any recoil mechanism, just fitted to a base plate in the park outside the restaurant . . . light in weight, disassemble after firing, dump it in the Gowanus Canal afterward . . . sink without a trace . . . put up a little smoke shell for cover first . . . every TV screen in the country going black . . . and everyone talking to everyone else and *reading* books and newspapers."

"Sam, may I borrow your pipe dream some time?"

"We can share it," he said.

The glowing candle on the table turned the last of the wine in their glasses deep amber.

"Television . . . you know what these networks are all about? Air and space. They sell what I was raised to believe belonged only to God."

She touched his hand.

"You know, sometimes I feel like an organ grinder with a monkey and tin cup. I keep turning out the same tune, year after year, and trying to make the monkey dance . . ."

"I'll put a coin in your tin cup anytime, Mister."

Across the river the antennae stood, under a satellite sky, sending and imprisoning signals from the squawking nightingales. Sam Linkum pointed his thumb and forefinger at the towers, winked, and said, "Bang!"